"YOU ARE ALWAYS THOUGHTFUL, MADAME."

That felt like groveling. James hoped she saw it that way. "The under butler has already arranged a supper for us."

"Very well." She stood looking at the ruin and finally glanced back at him. "I suppose I shall go." She made another curtsey as though to leave.

"I suppose you shall." He whispered it and saw her hesitate.

"You make it so difficult, my lord," She spoke with exasperation when he would have preferred amusement. "It may be that you are able to find privacy when you need it, and are not quite as practiced at asking for company."

"It may be, madame, that it is not lack of skill but lack of interest that keeps me from asking for company."

"Oh, my lord, you have mastered the veiled slight, truly you have." She laughed as she walked back toward him.

One of the things he liked most about Marguerite Voisson was how rarely she took offense at his insults. And she did not disappoint him this time.

"I have no doubt that you are capable of always making your wants known, my lord. And in this case I can see that you long for company and will not ask for it directly."

He would not admit to anyone, and barely to himself, that the only company he wanted stood before him . . .

HIS LAST LOVER

Mary Blayney

ZEBRA BOOKS
Kensington Publishing Corp.
http://www.kensingtonbooks.com

To
Elaine Fox,
Beth Harbison, and
Marsha Nuccio

A critique group
specializing in
honesty, inspiration,
and ice cream

One

West Sussex
Spring 1810

James Braedon stilled his horse and reached for his gun. Unrest filled the air, as tangible as the wind at his back. Searching the trees that shadowed the narrow track, he saw nothing untoward, heard nothing beyond the familiar rustle of animals foraging on a spring evening.

James urged a reluctant Parson forward. He knew this back way home from his earliest days, still, his uneasiness grew as the light faded.

It could be poachers. He drew in a deep breath and caught the smell of smoke overriding the earthy scents of spring. Gypsies?

Scanning the trees yet again, he noted the sun setting as a warm red glow against a threatening gray sky. Would there be rain? Did that make the animals restive?

James urged Parson into a brisker trot, turning his thoughts to Braemoor, as if that would speed his arrival. Until a few moments ago he had approached home with something more than a draining sense of obligation. A few days in London had been a true tonic.

Now he marshaled his thoughts. He would need to see Marfield as soon as possible and certainly the land steward would have news for him, too.

What mischief had his father brewed while he'd been away? Had he demanded the "chamber pots be emptied into the soup bowl" again? Did he still insist that "Marfield must sleep with the housekeeper"?

The Marquis of Straeford was recovering from his apoplexy. Oh yes, the force of his personality remained, but more often than not he was in some world other than this one. Amazing that a few days away made his father's behavior seem more amusing than annoying. He must do it again soon.

A swirl of air brought the stronger smell of smoke. His apprehension edged up a notch as Parson threw his head up with a snort.

James reached out to pat his neck, "Easy, boy. The stable is almost within sight." He urged the horse into a canter as they approached the last copse of trees.

He realized what was happening the moment he left the wood. The red ball was not in the heavens. The gray did not grow from a night darkening sky. Flames flew into the air. Fire close to home. Fire on his land. Was it the old cottages? The stables?

Twilight and rising smoke made it hard to see. He reined Parson to a halt, but only for a second. Horror pushed him forward at a breakneck gallop.

Great coils of gold and red swirled around Braemoor. Not the outbuildings, but the main house itself ablaze in a gaudy riot of fire stripping it to the rock of the old stone walls and foundations.

"Move away! Get out!" He bellowed at the top of his lungs as Parson plunged down the slope, nervous and eager to veer away from the fire toward the stable.

Were his people safe?

Had his father escaped?

Leaping from the horse, James raced toward Braemoor, mesmerized and sickened by the spectacle. He could make out people, backlit by the inferno, little more than silhouettes moving about like actors uncertain of their marks or their next line.

"Is everyone safe?" He called out even as he ran.

No one answered.

Could he even be heard above the roar of the flames? Or seen beyond the great billows of smoke sending Braemoor into the mourning gray sky?

James stopped running. "Where is my father?" he shouted heavenward, as though swearing at the powers above.

A few yards more and he joined the chaos. He grabbed a man by the arm and forced his attention. "How long?"

He recognized Harold, the hall porter. "Oh my lord, thank God you're here."

James shook the man. "How long? Where's my father?"

"Hours, Sir. Hours. Since teatime or before that even. The marquis? Not here, leastways not that I've seen."

"God damn it, man, is he dead or alive?"

Harold shook his head. Before he could explain another man stopped in front of them, just short of knocking them both down.

"There ain't enough water, my lord. What are we to do?"

James turned to Harold, "Find the marquis, come back and tell me where he is."

James started toward the blaze at a slow run, trying to focus on something besides the flare of fire and the long black scorch marks it made as it spiraled from window to window.

He tripped over something and that slowed him. Looking down, he knew fear to his core. Thank God it was only a piece of furniture. Other pieces of debris littered the lawn, as though some giant had thrown whole rooms from windows. If they had time to salvage furniture then the people must be safe.

"Is everyone out?"

"A crowd is over by the east wood."

Rounding the corner of the south wall he saw no flame, only wisps of smoke. The west facade remained intact. He broke into a run. At the corner of the west and north wall he found what he was looking for: Marfield directing the brigade.

His land steward nodded to him. "We dammed the lake for the new drainage project only two days ago. The stream is too low."

"What about the pump from the village?"

"By the time the pump was brought up the fire had too strong a hold." Marfield jerked his head toward the north facade. "I thought to save the North wing so I had them set it up over there." He shook his head doubtfully.

James tracked the long line of men passing buckets along, followed the line inside and saw it again up three levels, dozens of men working as one desperate machine.

"I have them wetting down the roof of the north and west wings. I feel sure the west wing can be saved."

A tumultuous crash of timber and a mighty shower of sparks stopped them all for a moment. Screams followed. From onlookers only, he begged.

James grabbed Marfield's arm to get his attention. "Is it safe for them up there?"

"So far." They both began moving toward the renewed blaze. "That was the interior wall of the east wing." Marfield looked at James with narrowed eyes. "Where it started."

James stopped. Where his father's rooms were. "Is he dead?"

Marfield shook his head. "He's in one of the cottages near mine."

James pressed his lips together and turned his back on Marfield, continuing his circuit of the building, moving toward the copse where he could see the biggest crowd gathered.

Even up close he recognized no one. Soot-stained skin and torn clothes, eyes white with horror. Did they even know him? They must have. People parted without comment to let him into the circle. He saw the housekeeper swathed in a rough blanket, her eyes closed and bruised looking. "Mrs. Lanning?" He knelt down.

One of the women nearby whispered. "It's the marquis' son, ma'am. It's Viscount Crandall."

When Mrs. Lanning opened her eyes and recognized him, her face lit with rage. "This is the last you'll see of me, my lord. Your own father began this and deserves to die."

The group gasped and a maid hushed her. "She be that upset, my lord. We thought her daughter, Hannie, was trapped. But we found her over a ways and quite safe."

"No thanks to him."

James had heard enough. He turned his back on her even while she spoke.

Halfway across the lawn, a man grabbed him without ceremony.

"We have to get them out, my lord. They thinks the paintings is worth more than their lives."

"How many?"

"I think only Prentice remains inside, my lord."

"The house steward?"

The man nodded. James recognized this man now as one of the gardeners.

"My lord, he'll save the silver or die doin' it."

"Prentice would think that a worthwhile trade." At the man's shocked look, James snarled. "I said Prentice would think that. I do not. Where is he?"

He pointed toward the edge of the north wing where smoke seeped from the ground level windows.

Prentice threw things from the window while several men below caught the miscellany.

James walked among them and shouted up. "Come out, Prentice. Come out at once!"

His voice did not carry over the din. A shower of sparks flew into the air and those outside moved back several steps. Prentice disappeared from the window and returned in a moment, making frantic gestures. The approaching fire held him prisoner.

The men turned to James, alarm in their eyes. "He'll die if he jumps, my lord."

James spoke over his shoulder as he ran back toward the crowd. "Tell him to wait while I get help."

Mrs. Lanning had not moved and the crowd around her had grown. He elbowed his way through and pulled the maid aside. "I need her blanket. I must have it and immediately."

"Her dress is in tatters, sir!"

"You do it or I will." He moved forward, but she was ahead of him. A moment later he had the blanket to hand and Mrs. Lanning's screeches echoing in his head.

The maid looked at him with disapproval. He grabbed the blanket without explanation and raced back to the men who had gathered below the place where Prentice would land. In a moment, most grasped what the viscount hoped to do. They surged forward, all willing to help. James waved them off. "Only four. We must be able to move quickly if necessary."

He chose the strongest of the lot, two footman and one of the under gardeners. He would be the fourth. His strength equaled any one one of theirs and he certainly had the most responsibility. Besides, if he were holding one corner of the blanket, it would be easier to direct any necessary movement.

It had taken less than five minutes to contrive the effort,

but already flames spouted from the windows closest to where Prentice stood on the sill.

"We need to get close!" he urged. "But not so near that the smoke blinds us." They moved close enough to be made uneasy by the heat. "The closer we can get, the better chance he has. Dropping is better than jumping."

The men nodded and moved into position. Prentice understood too. He eased out onto the ledge, lowered himself down five feet closer to the ground.

Unfortunately, at that moment a whoosh of fire-filled smoke blew through the window. Prentice released his grip instinctively and sooner than he might have.

He hit the blanket on his side, feet first. All four corners held, but the wool itself gave in and split up the middle. The steward hit the ground, holding out his arm to break his fall. The four closest heard the sickening snap of bone against ground. Prentice stumbled to his feet, cradling his arm. The rest of them moved away as quickly. They needed no urging for the thickening smoke made breathing a challenge.

James nodded to the men. "See to him."

As he moved away, James heard Prentice directing the removal of the rescued items to a safer place.

James slowed his steps, moving toward the line still handing buckets with energy and conviction. Marfield definitely had that under control.

Villagers had arrived, along with the surgeon. They tended to the servants who numbered among their friends.

He had nothing to do but wait until the fire burned itself out. James climbed the crest, heading for the cottages where they had moved his father. He stopped at the top and did not look back. He put a hand against the trunk of a tree and stared at the ground. The smell of smoke, the sound of fire eating wood, the ash raining down, filled his mind and scarred his heart.

He stared at the grass and tried to order his mind, to repress the wild swing of emotion careening from denial to terror to heartache. Braemoor burned to ash, his father still alive. He kept on staring at the ground not seeing the grass or any of the life hidden there, instead envisioning something he had not thought possible. A world worse than the one he had lived in yesterday.

He heard no sound of approach. His first awareness of her presence was a voice of quiet urgency.

"Can I help you, sir?"

The voice was such an invasion of his very personal hell that when he looked up and saw a woman, dressed in gray, he thought she must be a ghost.

"Maddie?" He said the word out loud and immediately shook his head. Of course it could not be his sister come to haunt him.

"No, sir, I am a visitor and want to help. Are you all right?" She spoke with great calm, even though emotion colored her words.

He turned back and nodded toward the flaming wreckage. "There is no help for it now."

She walked closer and stood a half step behind him. They both watched for a very long minute until she shuddered. Did the shiver come from cold or fear? He glanced at her and found her regarding him steadily, ignoring the fire.

He felt her hand on his arm and knew two things. Her shudder had come from fear, for her hand shook. And she was no ghost. The light touch of her fingers sent a warmth through him that only a woman could. Her touch tightened a little.

"No one died, sir? No servants? The family?"

She spoke these words as though they were hard to say, as though she feared the answer. He covered her hand with his and her trembling eased.

"No one died. They are all quite safe."

She pulled her hand away and stepped back farther into the shadows. "Then it is not such a terrible loss, is it?"

Her words so shocked him that James turned sharply to look at her, more carefully this time. He could not see more than a pale oval of a face and dark hair covered by a shawl.

She shook her head slightly. "I know it sounds unfeeling, but a house is filled with things, nothing more. The flames will have them, destroy them as easily as we would eat a sweet. But your family has survived. That is the greatest treasure and your happiness with them the foundation of your true home. You still have them. You are truly blessed."

She spoke with such feeling that he almost believed it. "In the case of Braemoor, Madame, that is hardly reassuring. Your father may have been your greatest treasure. Mine is not."

He turned away from her and wished she would leave. She was silent so long that he thought she might have. He glanced back. She was still watching him though her expression had changed from sympathetic to considering.

"Perhaps, my lord, you've been given this fire as a chance to rebuild not only the house but your family's happiness." She leaned slightly toward him as she spoke, her hands folded in entreaty.

"Why are you trying so hard to find good in this?" He turned towards her fully, but still could see little more than an encouraging look in her dark eyes. "Are you sure that you are not my dead sister come back to tease me? Your optimism is wasted here. I assure you it is hopeless."

"Oh dear, am I lecturing? Then it is, most assuredly, time to bid you goodnight." She angled her head as though it would give her a different image of him. "I do beg your pardon and am much relieved to hear that everyone is safe."

She curtseyed slightly and turned before he could respond in kind. She walked with a slow, measured step. It was an effective exit until she stepped on a sharp twig. Her

"Ouch!" was involuntary and made him realize her slow steps were because she could barely see her way in the dark.

He turned back to the scene playing out before him, dismissing his visitor as some naïve girl who read too many novels. Her insistence that nothing was more important than family struck no chord with him. He did not love a single soul at Braemoor and no one loved him.

Two

As he moved through the cold, wet wreckage, James wondered if his father's illness could be contagious. He felt as though madness lurked a heartbeat away. Without closing his eyes, he rubbed at his forehead, willing the headache to subside. The pain refused, persisting as a dull ache behind his eyes and at the back of his head. It radiated into his neck muscles and down his back so his entire body felt the insult.

He eyed the doorway, tested the floor, and stepped carefully into the remains of the library. This room had burned with spectacular fury, the flames fed by the books, maps, and paintings. All lost.

Mixed with the charred wood were the ashes of the book he had been reading before he had left for town. Rousseau, he recalled.

He sat heavily on the rock foundation. Yesterday he'd found this place ablaze. Only yesterday. He felt years older, felt as tired as a man could and would not deny the guilt that made his pounding head a kind of just dessert.

If he had stayed home this would not have happened. He had needed to meet with the trustees, but his trip to London had been nothing less than an excuse to run. And it had worked. The trip had tilted his world to a more appealing angle. With the help of the voluptuous and generous Henrietta he had managed to forget the responsibilities of the

estate for hours at a time. He had traded three days of pleasure for this catastrophe.

James kicked at a scorched and empty frame and wondered if they would find anything worth salvaging. Not
here. But there could be bits and pieces in the other wings,
the ones that had escaped complete destruction. He looked
around the room, up toward the place where the ceiling
mural had once been. Verrio's months of long hard work destroyed, as were the world maps and globes his father had
collected, the three marble busts of the Greek gods his
grandfather had commissioned from Italy. Did marble burn?
He supposed anything would if the fire grew hot enough.

He stood up, started to shake his head and stopped as the
headache rose up again. He walked down what he thought
was a hallway and through what he recognized as a doorway
and then realized this opening had once been a window. He
stood in the inner court in the shade of the burned-out walls.
The sun beat down with merciless brightness. What he
wouldn't give for a little rain, or a cloudy day? Something
that would ease the dust and the smell.

He heard footsteps and turned towards the sound. Simon
Marfield approached, his expression full of apology. He
might be the bearer of bad news, but James felt a spurt of
relief at his arrival. Seeing Marfield reminded him that life
went on. Somewhere beyond this, the world smelled of
more than smoke.

Marfield looked around, shook his head but forbore to
comment on the wreckage. "My lord, several items have
come to my attention this morning and they will not wait."

James nodded. "And I have news of interest from London."

Marfield nodded in encouragement.

"First, the good news."

Marfield's smile grew.

"The trustees say that the marquis can rail all he wants.

He can send a notice to every newspaper in the land. Any threat to the succession is impossible. I am his heir, his marriage to my mother is valid despite what happened after. He can do nothing to keep me from inheriting."

James looked at the charred remnant of frame dangling from a wire. "And, should I ever marry, my sons are the legitimate heirs, regardless of his intent not to recognize them."

"Very good, my lord." Marfield spoke the words with emphasis.

Simon Marfield currently viewed marriage as the most wondrous of estates. James did not share that opinion. From his vantage point, marriage promised little more than a nightmare of deceit and dominance. It was enough that his father could not disinherit him. He had decided long ago that he would have no wife, no sons. His brother's children would inherit the title. He and his father might agree on nothing else, but in that they did find common ground.

"Further than that, Simon, the trustees will not go. Since the Marquis continues to recover from his apoplexy they are unwilling to formally turn the estate over to me. To quote Beaufort, 'we would need more compelling proof of permanent incompetence.'"

Marfield shook his head.

"Those were his exact words. They would need something more before they wrest control from him and give it to me."

Marfield pursed his lips and nodded. "Do you think that they would reconsider after this?"

"He really did start the fire?" The ache in his head thrummed more urgently.

"We have no proof, my lord, and no one has tried to question him, but his bed in flames roused his nurse from her stupor. She said that she saw him standing by the bed, staring at your stepmother's portrait with flaming bed curtains behind him and an empty candle holder in his hand."

With a grunt of exasperation, James pressed his fingers to his forehead. "Yes, and we have no true way of knowing the truth of it. Though she did save his life. That nurse presents another matter we must resolve. God knows that most of them drink to excess. It's her superstitions that are intolerable."

"I can watch out for her, my lord, especially with the marquis in the cottage near mine."

"You have enough to do without becoming a guard dog." James leaned against the rocky wall outcropping. "I must admit I have more than a little sympathy for the royal family. At least we Braedons are not in the public circus. With a quiet nod from the trustees, I am the one who runs Braemoor."

"Yes, my lord and I see no reason for it not to continue that way."

Oh, how he appreciated that loyalty. Simon had the heart of true gentleman, more so than half of the ton. "My only worry has been that my signature would not be binding on any agreements that I might consider."

"Like the land at Highton Rock you are trying for?"

"Some day I will grow used to the idea that there are no secrets here." James shook his head in a long-suffering gesture of resignation. "How did you learn of it?"

"Collington asked me what you could want the land for. He always thought it worthless and has been trying to find a use for it for nigh on thirty years." Marfield looked disgusted. "As if I would tell him why you wanted it even if I did know."

"My brother Rhys has a need for it, but let that be our secret, eh, Marfield?" When Marfield nodded, James smiled. "I will call Collington's confusion a triumph, even if it is a very small one. I must take my pleasure where I can."

He looked around the ruin.

"And you, Marfield, have some news for me." He gestured to the crumbling wall. "My new study."

Marfield was an intense sort and James could tell that he saw no humor in the suggestion.

"I thought that since the estate office is still useable, my lord, you might prefer to move your work there."

"Very generous of you." James stood up, turned his back to Marfield and stared up at the sky visible through the jagged beams overhead. "Or is it that you think I have wasted enough time in self-pity?"

He wheeled back to face Marfield who shook his head in urgent denial. James waved off his embarrassment.

"You might not think that, but I do." He nudged a toe through a pile of ash and shards of porcelain. "I really came here to see if anything could be rescued."

Even as he spoke he bent over and picked up a box he had unearthed. Gaming counters, the white of the ivory box only a little streaked with soot. He dusted the top and flipped open the lid. The counters inside rested on unmarked velvet. He held it out to Marfield. "How can it be that something this fragile survives and there is not a trace of the statuary or even the library ladder?"

Marfield's face lit up as he took the box. "Huzza! my lord, how encouraging! Who knows what else lies buried here?" He looked around as though several other items might magically appear. "We will have to organize a careful search before we clear away the debris."

They began to walk along the outer wall, toward the estate office. "Why do you speak as though you were in charge of this? Prentice is abed with his broken arm but surely the Lannings, both Mr. and Mrs., will want to supervise." Indeed he would have thought the housekeeper would be here right now, glorying in her seniority.

Marfield did not answer. His silence stretched to a full half minute.

Finally, James stopped walking and looked directly at him. "Come on, man, it is not possible to make this ache in my head any worse."

"My apologies, my lord." He began worrying the crown of his hat with nervous hands. "There is no easy way to say this. Mrs. Lanning has left her post. She told me today that no respectable housekeeper would tolerate the marquis' behavior. And, according to her, a fire started by him was the final insult. She took her husband and her two daughters with her."

"She quit? Lanning too? Good God, Lannings have been here for generations!" Why did he feel surprise? If he had an option, he would be long gone himself. "Did you offer to increase her pay? A housekeeper and butler will be difficult to replace."

"She said it would take a fortune to keep her here."

James leaned forward. "Did you ask what she considered a fortune?"

"No, sir," Marfield shook his head decisively. "That would only set a bad example for the others. If we pay the Lannings to stay, the rest will find out quick enough and think loyalty inadequate compensation."

"True enough. Still, there is a message here." James rubbed his forehead. "Pay a bonus to the staff who remain. That will convey, I trust, the value that we place on their continued service and include the house steward. Prentice may be abed awhile but he is still a valued employee."

Marfield nodded.

"I suppose the under butler can assume the butler's post, but where will I find another housekeeper, especially with Mrs. Lanning's daughters gone with her? Is there anyone

else on the staff who is prepared to move up? Do we even need a housekeeper? There is, after all, so little house to keep."

James had meant that as a joke, granted a morbid one, but Marfield took it as seriously said. "My lord, if I could help I would be happy to. I can organize some of the servants." He looked back toward the burned out shell. "First, we would have to make sure it is safe for them to work. After that we must make an inventory of the loss and arrange some living space and items essential for your comfort."

"My rooms are untouched, Simon, and as for the rest, comfort is the last word any of us would use to describe Braemoor. Why should that change? My father's second wife used to say that the only thing Braemoor did well was breed ghosts. Unhappy ones."

"Yes, my lord, but you will need some place to work and we must arrange some room for dining."

They turned the corner. The smell of burnt offerings lingered, tickling the nose and poisoning the air, but the west wing had escaped any damage. Marfield pushed open the door halfway down the wall and held it for James. The land steward followed him into the office that until this moment had been his.

"Please sit there, my lord. This is yours now." He gestured James to the seat behind the desk. Marfield took the seat opposite and placed the box of gaming counters on the desk between them.

What a generous soul you have Simon Marfield, James thought, as he sat carefully in the creaking leather chair. "Simon, you might have to sacrifice your desk to the estate's greater good." James noted that Simon had already cleared it of papers and ledgers. "But I will not have you give up the work you do so well. Continue with the planting. We are all depending on you. A good crop, healthy sheep, and a good price for wool will do more than anything else to convince everyone that Braemoor and the Braedons are not living under some ill star."

"But who will direct the indoor staff?"

"I suppose we must send to one of the agencies in London."

"Yes, but the Season starts shortly and town fills rapidly. Besides the situation here would require a personal interview." Marfield's voice trailed off at James's questioning look.

"Exactly how would you describe the situation here?"

"Difficult." Marfield spoke without a moment of hesitation, ruining his conviction with a stammering apology.

"For God sake, stop the apology man. Calling this a 'difficult situation' is like calling the war with Napoleon a slight misunderstanding. You are too kind."

They sat in glum silence. James looked at Marfield and nodded, ignoring the wince of pain echoing in his head. "You are right, Simon. There is little likelihood that the agencies will be able to find anyone acceptable at this time of year, especially on such short notice." James rubbed his forehead.

"Sir, could you ask some of the ladies in the neighborhood for assistance?"

James nodded, but who to ask? Who would help and not consider the request a general invitation to involve themselves in Braemoor? "Most have gone to London. There is Mrs. Heron."

Marfield straightened and shook his head slightly.

James nodded and did not even consider asking why Mrs. Heron was not a wise choice. Who else had not gone to town?

"My wife, my lord?"

Marfield mentioned her so tentatively that James was loathe to say no. Jenneth Marfield hated him. It had been all his doing and seemingly impossible to resolve. He was still

trying to find a way to gently refuse and save all three embarrassment when Marfield spoke.

"I'm sorry, sir, I spoke without thinking. That would not work at all." Marfield grinned at some private joke. "She would help in any way, my lord, but her housekeeping skills are too new and she is still confined to bed most mornings. Our child makes his presence felt even before he takes a breath."

James sat back in the chair and pressed his temples.

"My lord?" Marfield's tentative voice had James looking at him with a sideways glance, nodding slightly.

"Could you ask the widow in Penfield?"

"No." Marfield knew of Janet? Of course he did. They all did. Never mind that he and Janet had both been discreet. Their relationship was of many months standing, certainly more established than his recent distraction with Henrietta in London. Everyone would know of his regular visits to the "widow in Penfield." Still, he would do nothing to encourage his mistress to think of their liaison as anything more than temporary. "No, Simon, I will not ask her."

"Yes, my lord. I beg your pardon." Marfield blushed. His embarrassment was vaguely irritating.

"One year of marriage has turned you staid, Simon."

The steward raised his shoulder in a half shrug of agreement.

James could almost hear the man speak, though his lips remained pressed in a tight line: *The Braedons live by their own code, my lord, and I want none of it.*

"Your loyalty and obvious affection for your lady is everything that is admirable, Simon Marfield. Please let me blame the headache for my meanness."

Marfield nodded and the tightness left his lips. He looked away for a moment and then spoke with enthusiasm of a new discovery. "There is a French woman staying in the village with the Vicar. Mrs. Marfield tells me that she came in hopes of a post at the Young Lady's Academy in Little Madison. However it appears that they did not wish to hire a widow. She might be available for an interview."

"Your theory being?"

Marfield shrugged. "I thought that since she's French she might be more accustomed to dealing with our difficult situation." Marfield's self-satisfaction increased as he repeated the phrase and claimed it for his own.

James smiled with genuine humor. He wondered in what way Marfield considered a French woman better equipped to handle this household. Because everyone knew the French were an odd lot or because they were actually able to speak that nonsensical language? He'd heard both explanations more than once as the *émigrés* from the Revolution had moved from London and into the countryside. "I wonder, but it is at least a possibility."

"I could speak with the Vicar and see if he thinks she might be suitable."

"I think the suitability of our all-male household may be more to the point. Mrs. Lanning had age and that hulking husband of hers to protect her. I hope this Frenchwoman is as desperate for employment as we are for help."

"Oh, my lord, no one has ever implied that this household is not a safe one for any maid or lady. Your father is ill, everyone knows that, most especially the Vicar."

James considered his options for a moment. There were damned few. "Be sure she does not drink." Though how anyone could tell that in advance, James had no idea. "We can already lay one disaster at that door. If she is not too old or feeble, we can only hope that she finds the Vicar, his wife, and all those children as boring as I do and is longing for an escape."

Three

Marguerite loved children, she truly did, but if this infant threw up on her one more time she would cry in vexation. *Eh bien,* she could only fault herself. The fire at Braemoor had awakened memories she had thought long gone. With her sleep a mix of dreams and half waking reveries she had used her best gown to cheer herself up.

So far her dress had survived Baby's attention. But if his colic persisted it would be no time at all before her shoulder wore a badge of motherhood that she had not earned.

She shifted her light burden so that he could see the garden. Had spring come at last? Days of warmth and the softest of rains gave her hope. In the north it would be a lie. Here in Sussex it might be the truth.

Marguerite sighed in appreciation as a warm breeze brought the scent of spring to her. The snowdrops had come and gone and color bloomed everywhere. Did Baby find as much pleasure as she did in the primroses? Perhaps he did, though his sigh turned into a yawn that ended in an indelicate hiccup.

"Ma'am?" A maid tiptoed into the garden, using the tentative voice Marguerite had grown used to. Yes, she came from France. Yes, if she spoke without care her English would be tinged with the slightest of accents, but she had spoken the language since childhood. She could grasp complex sentences. The maids had yet to be convinced.

She turned to young Betty. "Yes?"

The maid hurried forward and lifted the baby into her arms. She looked at Marguerite, speaking slowly. "Someone from Braemoor wishes to see you in the study. The Vicar is with him."

Could it be the man from the other night? How had he found her? She had tried so hard to be as anonymous as the spirit he had accused her of being.

It had been no less than impolite to rush over to view someone else's misfortune. Still, it had been rude, not wrong. Her mortification eased. If the Vicar found out, she would be terribly embarrassed. But the Vicar knew her circumstances. He understood her need to go, to see for herself that everyone was accounted for, no one lost.

What could the man want? Had he thought of a way for her to help? She had offered.

Betty must have misunderstood her silence because she began the sentence again, this time speaking in a louder voice and even more slowly. "There—is—a—man—to—see—you."

Marguerite raised her hand. "Yes, I do understand and thank you, Betty. Why do you think someone from Braemoor would wish to see me?"

The maid clearly had a dozen ideas but seemed hard pressed to translate them into words of one syllable.

"I suppose I shall go and find out." Marguerite rose from the bench and started toward the door, still lost in her worrisome speculation.

"Ma'am?" Betty's voice called after her.

When she turned the maid patted her own shoulder and Marguerite realized she still wore the cloth she had used to protect her dress. With a laugh she brought it back to the maid. "Thank you, Betty. That would not impress anyone would it?"

They laughed together at the image and Betty used the cloth to wipe the new spurt of white dribble on Baby's chin.

Marguerite hurried toward the garden door. Before she reached it, Abel and Aaron jumped from the nearby bushes. Yelling their loudest, the boys brandished the wooden swords they used to threaten anyone who came too close to their hiding spot.

She held up her arms in surrender and they stepped aside in silence to let her pass. Boys were the same everywhere, were they not? Never enough space to contain them, never possible to talk quieter than a shout, and always, always into mischief.

She paused at the mirror in the hallway long enough to tidy her hair and straighten her cap. She smoothed her dress and went to the library door. She could hear voices within, including the high timbre of Mary's fourteen-year-old version of a lady's conversation. She must be acting as hostess for her mother. The clock had not struck noon. Mary's mother would still be abed.

Marguerite loved children, she truly did, and dear Mary was the exact reason why. The Vicar's only daughter tried so hard to be precisely what she thought her parents expected and was blossoming before their eyes.

No doubt Baby would be even more endearing when his digestion improved. And someday Aaron and Abel's imaginations would be more entertaining than vexing. Mary, however, glowed with the perfection of childhood, at that moment when maturity beckoned. Everyone rose as she entered the room. Mary gave her a huge grin. *"Bonjour,* Madame Voisson."

"Bonjour, Marie."

The tea tray stood nearby and Mary moved to pour her a cup.

"None for me, my dear."

With a nod, Mary returned to her seat. They all ignored

the sound of a tear as Mary stepped on her hem and a rip echoed through the room. Perhaps it was a seam and easily mended.

In an effort to control her nerves, Marguerite assumed her best-practiced look of polite interest and turned to the man seated next to the Vicar. He was a stranger. *Thank you, Lord.* He had the look of a gentleman though she recognized his clothes as one step away from well-made.

It took a few minutes for the Vicar to make the introductions and for Mr. Marfield to acknowledge her.

She sat in the chair and settled comfortably. The Vicar's sonorous voice was suited to the pulpit. Marguerite loved listening to the bass music of it. She would watch his lips move and enjoy the rumble of sound without hearing more than a word or three. Unfortunately when she heard the words "looking for employment" and "housekeeper" she knew she should have listened to the words much more carefully, not merely admired the sound.

She looked from one to the other of the gentleman hoping for a further clue but they both watched her, and waited.

"You have heard that I had hopes of finding a position teaching French at the Academy?" she said.

Mr. Marfield nodded politely, apparently equally aware that she had been found lacking.

After a few more moments of conversation, to which she now paid close attention, Marguerite found that Braemoor needed a new housekeeper and Mr. Marfield hoped that she might be willing to help them—for a time.

The Vicar added that last phrase. He spoke with such decision that Mr. Marfield accepted the limitation without demur.

Or were they so wretched at Braemoor that any conditions would be acceptable? From what the man had said the other night, that could be the truth. *Bien,* even if they had hoped for someone with more experience, there was a mischievous angel at work here. For no matter how great their need at Braemoor, her need most certainly exceeded theirs.

She had originally thought that she might stay on with the Vicar for as long as she could help with the children and whatever else might need her attention, but the situation had grown awkward. She enjoyed the children and yet the Vicar's wife had only grudgingly welcomed her, and lately the Vicar himself had been growing more constrained and less at ease in her company.

As the two men prattled on about pay and days off and the "unusual needs" of Braemoor, Marguerite considered her situation. It would mean seeing that man again. That should pose no problem. Despite his intimation that she lectured him, she had meant to give sympathy. Surely he would not fault her for that.

And who could be better suited than she to such a task as Mr. Marfield described? True, she had never been a housekeeper, but was more than familiar with the duties even if she had undertaken them in a smaller house and had she not watched her *chère Maman* direct a much larger house in the early years? How difficult could it be?

None of her inadequacies seemed to have come up in Mr. Marfield's earlier conversation with the Vicar. Marguerite decided she would be a fool to mention them. Besides, the Vicar seemed relieved to be rid of her. Was it because she was French that he saw her as temptation?

He certainly had done nothing to embarrass her. And she had done nothing to encourage him, far from it. She had spent most of her time caring for the baby, working with Mary on her French accent, even helping in the kitchen.

It hardly mattered anymore for she could see God's hand in this. Perhaps she had finally found her place.

* * *

Two hours later she sat in the chaise with Mr. Marfield, her belongings tied to the back and her future before her.

"You understand, Madame, that Viscount Crandall must interview you?"

"Oh, yes." Marguerite lied. She had never heard of a Viscount Crandall, though she had a dreadful feeling she had seen him before. If her employment was uncertain then why had they brought her trunk along?

Why had she not listened more attentively when neighbors had come to call on the vicar's wife? She loved a friendly gossip, but here it had little meaning since all the names were unknown to her. Now she did know a name and had no one to ask.

She had tried talking with Mary about Braemoor as she packed and changed into her most serviceable black gown. After her things had been taken downstairs she insisted on repairing the tear in the hem of Mary's dress.

Mary stood admirably still for the brief time it took. Even with those extra few minutes, all that Mary could tell her was that since his illness everyone knew the marquis for a madman, kept in a straitjacket under lock and key exactly as the King had been. That sounded more like the forbidden novels Mary read than the truth.

At the last, Mary gave her a fierce hug and begged that she be allowed to come visit soon. Marguerite promised to invite her, aware that once her mother understood Marguerite's change in station, their acquaintance would end.

She glanced at Mr. Marfield. "Viscount Crandall is related to the marquis?"

"Yes, ma'am, the viscount is his son and heir. He is handling the business of the estate while the marquis recovers from an illness." Mr. Marfield blushed and asked. "I beg your pardon. Would you prefer to be called *madame?*"

"Ma'am is quite acceptable. I live in England, as I have

since childhood. And while I will never be English I like to think that I have learned to blend in."

Marfield spared her a quick look, and then turned his full attention back to the horses.

"What is it?" With a huff of annoyance, Marguerite turned fully towards him. "You do not think I blend in? Why? You must tell me. I have been here more than fifteen years. How can I still appear French?"

A commotion in the road spared Mr. Marfield the pain of answering. Two conveyances vied for the right of way and the sound of the quarrelsome voices distracted both of them.

"The greengrocer from the village." Mr. Marfield said. "And I suspect the other is yet another group of people come to see the result of the fire."

He hesitated only a moment and apparently decided not to become involved in a discussion that showed signs of turning violent. With a flick of the reins, he turned onto a track located conveniently to their left. Though not well maintained, it *was* well used. The chaise moved as quickly as the rutted road would allow.

"If you do not mind, Madame Voisson, I should like to introduce you to my wife. I am sure she would be very happy to give you any support that she can."

Oh, thank you, God, thought Marguerite, finally acknowledging the nerves that named this adventure as more of an ordeal. *Please, let Mrs. Marfield be someone I can talk to, someone who has some idea of exactly what this position entails.*

Shortly they came upon a series of picturesque cottages lining a path. Trees clustered in front of them along a rise to the east and behind them lay a scattering of trees and the rolling expanse stretching away to the Sussex Downs. She could see sheep grazing. She sighed in appreciation of the serenity of it all.

The door of the end cottage swung open and an incredibly pretty woman stepped into the tiny yard. She had been wearing an apron, which she now had in one hand. She raised her other hand in greeting. The smidgen of dirt on her face attested to her activity. The blue hollows of fatigue around her eyes looked completely misplaced in a face otherwise unlined.

None of that detracted from her greeting. "Simon, how lovely. And you have brought a guest. Please come in for some refreshment."

Ah, how beautiful, Marguerite thought, *this is a true love match. Someday I hope to hear every romantic detail.*

Mr. Marfield leapt down from the seat and turned to help her down, while looking over his shoulder, addressing his wife. "I am so sorry, my dear. I am pressed at the moment. It appears the gawkers continue to abuse the road to Braemoor and I must clear them away for the goods we need must have easy access. Can Madame Voisson stay with you for an hour or so? I will come back as soon as Lord Crandall can spare time for an interview."

Mrs. Marfield nodded, though her husband barely waited for an answer. He leapt up to the seat and urged the horses into motion before his wife could do more than acknowledge the cursory introduction.

Marguerite found the cottage as tidy as she had expected and much brighter. There was more than one room and she could hear someone in the kitchen, a maid most likely. As soon as Mrs. Marfield had seated her in the chair closest to the fire, she excused herself "for a moment" and disappeared through the door to the back of the cottage.

Marguerite tried not to be obvious, but looked around with cautious interest. It was surprisingly spacious.

After a few moments the reason struck her. Clearly, two

cottages had been converted into one. Outside it looked like two. From the inside she could see that where there should be a door someone had placed a large dresser standing against the wall. The interior wall perpendicular to it had been removed and the ceiling and floor patched with real skill. So, the marquis was not mean with his funds, or, at the very least, wished to keep his steward happy.

Mrs. Marfield returned and took a seat next to her. Marguerite's nerves stretched closer and closer to pure anxiety as the silence lengthened. "Your cottage is very cleverly contrived."

"Yes, yes, it is." Mrs. Marfield spoke as though her thoughts had been elsewhere. "It will suit a family quite nicely. There are two bedrooms and it is much cozier than the dower house would have been."

"There is a dower house?" She would do her best to make polite conversation and hope for an opportunity to ask her other, more personal questions.

"Yes, there is. Mr. Marfield asked me if I wanted to live there when we first came here from London. He said it could be made livable in a trice." She gave Marguerite a totally feminine look. "He can be very impractical."

"Only in your best interests, I am sure." He had seemed most judicious to her, but marriage surely gave one a different perspective.

While Marguerite waited for Mrs. Marfield to speak, it occurred to her that this interview might be more important than the one with Lord Crandall.

"Madame Voisson, Mr. Marfield tells me that he is bringing you to Braemoor in hopes that Viscount Crandall will offer you the position of housekeeper?"

She might sound all business but Marguerite heard a nuance of dismay.

"Yes," she replied, careful to remove all the accent from

her words. "We both hope that I will prove suitable and even the Vicar and his wife send their support."

"I see." Mrs. Marfield sat silent again for a long moment. "I am so sorry, Madame. So very sorry." Mrs. Marfield shook her head with earnest regret. "I must be honest with you. Yes, it is true that they are in great need of a housekeeper at Braemoor." She sighed in disappointment. "But, Madame, you will not do at all."

Four

"You see Madame Voisson, you are much too young."

Marguerite raised her hand to push a lock of hair behind her ear. "Mrs. Marfield, I am twenty-nine years old." Or she would be in less than eighteen months. "I am a widow. I am not young. It is only that I am so short. That is the reason. If you look closely you will even see that I have some gray hair." She rather hoped that was a lie, but trusted that Mrs. Marfield was too much of a lady to actually inspect her.

"I have never yet seen a housekeeper who is under forty." She shook her head with sincere regret. "And there is no way you can stretch your age to that extent."

Marguerite tried to speak, but Mrs. Marfield had not finished. "Be that as it may. Gray hair or none, there is an even greater obstacle. You are much too lovely."

"Oh, Mrs. Marfield, that is unfair. I will tell you that indeed I have been refused employment for a number of reasons, but never that one." Indeed her looks could not compare to Mrs. Marfield's or her own *Maman*. No, she would describe herself as no more than passably pretty, the overall effect influenced by the fact she still had all her own teeth, strong and white, and the pox had not marked her face.

"It would be false of me to say that this is the employment I had hoped for, though I think I should be quite good at it."

She bit her lip. "If you are being frank with me then I must be honest with you."

Marguerite looked down at her hands, clenched in her lap. She forced them from their death grip on each other and tried to think of something that would turn this woman into her champion.

"I have no means and no prospects, Mrs. Marfield." She looked at her hands again and hated telling the truth. "If I must return to London, I have no more than two guineas between myself and starvation."

She could go on and explain that there was not a soul in the world who gave a thought to her welfare. That none of her previous employment had been satisfying. That she wanted and longed to find some place for herself where they would welcome her, where she could contribute something, where they would mourn her when she died. But who needed to hear such thoughts on a lovely spring day?

It occurred to Marguerite that Mrs. Marfield had not responded. She looked up, prepared for the hardening of her eyes that meant rejection. Instead she saw tears. Mrs. Marfield looked down quickly, her cheeks pinkening with embarrassment.

"Oh please, I am so sorry." Marguerite reached over and touched the woman's hand. "Do not be distressed. I must simply trust in God. He has some wondrous plan in mind for me, I am sure. 'Tis only that I felt certain that this situation was intended for me."

Marguerite looked about for her bonnet, suddenly determined to put this very bad idea from her mind. If she left quickly, she could walk to the village and be bound for London before evening. They would surely send her clothes later.

She made to stand when Mrs. Marfield looked up. Her eyes were clear and filled with a mischievous determination. Curious, Marguerite leaned closer, inviting her comment.

"It seems my years as an actress will stand me in good stead, Madame." Mrs. Marfield smiled with a conspirator's glee. "Who would ever have thought it? If you wish to be a housekeeper, we shall give you the look of one."

"You were on the stage? What a surprising coincidence. I did consider it myself, but decided my looks would not make up for my lack of true skill nor did I have the nerves to face an unknown audience every night."

"Believe me, my dear, the unknown audience is the least of the challenges."

Marguerite nodded. "Your story appears to have a happy ending."

"Yes, it does." Mrs. Marfield turned suddenly very serious. "And, please God, I will never take the gift of Simon and this life for granted."

Marguerite's eyes now filled with tears and Mrs. Marfield laughed. "I see we have at least one thing in common. However my inclination to tears I can blame on my condition." She patted her stomach and Marguerite understood that she was increasing.

Marguerite gave her the smile she was looking for. "How lovely for you and Mr. Marfield. We can blame my French heritage for all my extremes of emotion."

With a nod that came close to sealing their friendship, Mrs. Marfield made her decision. "In the London theatre we did not use makeup much." She rose. "But come with me and I will see what I can do to make you appear closer to forty than twenty-nine."

The person who stared back at Marguerite from the mirror an hour later looked surprisingly like her last memories of her mother. Her hair, streaked with flour that made it a vulgar if effective gray, was drawn into a tight unbecoming knot at the back of her head.

Maman's gray had looked quite beautiful streaked through her black as it was. How Marguerite longed for hair that dark. Hers was a poor imitation of *Maman's* raven-winged sheen.

And the lines around her lips and eyes were very convincing. Jenneth, for by now they had progressed to first names, had shown her how to apply the shadow beneath her eyes. That seemed easy enough to master, but the lines around her lips and eyes took a delicate hand. She was not certain she could manage it.

"When I first joined a troupe we played near Bath. We were only five and had to devise ways to age both men and women so we could play multiple roles." Jenneth stood back and examined the results. She nodded. "I do believe that this is subtle enough to be convincing." She added a light dusting of powder to set her efforts and nodded once again.

"Madame, I am not sure that I am doing you a favor. The Braedons are a difficult lot and Lord Crandall the most difficult of all."

Marguerite nodded, hoping for more.

"It is not that we are more than mere acquaintances. We do not move in the same circles in spite of my husband's employment here."

Mrs. Marfield's apparent satisfaction with that did nothing to ease Marguerite's growing anxiety.

"I will tell you this. Never feel you have no friends. If life becomes too . . ." she paused searching for a word; "If life becomes too complicated you can always come to me. I vow Mr. Marfield and I will help you."

Marguerite did not find her promise reassuring. What was so difficult? What was so forbidding?

They both heard the carriage crunch to a stop. No more time for questions. One more chance to reconsider. They looked at each other and with mutual nods began the charade. Mr. Marfield would be the first test.

It turned out that he barely noticed her. He was still in a rush. Beyond inquiring after his wife's health, he did no more than hurry Marguerite into the chaise and turn back toward Braemoor.

As they entered the gates they came upon a dilapidated-looking house. Vines crawled up the front, more menacing than appealing, and cracks had damaged at least one window.

Mr. Marfield urged the horses past the short drive and gestured towards it with his whip hand. "The dower house. You can see that it is not so very old. The current marquis' mother lived there, I believe. No one has used it in years."

Yes, she could see it now. Neglect rather than disaster made the place look shabby.

As the carriage moved on, panic gripped her. She could not do this. She could not manage a house, even if it were only the size of the dower house. And Braemoor was so much larger. It would have servants and a cook and a garden and not one but two lords.

She almost blurted out her confession to Mr. Marfield, when Braemoor came into full view.

The breeze shifted at the same moment and with it came the acrid smell of charred wood. Suddenly engulfed in a nightmare recollection of fire, chaos, loss, terror, Marguerite pressed a lid on the Pandora's box of memories.

At that moment someone called to Mr. Marfield, and with a word to Marguerite, he excused himself and leapt to the ground.

Wicked stains of smoke and fire marked every window opening, no glass remained, and the gaping holes looked like outlets of hell. Marguerite began to shiver.

The fire here had brought no death. All the same, these windowless holes spoke not of opportunity but of pain and resignation.

Even with no flame she could imagine Satan making the rounds of his handiwork checking the beds in each of the soot-darkened rooms and wondering where all the tenants had gone. At that very moment Satan did appear.

Marguerite covered her mouth with her hand, almost crying out at the incarnation of her worst childhood nightmare.

It took only a moment for her to realize that this was no devil, or at least not like one she had ever dreamed.

She lowered her hand and leaned forward for a closer look, almost sure it was the man she had met on the rise.

He stood back a step or two from the window, but she could see golden hair and a virile body. Indeed his white shirt and cravat contrasting against the dark of the window hole was what made him visible. She watched him scan the surrounding area and then his gaze settled on her.

He did not smile. Indeed his face remained cool and impassive. Yet, something in him reached out to her as though he were a tempted angel who had not yet fallen. As though she were the one who might be his redemption.

"You are seeing the worst." Mr. Marfield recalled her attention with a start. He climbed up to the seat as he went on. "The oldest wing was not damaged at all."

The horses moved toward the back of the building and Marguerite looked up at the window once again. It was empty. He was gone.

As quickly as doubts had assailed her, they disappeared. This was not France. She was not a child. That person in the window had been a man, not the devil.

With those certainties came the conviction that she could manage this ruin. It might look completely unlivable but had she not lived in just such a place for years? She might not have the experience of a traditional housekeeper, but this post could hardly be described as traditional.

With newly restored confidence she turned her attention back to the building and tried to see beyond the destruction. This must once have been very impressive. It was very old, though not a castle, most likely built to impress rather than protect. The later additions only added to the grandeur.

The grandness persisted even though most of the building was nothing more than scarred stone walls and burned-out timber.

She turned to Mr. Marfield and found him watching her. She gave him a reassuring nod and he looked relieved.

"If you have seen enough, Madame, I should like to escort you around the rest of the building on foot so you will understand the terms of your possible employment."

She waited as Marfield passed the reins to a groom. The boy stared at her from beneath lowered brows as though that made his interest less obvious. *Bien,* she thought, *for I am interested too.* She nodded pleasantly at the boy and he turned beet red, which surprised her. Surely she appeared old enough to be his mother, perhaps even his grandmother.

As they made the circuit, she found it as Mr. Marfield had said. Two sides of the square building were totally destroyed; the third appeared to have significant smoke and water damage.

There were piles of wood and debris, scraps of fabric and frame. No one had yet made any effort to sort through the charred remains. There was activity however. A group of men in the midst of the courtyard worked at erecting a scaffold to support the inner wall of the least damaged end of the north side.

She turned to Mr. Marfield who explained, "The viscount thought it wise to add some support until we can determine if it is structurally sound."

"Yes, that makes good sense. You will want to reclaim as much as possible from this wing before it is exposed to the elements, but not at the expense of safety."

He nodded and they moved around to the undamaged west side of the house.

The afternoon sun bathed this wing in light. Sunbeams

glazed the windows and warmed the gray stone. This was as welcoming as the place could be, she decided, and tried hard to let this image take the place of her first.

Mr. Marfield led her to a side door. It led into a roomy office, with walls of the same stone as the exterior. Those walls were, for the most part, insulated by shelves and high dressers, the shelves and drawers filled to overflowing with papers and books. There was a desk with a chair on each side of it and a fireplace that was not in use. The room was empty.

With a brief apology Marfield opened an inner door and, leaving it ajar, moved down the hall obviously looking for the viscount.

Marguerite rubbed her hands together and pretended that the chill came from the remains of winter that had seeped into the walls, not yet warmed by the spring sun. The smell, dust, even the beginning of mold, tickled her nose a bit short of a sneeze.

She walked to the one window, framed by shelves. Five books lay on their sides, edging over the shelf encroaching on the window as though coveting the empty space. She put her hand on the bindings and found them warm to the touch. *Are they as greedy for the heat as I am?* She left them where they were, even though the sun would surely damage them.

She debated reopening the outer door to let in more light and warmth. Instead she stood at the window and closed her eyes basking in this *soupçon* of summer. She heard the door open and spoke to Marfield without turning, her head still raised. "Even with a fireplace this room must be cold in winter."

"Until yesterday, warmth has never been a part of life at Braemoor. I thought I made that clear when you visited me on the hill last night."

The voice was not Marfield's.

Marguerite turned with a start. He was even more appealing than he had been when shadowed by dust and soot or framed by the ruined window. That wonderful bright golden hair, swept back from a high forehead, the enigmatic gray eyes, the mouth, so unforgiving. Put together they conveyed an arrogance more tempting than intimidating. What would make him smile? What would it feel like to hear him laugh? *Oh my,* she thought as she recalled Jenneth's words. *Truly, he could complicate my life.*

Five

Thank heaven for her disguise. He would not find her half as interesting as she found him.

She curtseyed. "I beg your pardon, my lord. I thought Mr. Marfield had come back."

He bowed in turn. "He sends his apologies for a less than formal introduction, madame. Unfortunately, the scaffolding will not cooperate and he hopes to give it and the workers the guidance they need. It is quite urgent." He spoke without a trace of humor and no real apology despite the formal words. His superiority diminished the appeal of his amiable looks. This was just as well, she decided. Living with temptation would not be pleasant at all.

"I am Madame Marguerite Voisson, recently arrived in Sussex from Yorkshire, applying for a post as house-keeper."

The viscount spoke in his turn. "I am Viscount Cran-dall. I represent my father, Marquis Straeford, who is ill and unable to conduct any business."

How odd to have no one perform the introductions. Marguerite took it as a sign that none of the conventions applied here. She hoped that would work to her advantage.

The viscount held the chair for her and seated himself behind the desk. The chair creaked ominously and he paused before settling. Marguerite ruthlessly curbed her amusement and made a mental note to find a chair better than this one as soon as possible.

The viscount looked at her for a moment and then massaged his temple.

Ah, she thought, *his head aches. And whose would not under these circumstances?*

"Could you tell me, Madame, what brought you to Sussex?"

"I came here in hopes of finding employment as a teacher of French at the nearby Academy for young ladies." Marguerite moved her hands from their death grip on the arms of the chair and folded them neatly in her lap.

"And you were not able to come to an agreement there?" He narrowed his eyes only a little, turning polite curiosity into an inquisition.

Obviously, she thought with some asperity. *If I had a post there, I would not be enduring this torture.* She swallowed that sentence and spoke carefully, wishing for the sense of excitement she had felt only a few moments ago. "No, the headmistress seemed quite determined to find an older woman."

"Older?" He looked puzzled.

"I think, my lord, that I must have used the wrong word." She realized her mistake instantly. "They were looking for someone with more experience as a teacher." She hardly wished to imply that she had a problem with the language, what else could she do? At least it was a sign that Jenneth's makeup was convincing.

He nodded with a considering twist of his mouth. "You were staying with the Vicar?"

"Yes, my lord. He was a friend of my uncle in Yorkshire and his wife offered me a place to stay while I sought employment."

"Is there any point in my asking what experience you

have as a housekeeper?" The viscount looked down at the desk, picked up a letter opener, tapping it on the blotter.

"But of course." Marguerite straightened in her chair, her anxiety fading. There was a difference between arrogant and insulting. "I may not have worked as a housekeeper, not precisely, that is. As you may have been told, I come from France. I spent my youth on an estate similar to this one. It was burned to the ground during the Revolution and still I lived there a good while after that even though the family was gone."

Pleased with the practical sound of that explanation, her confidence grew.

"I have very particular experience in dealing with a house in such a state as Braemoor, which may be even more to the point than my experience as a housekeeper."

He would have spoken, but Marguerite held up her hand.

"A moment more, my lord." She would tell the truth, but to do so she must speak her piece exactly as she had practiced it. "I came to England with my aunt and we settled in Yorkshire where she soon married a surgeon. As they aged, I kept house for them until they both passed away."

"A touching saga, Madame." He continued tapping the letter opener against the desktop. "I still would like some assurance that you will be able to manage a staff of this size."

Marguerite pursed her lips, erasing the smile that had crept out when she spoke of the Osgoods. She could practically feel the chill that kept his heart so safe.

"Mr. Marfield tells me that the house steward suffered an injury last night." She matched his formality. "And that the butler left with the housekeeper. Mr. Marfield said that there is an under butler prepared to move up. With the house steward recovering, I can assume that I will by default direct all the servants for the time being. I will care for the furniture and linen. Food and condiments, candles and stores of all sorts. And in addition to the regular list of responsibilities, I will supervise the salvage and restoration of items from the burned-out wings of the house. I assure you that I have had years of experience doing all these things and with far fewer resources than Braemoor commands."

"Does the wisdom you so generously shared last night come from the same experience?"

Oh, she wanted to stand up and walk from the room. His insults could drive patience from a saint.

"Last night I wanted to be sure that no one had suffered the same kind of loss I did, my lord." She looked at him with anger in her heart. "No one deserves that kind of pain." *No matter how insensible he is.* She added the last silently to herself, only with the greatest of effort.

"You are right. No one deserves it. Least of all a woman who is without protection."

She looked down at her hands clenched in her lap, her eyes filling with tears. Better he should insult her. Sympathy would be her undoing.

"Your references?" He held out his hand for them. "I assume you have some."

"But of course." This time she did smile, with as much patronizing disaffection as she could muster. "They are for my hoped-for position as a French teacher, however you will see that they address my flexibility and enthusiasm which are more pertinent to this post."

It was as insolent as she dared be. Marguerite handed him the packet of papers and waited while he perused them. He looked at her once with sharp assessment and returned his attention to the third letter.

Why that look? she wondered. She had not included the letter from the modiste she had worked for last winter.

Her letter hardly cast her in the best light, but that post had not suited her at all. They had both agreed on that.

It would be different here. She would be doing something important at Braemoor, more important than helping vain women with more money than taste. One need not look farther than the burned out walls to see that. It would be the perfect place for her. She was certain of it until she looked carefully at the man for whom she would be working.

While the viscount read the last of her references, Marguerite tried to imagine dealing with him on a regular basis. Without a lady in the house she would discuss menus with him and could not imagine that he would care a jot for what he ate. Would he have a preference for lavender water scenting his bed linen, would he even notice if it was missing? With the house steward unavailable would she be expected to maintain the wine cellar? If there still was a wine cellar.

He stood up and walked the length of the room. Then turned toward her with his back to the window.

He stared at her in a most impolite way, and with the sun full on her face, she knew he could see past every *faux* line and wrinkle, right to the heart of her deception. He shook his head slowly and the panic welled up. He had no intention of hiring her.

The silence lengthened while he considered, but until he spoke the words, hope remained. Surely she could convince him that Braemoor needed her, even if he did not.

"My lord, if I can prove to you that I have skills most housekeepers cannot provide, will you consider offering me the post?"

He welcomed her suggestion with the first sign of emotion she had yet seen on his face: a narrow, very small smile. It might be at her expense, but it was real.

What had she said? What had she suggested? The speculative gleam in his eyes had nothing to do with respectable employment. She lowered her face and tried to recall her exact words.

"I think, madame," he cleared his throat as though trying to control his amusement, "I think, madame, you do not mean precisely the intimacy you implied."

She glanced at him, immeasurably relieved by this gesture of understanding. "My lord, what I meant was that I would be willing to work without pay for the first month, until I have proved my value to the household."

He narrowed his eyes, his good humor gone, and somehow that closed the space between them. "Madame, although you speak English beautifully, it is exactly such a misspoken phrase as this that indicates how unsuitable. . . ."

A resounding slam startled them both as the outer door smashed against the bookcase. Marguerite jumped up from her seat as several volumes pitched to the floor. An old man stumbled into the room, throwing a walking stick ahead of him and grabbing hold of the shelf nearest for support.

Dressed in breeches and a shirt, he wore no cravat and no jacket. His bald head shone with sweat and he panted with the effort of escape. Not that he could run. One side of his body sagged noticeably as though his bones had aged out of all proportion to the other side. As he moved into the room, he dragged the aged part of his body with effort. Looking around the room, he espied the viscount, and swore. At least it sounded like swearing to Marguerite, though the words were a jumble of sounds that she did not understand. When he had finished the diatribe, the old man turned his attention to her.

"Who are you?" he demanded.

She curtseyed, for surely this was the mad marquis. "I

hope to be the new housekeeper, my lord." She kept her words simple, unsure of what he could grasp.

"You ain't ugly enough to take Mrs. Lanning's place."

The viscount moved forward. Marguerite raised her hand as if to stop him. "I am old enough, am I not?"

"Stupid question to ask me. Can you make a pastry?"

"Yes."

"Can you preserve fruits?"

"Yes, I have a particular fine receipt for preserving candied orange flowers."

"Can you brew coffee?"

"My lord," she bowed, "Of course I can."

"Rotgut." He cackled at his version of a trick question. He turned to his son. "Take her for a week, beat her, and see if she is up to the work."

"My lord!" Had he said that the viscount should *beat* her? No one beat employees in English households. She found some reassurance when she noticed that the viscount looked equally appalled at the suggestion. She turned back to the marquis. "Surely, my lord, you mean that the viscount should *hire* me to see if I am up to the work?"

"That's what I said." The marquis worked his way over to the chair behind the desk and thumped into it, losing much of his authority as he sank deep into the leather and let his body go limp.

It reminded her so forcibly of Mr. Osgood on one of his bad days she knew, despite the rumors in the neighborhood, that madness was not what ailed the marquis.

A hurried knock at the door distracted all three of them. A woman and two men fell into the room. They began a barely coherent explanation, but when they saw the marquis, they stopped and lunged at him. From their behavior you would guess him four times faster and twenty years younger than they.

Marguerite stepped forward, blocking their progress. "Please, you will upset the marquis. He came to assist Viscount Crandall in this interview."

She turned to the marquis and putting her hand under his arm encouraged him to rise. "We are finished, are we not, my lord?"

Her face was close to his and he started back for a moment. Did he find her touch an insult? But no, he raised his good hand to cover hers and narrowed his eyes as if to focus on her. "Gwynie?"

Her heart ached for him. He looked so confused and as if what he asked for would set his whole world right. It sounded like "gimme" to her. Perhaps he meant, "Give me?"

"Tell me, my lord," she urged with as gentle a voice as she could command. "What can I give you?"

He shook his head and reared back. "I want a cup of cattle dung and I want it now."

She laughed out loud. One could not call it the most polite thing to do, but she could not contain her relief. She knew what ailed him. How odd that her Mr. Osgood's lingering awful illness should prove a boon to her.

Marguerite knelt down next to him, since he showed no inclination to rise. "Is it a cup of tea that you wish, my lord?"

"Yes, exactly."

"I am sure if you will go with. . . ." she turned and looked at the three and the woman stepped forward.

"I'm the nurse, Mrs. Beecher."

Marguerite nodded approval and ignored the woman's dirty apron and unkempt hair. "Why, you must be the one who saved his life?"

The woman nodded with a jerky pride.

"The viscount will know his father is in good hands."

Marguerite stood up and tried, a little harder this time, to get the marquis to stand.

"Here, my lord, will you allow Mrs. Beecher to take you to a warmer room and then she will bring you your tea?"

He gave no answer, though he did not resist the urging of the nurse. Marguerite stepped back and let the threesome move him. He treated them with a stream of words that once again sounded like cursing though they had no coherence. Marguerite stood at the door and watched them a moment, remembering, and doing her best not to let sensibility better her sense.

She turned to the viscount. "Did you plan that test?"

Six

The viscount watched the troupe leave from the window. Without looking at her, he shook his head. "I wondered if you had, madame."

He turned his attention back to her. When he gestured her to the chair Marguerite understood that the interview had not ended after all. The viscount did not sit. He walked behind the desk and stood with his arms folded. "How did you understand what the marquis wanted?"

Marguerite settled in her chair, her nervousness fading. *Bien,* she thought, *this I can answer so much more easily than more detailed questions about housekeeping.* "Mr. Osgood suffered an apoplexy. . . . "

"A moment, Madame. Who is Mr. Osgood?"

Precisely how many details did he want? "Bien, my lord, I believe I told you that the woman I called my aunt married a surgeon. Miss Morton, my aunt, brought me to England and raised me here. When she became Mrs. Osgood I went to live with them and they are the couple that I mentioned earlier. I kept house for them and then for Mr. Osgood after his wife died."

Marguerite stopped abruptly. The viscount sank into the chair, no doubt exhausted by the effort of following the convolutions of her childhood. She wished for the hundredth time that she could think of some efficient explanation for the chaos of her life. "Am I telling you more than you wish to know?"

"Yes." he answered with an accompanying nod. "And I listen only because I hope I have a personal stake in your monologue. Continue."

"My lord, I am sorry for the boredom, but this next is important. Please do listen." She could almost admire his ability to insult and decided not to take it to heart. Besides, two could play at this.

He gave her a slow nod and she continued.

"Mr. Osgood had his seizure three years ago and I spent these last few years with him, caring for him and praying for a complete recovery. I truly thought it would happen. He recovered his speech, even if he did have some confusion. And he learned to walk again. He even mastered the stairs if he had a hand to help him. But he did not complete his recovery. He died not six months ago, from an inflammation of the lungs."

She paused a moment.

"Continue, Madam, for I suspect you are about to reach the part that will actually interest me."

Oh! she thought, *he badly needs a set down.* She allowed herself a very discreet huff and continued as instructed. "When Mr. Osgood could speak clearly again, he reminded me of an article I had translated for him from the *Histoire de l'Académie.* It describes one man's observations of his problems with speech following a mild apoplectic seizure. In this case the man, a learned scientist, found that he could not pronounce the words that he wanted though he knew exactly how he wished to reply."

She leaned forward. "My lord, this is the important part, for this scientist wrote that he would speak other words than those he intended and that he did not always realize his misstatement."

She spoke the last sentence with particular emphasis and

saw with satisfaction that she had his full attention. She relaxed. "I see that your father will use a wholly inappropriate
word in an otherwise normal sentence."

The viscount nodded.

"Mr. Osgood had a similar affliction and found it a great
burden, though once I grasped the problem it grew easier to
arrive at an understanding of what he wished to say. My
lord, does your father fly into unaccountable rages?"

James nodded, this time with emphasis.

"Mr. Osgood felt extreme frustration and would occasionally throw things in anger. It surprised everyone when
he did as he was well known for his patience."

"No one has called my father patient."

"But you must see how awful it would be to wish to convey an idea and be denied the words. Especially if one were
accustomed to being in charge."

"And being in charge is something that the marquis has
perfected." James drew a breath and looked at her in a considering way. "You amaze me, madame, for you have
explained it to me exactly as his physician did when the
apoplexy first came upon him."

"You knew all this already? My lord, it is vastly annoying
to tell a story one's audience has heard before."

"And, I assure you, even more annoying to listen to it. But
your knowledge of his condition and your willingness to
deal with him is the very thing that will set you apart from
almost everyone else in the place."

He began toying with the letter opener again. "So nursing
is another of the talents you have acquired in all your years
and experience."

"Yes," she replied cautiously, unsure if he meant this as
an insult. She had seen the marquis' nurse and heard tales of
others from Mr. Osgood. "Yes, I have cared for the sick, but
Mr. Osgood was as family and I am not so reduced in circumstances that I would hire myself as a nurse. Well, yes, I

am so reduced in circumstances that I should consider it, but it is, beyond anything, demeaning. And how is it you have no chamber nurse?"

"We have had no need of one these last fifteen years so when the last nurse left service she was not replaced. And then it proved a challenge to find someone willing to care for a man as confused as the marquis." James finished with a nod. "And although Mrs. Beecher may have saved the marquis' life, it is equally true that she drinks too much and beyond that has an inclination to superstition that produces ghost and evils at her every turn."

"Surely one must expect ghosts in a place as old as Braemoor." He would not frighten her with that prospect. "You yourself mistook me for one last night. Perhaps there will be fewer apparitions in the cottage where the marquis lives now."

"One can only hope." He leaned forward slightly. "Ridding her of her superstitions is the least of two evils. I want you to instruct her in correct behavior. What your Mr. Osgood would expect from a nurse. I will hold you responsible for her behavior. Do you understand?"

"Yes, if there is another disaster involving the marquis, the nurse and I will be fired without consideration."

"Oh excellent, Madame. You do show a complete grasp of the situation."

"Thank you, my lord, however if that is so, might I remind you that you threaten to fire me before you have actually given me the position."

He stood up and so did she, only a little afraid that her impudence would cost her the offer.

"You are hired. For a month." He walked over to the window and looked out a moment with his back to her. "And after that time, if I am satisfied, your temporary status will be suspended."

Marguerite nodded. She walked a few steps closer to him

and picked up the books that had fallen to the floor. The first was a volume on sheep breeding and another on how to treat fruit blight.

"How eager you are to begin your work. I warn you that I do not impress easily."

Let him think what he will, she decided, as she placed the books on the shelf. The task gave her a much-needed moment to control the elation that made her all but dance with delight. Her joy was out of all proportion to the situation.

She turned to face him once again, pleased that she had control of her expression.

He mentioned her salary, a generous thirty guineas per annum and then dulled the pleasure by adding, "If you survive your temporary term."

"And accommodations, my lord?" Indeed this did worry her, for any number of reasons.

"I am sorry to say that the housekeeper had her suite in the north wing and it is beyond use of any kind. Marfield will contrive an office for you in this wing where you will be able to interview and deal with the staff as needed."

Marguerite nodded. It had a satisfying air of substance.

"But as for a suite of rooms, I think you must be satisfied with one of the cottages. The one between the Marfields' and the one the marquis is using. That will allow you ample opportunity to supervise Mrs. Beecher."

She nodded again, more in charity with him than he might suspect. She already knew the cottages were clean and solidly built. Living apart from this all-male household would ease any sense of impropriety if her true age were ever discovered.

"You will begin immediately."

"That will suit me perfectly, my lord." She spoke as if she had a choice.

"Marfield will show you to your cottage and introduce

you to the rest of the staff. After that he has his own work to do. You are not to bother him at any time."

"But of course. That is understood." She spoke with authority and liked the feel of it. "May I arrange to speak with the house steward when he is able?"

He nodded and turned back to the window again. Marguerite assumed that she had been dismissed. He turned abruptly and spoke again as she moved to the door

"Before you go, madame, there is one other thing."

He walked closer to her and raised a hand as if to touch her face. Shocked by the gesture, Marguerite swung her arm up to stop him.

He took the raised hand and very gently turned it over as if he would kiss it. The intimate feeling of his fingers on her bare hand had an amazing effect, much too intimate, but impossible to ignore.

As quickly as pleasure filled her, dread overcame her. Would familiarity of this sort be a condition of her generous salary? She had heard such arrangements existed, but the Vicar had insisted that the Braedons were not so inclined.

"You are not ugly enough for a housekeeper, Madame."

Mon Dieu, she thought, *what am I to do?* She tried to pull her hand from his, but he held it with more pressure than before.

"The marquis said that you were not as ugly as Mrs. Lanning and showed his eyesight is improving. But, madame, neither are you as old as she is."

They stared at each other for a long moment as Marguerite grasped that this had nothing to do with seduction. Her recovery was slow, the touch of his hand too much of a distraction and Marguerite's eyes fell first, as good as admitting the lie. But all was not lost. Had he not already promised her the post?

She gave a slight curtsey. "*Eh bien,* I did not expect my disguise to work forever, but had hoped it would be convincing for longer than twenty minutes." She wanted to smile but thought better of it. He still held her hand and he might interpret a smile as an invitation.

"If you please, my lord, how could you tell? I thought it such a fine effort."

"Indeed, Madame." He raised her hand. "However, these are not the hands of a woman in her middle years and, if that were not enough, your second reference letter refers to you as—and I quote—"a young woman suited to a post of a mature nature." Besides that, you said that you were a child during the Revolution. If I wanted to trouble my mind with the arithmetic, I am sure I would find that you could not be much above your mid-twenties."

He looked at her with a leveling stare. At best, she would describe it as uncertain, and at worst, skeptical. "One month, Madame Voisson. I trust you harbor no more secrets?"

She shook her head, still holding his gaze, not looking away this time.

"I will not tolerate dishonesty in an employee, and certainly not in one on whom the harmony of this household depends."

"Thank you, my lord. I appreciate your consideration and must tell you that I am optimistic. I see a future filled with opportunity."

"Tell me in a month if you still see it that way, Madame. If you do, I will be convinced that my father is not the only imbecile in residence."

She laughed out loud and knew some gratification when he joined her with the smallest of sounds that she was sure was laughter.

James walked toward the cottages. Beyond the crest and with the trees as a break, the air felt cleaner. He drew a deep breath, welcoming the smell of anything not tainted with smoke. There were lights from several of the windows but none from the cottage that his new housekeeper would be using.

Madame Voisson. He shook his head. Did she still have a husband somewhere? Or had she chattered him to death?

Oh, that was unfair. She was talkative, but not thoughtless. Pretty, but hardly beautiful. Young, but not immature. And his headache had evaporated for all of an hour. James could hardly credit her for that, but having one less thing to worry about had helped.

And why was he not worried about this new employee? Because one thing she did have in excess was charm. He had never thought to require that in his staff before. It would be worth watching to see if she could use it successfully to sidestep her more obvious lacks. Time would tell. And it would not take much time at all.

He stood outside the door to his father's cottage. He heard no voices, no shouting; and he hated to interrupt a rare moment of peace. He would inspect the place some other time.

James stepped away from the door, aware that he'd used the quiet as an excuse to leave. He would most likely have done the same if there had been a tantrum in progress.

He walked down the narrow lane and stopped at Marfields'. Despite the sturdy front door, he could hear laughter inside and a loud voice as though someone were calling from one room to another. He hardly wanted to intrude on this scene either, but for entirely different reasons.

He raised his hand and knocked. The door opened almost immediately and Mrs. Marfield's spontaneous welcome grew at once more formal. She stepped back and invited him in with a curtsey, "Lord Crandall."

He stepped into the room as her husband came from the kitchen wiping his hands on a cloth, speaking through his laughter. "Jenneth, joy, you must learn not to take the. . . ."

He broke off when he saw they had a caller. His laughter stopped but his smile remained, his greeting more sincere than his wife's. "My lord, how good to see you, but I would have come to your office."

"I needed the walk." James knew he sounded curt, but he wanted to do his business and leave this cozy domestic scene far behind as quickly as possible.

He felt out of place. With good reason. He no more belonged here than Jenneth Marfield did. "I came to tell you that I have hired Madame Voisson. She is much too young." He avoided looking at Mrs. Marfield but caught a slight grimace. *Ah,* he thought, *so she had been party to that effort.*

"She is too young," he repeated, "but she has the most amazing way of handling the marquis. For that alone I will give her a month's trial."

"The marquis?"

He could tell Marfield had no idea how his new housekeeper had met his father. James explained the interruption and madame's own experience and finished it all by saying: "She will move in next door to you. Introduce her to the staff. Then return to your work and let madame do her job as you will yours."

"Thank you, my lord. It will be exactly as you wish."

James looked around. He had not been inside since the two cottages had been combined into one. "The renovation of the cottage seems to have been a success." He looked directly at Mrs. Marfield. As he did, she moved closer to her husband. "Are you comfortable?"

She stared back at him as though what he said had a double meaning. "Yes, my lord. This is our home and I am very comfortable here."

He nodded. The floor alone looked clean enough to eat from. Is that what she did all day? How long could it last? How long before she missed the excitement of London? Until that happened, he had determined to do his best to accept her for Simon's sake and the good of the estate. The ache in his head edged up a bit.

"The truth is, ma'am, that I have no idea what shops Braemoor has used in the past or even from whom we get our meats and fish." He bowed to her. "I had hoped that I could impose on you to share your expertise with our new housekeeper."

She hid her surprise, but he could read the confusion in her eyes. "I would be happy to help her, my lord."

He seriously doubted that she would ever take what he had to say as straightforward, with no hidden meaning. Indeed, she had come by that dislike honestly.

His modicum of business complete, James hurried away from the cottage, then forced himself to slow. You would think he ran from pestilence. That was as good a term as any for the kind of wedded bliss Simon Marfield had embraced with such enthusiasm.

Like a disease, it came on strong, often with little warning and left disaster in its wake. He knew that would happen as soon as Mrs. Marfield tired of this performance, grew bored with Marfield's ardor and longed for London.

Love did not endure no matter what Robert Burns's poetry might claim. His mother had proved that. Running away had been her solution to a loveless marriage.

The marquis had not fared much better. True love might change someone, as it had his father in his second marriage, at least until Lady Gwyneth had died. But the changes she induced in her husband had not survived that trial. He might not be able to avoid the consequences of his father's bitterness, but he could surely learn from his experience and avoid the same trap.

He was sorry that someone as trusting as Simon Marfield had been caught in love's clutches and would have to learn the hoary lesson.

James looked back down from the rise that he claimed as

his favorite spot. Braemoor looked viciously unwelcoming. Someone, indeed it looked like Madame Voisson, walked along the wall of the east wing, peering in window holes and testing a door that had melted shut.

God help him, he had hired her out of pure desperation.

She bent down to pick something up and dropped it almost as quickly. After looking around for a cloth to wipe her hands on and finding nothing, she shrugged and wiped her hands down the side of her dress.

It was only for a month. Would she even last that long? At that very moment, Marguerite Voisson looked up, saw him, and raised a hand in greeting.

Seven

James stood at his dressing room window, watching the activity below. With the window closed he could only hear the buzz of her words, but Madame Voisson spoke with such animation that he did not need to open the window to make out her intent.

At the very least he could credit her with early hours. The garbled voices from below had awakened him twenty minutes ago. Seven o'clock and they were already beginning the clean up.

The group clustered around her listened with complete concentration and he finally gave in to curiosity and pushed the window open a few inches. The courtyard remained an echo chamber even with two walls completely destroyed.

"You see, *mes amis,* this is very much like a treasure hunt. It appears that there is nothing here but ashes, however we do not know for certain what lies underneath. Perhaps more ash. Perhaps something as untouched as this."

She brought out the box of game counters he had uncovered the other day and the group moved closer with a unified breath of surprise.

"So we must all be very careful to move slowly as we collect the ash into the baskets. I know how much we would like to rid ourselves of the whole of any reminder of the fire, but we must move with caution. Is that understood?"

They nodded, again as one.

"Very good. Since you understand that this will be slow, dirty work, I ask if any of you would prefer to work elsewhere? There is much to be done in the north wing, clearing the useable rooms of the smell of smoke."

No one raised a hand.

"Very good. This will take time. Please though, think of it as the first step in rebuilding Braemoor, restoring its beauty and our home. We will begin as a group, working one specific area at a time. Robert, you start over here. . . ."

James pulled the window shut and walked back to the dressing table. Treasures? She thought they were going to find treasures. He laughed in a soft breath of sound. If she were not so charming he would call her a fool.

He walked back to the window and glanced down once again. They all worked diligently, including madame herself. The dust that rose would soon make the work unpleasant and even as he had the thought, one of the younger maids arrived on scene with strips of cloth. Under madame's direction she passed them out to the six workers who paused long enough to tie them around their noses.

By the time he had finished dressing, two hours later, the group of six had dropped to five. Madame Voisson moved from one to the other encouraging each, eventually returning to her own task. Using a part of the foundation as a worktable, he watched her sort through a collection of something that looked like burned papers. With a gesture he read as frustration, she tossed the wad into one of several baskets, completely filled with debris.

How long would optimism endure in the face of constant disappointment?

Even as he watched, all work efforts stopped at an exclamation from one of the men. The rest pulled off their masks and clustered around as he held up a child-sized chamber pot.

Madame took it as though it had some value and placed it in a basket of its own.

James shook his head. A box of counters and a chamber pot. Hardly treasure, but enough to keep them working.

Which he had best do. He left his room and hurried down a back staircase and into the new breakfast room. He could smell coffee and counted three different kinds of muffins awaiting his attention.

James turned to the footman. "Yesterday I had bread and cheese for dinner. How did cook manage to clean and reclaim his kitchen so quickly?"

"Madame spoke some French to him and he worked like the devil all night, my lord."

"So much for his delicacy." According to Mrs. Lanning, the chef had complained constantly of his head or his sore back. More than once James had been tempted to give him something to complain about. With Mrs. Lanning between him and the temperamental Frenchmen that moment had never come. And the chef always managed to assuage ill will with impressive food.

"Delicate he is, my lord. The housekeeper let him cry all over her and forever. When he finished she made him a cup of tea, *your* tea, my lord, and when he finally went to work, she called four to help him and took a hand herself."

When did she sleep? She could not have settled into her cottage much before dinner and Marfield's introductions would have taken a good while. According to Simon, she had spent an hour with Prentice and still found time to work into the night with the chef.

If she did not pace herself there would be true circles under her eyes and gray in her hair.

He ignored the morning paper. There had been no serious fighting in the Peninsula since Talavera the previous spring and a quick glance showed little true news. He looked through the post and saw nothing save invitations he had neither the time nor the inclination to accept. He turned his full attention to his breakfast.

Did her face feel as soft and delicate as her hands had been? They were the hands of a lady, not someone who had spent her last years working.

With her face scrubbed free of makeup and her hair washed of gray, he expected he would find her every bit as appealing as her hands had hinted. He could still feel her fingers in his, the way she gave up the small struggle and let them rest in his, the way they trembled, the way they curled around his when he ran his thumb over her knuckles. He wanted to kiss them and almost had.

"Damnation!" He tossed his napkin aside, startling the footman and upsetting the toast rack at his elbow. She was his housekeeper, not a potential mistress. For God's sake, he didn't even know what she looked like. And still he daydreamed about kissing her hand? He needed to visit Janet, he decided. He would. Tonight.

When he reached his office he found Marfield loading books into a small trunk, with two of the stable hands carting a second out the door.

"Good morning, my lord. I thought to be finished before you came."

"Yes, well, madame's enthusiastic efforts had me awake earlier than usual." James looked at the bare shelves. "What is this? There is no need to make space here for me."

Marfield nodded as he removed books and reached for more. "Madame found a room for me to use as an office. The workmen have even contrived some shelves."

"Already?"

"Madame Voisson convinced them that the scaffolding was. . . ." Marfield paused. "Let me see if I can quote her exact words. The scaffolding was a 'monumental tribute' to their skills." Marfield turned to look at James. "She had them so puffed up, my lord, I suspect that they would have worked all night if she had asked."

James moved behind the desk and made to sit with his usual caution. He jumped up and looked accusingly at the chair that had welcomed him without protest.

Marfield's cough did not cover his laugh. "I believe Madame found that chair in the west wing store room. Or at least she sent one of the maids to hunt for one yesterday evening before the light faded."

James gave a long, slow nod and turned again to take his seat. The leather had been renewed with a careful hand and welcomed him with the promise of ease.

He smiled at Marfield and Marfield smiled back. "She is amazing, is she not, my lord?"

"Time will tell, Simon. This is only her first week."

Marfield sobered and began to list the items that made up their regular discussion, with James only slightly distracted by his newfound luxury.

By the time Marfield left, James had a thorough understanding of his plans for planting and the needs of the sheep-breeding program that they had discussed months ago. To act on it this year, they had to begin the process within the sennight. Marfield left with the authorization he'd hoped for, both of them pleased with the morning's work.

James found satisfaction in a staff that did work with minimal direction. Marfield's interest in husbandry and land management relieved him of the responsibility, thank goodness.

Could it be that despite her lack of experience, his new housekeeper would prove as valuable an employee? Despite her late hours last night and the work she did today, she had still found time to make him comfortable. He leaned back in his chair and looked at the desktop. It had been polished and though it hardly looked new, it was as clean as a healthy hand could make it. It held blotter, pen stand, paper and, placed to the side, a carefully written list in an unfamiliar hand.

Madame had written,

> *Please, my lord, both Mrs. Marfield and Prentice assure me that these items must be ordered from London. If you could arrange their delivery, or tell me how to contact your man of business, I would greatly appreciate it.*

There followed a list, with careful description and quantity. It was long, though not extravagant.

Immediately after the last item: *white cotton gloves, three dozen pairs in various sizes.*

It ended with a long note.

> *Prentice remains abed, his recovery slowed by a cut that shows danger of infection. The surgeon from the village expresses concern for its effect on Prentice when he is in such a weakened state.*

It would be easy enough to send one of the older grooms to town with the list and a message for the doctor. Even as he had the thought, James pulled a piece of paper from the stock in the tray. He could assuage the physician's affront at being called to treat a servant by telling him of his father's latest fiasco. Bakerton would move faster than a hare if he thought the marquis needed his attention. Would the physician's opinion move the trustees to a final decision?

While the groom delivered that message, one of the staff from the town house could be sent to the shops with madame's list. He added two or three items of his own and had the groom on the road for town before noon, advising him to return as quickly as possible. Surely, that would impress his oh-so-efficient housekeeper. She would have her three dozen pairs of white gloves before she found a clean place to store them.

He heard voices in the hallway, a laughing, chattering group moving to the kitchen. He rang the bell on his desk and instant silence followed. The footman who stood outside opened the door, but it was madame who entered.

She waited a little inside the door, her face composed, though barely controlling her excitement, longing to share something that she obviously had hidden behind her back.

Her hair had no need of makeup to appear gray and her red-rimmed eyes were sunk in shadows of dirt smudges. Apparently a few hours of such work would age her more effectively than Jenneth Marfield's skilled hand.

"You look terrible."

"We all do, my lord." She let her pleasure show, no less than a grin, her white teeth a marked contrast to the soot on her cheeks and her red-rimmed eyes. "It is a true chore, this sifting of the wreckage. I apologize if their *bonhomie* disturbed you. I thought an early break for dinner would restore their energy and this is the quickest way to the kitchen."

He waved away that interruption.

"I have some things for you." Without waiting for further invitation, she came to him, bringing her hands from behind her back, lifting a basket onto the desk. "I expected that you would like to see what we found this morning."

Before he could tell her he had no interest in her discoveries, she handed him the first item. "The hall porter tells me that this is the tray which held the post. You can see that it is dented and tarnished, but the silver has not melted and it could surely be restored."

He shrugged.

She pulled out a piece of linen and carefully unwrapped the contents, pieces of charred paper, the writing on them virtually illegible. "Harold tells me that there were several letters and other items on the tray awaiting your return from London. He estimates a dozen. This is all that is left."

He looked at the fragments.

"I thought, my lord, that you might like to examine them to see if there is any way you can determine the correspondent and reply."

He said nothing, trusting his long hard look answered her as well as words.

She bristled a bit and her happiness faded. He almost reached out and accepted the letters as apology. Before he could give in to the weakness, Madame Voisson refolded the fabric around them. *"Bien,* my lord, if it is important they will write to you again."

"Exactly. Tell me, madame, how many more bits of household trivia are in your basket?"

She glanced in the basket and then at him. "I think that is all for today. I see that you are busy and there is one other thing I would ask you."

He raised his eyebrows.

"You see, my lord, there is a certain disadvantage to my not knowing the staff well. I would like to let them work on their own while I attend to other of my duties. In order to do that I must know who the most trustworthy are."

He knew the senior servants; their families had been part of Braemoor forever. He knew them and relied on them without conscious thought. But less than a week ago that faith had been destroyed, for despite their ties, every one of the Lannings had left.

He was about to tell her to ask Prentice but apparently he had been quiet for longer than she could tolerate.

"Surely, my lord, some are more trustworthy than others." She looked at him with a sidelong glance. "For that matter, you do not know if you can trust me."

She turned her head so that she looked at him directly.

"Trust you, Madame?" He wanted to laugh and made himself hold it back. "I most certainly do not trust you."

She looked more shocked than offended.

"You come from nowhere or, as you said, Yorkshire, which is as near to nowhere as makes no difference. You pretend to be older than you are and then use your charm to inveigle me into hiring you. Within a day you prove your worth by coaxing the chef into cooking something edible, somehow find a comfortable chair among the ruins, and have the staff enthusiastic about a job that is dirty and unrewarding."

He shook his head on a sniff of disdain. "Of course I do not trust you."

She absorbed his words with narrowed eyes and stood up.

"But I do appreciate your ability as a housekeeper."

"Bien, my lord, then I perfectly understand your regard for me." She spoke with no rancor, without even a hint of offense, but she did not smile. "I will endeavor to give satisfaction." She curtseyed slightly, showing she had mastered the small insult as well as he had, and made to leave the office.

He remained seated, watching her stiff back and fought the urge to get up and open the door for her. She was a servant. She should not have dared to leave the room without his permission.

He could call her back, but what good would that serve? He had seen her upset and he knew that it had nothing to do with his lack of interest in chamber pots and letters reduced to ash.

He had not handled that very well. How could he expect loyalty from someone who worked hard, set a good example, and received no praise? For it was entirely possible that despite her impressive energy and verve Madame Voisson might need encouragement too.

Eight

By the time James found a few minutes to visit the salvage site, daylight had faded considerably. A mass of clouds covered the setting sun and hinted at rain to the west. He passed the staff as they made their way inside. The afternoon sun had made the work hot, tedious, and dirty.

The good spirits of dinnertime had disappeared, replaced by the stolid, mechanical movements of five people who had worked all day with no great success. They bobbed and bowed as they approached him. The footman, Robert, was the only one who looked him in the eye.

"Well done."

The group stopped as one and stared at him with a surprise akin to shock.

"I appreciate that this is hardly the work you are accustomed to at Braemoor." He cleared his throat. "Madame has told you of your bonus?"

They nodded with enthusiasm though their expressions were still guarded.

"Good." He rubbed his hands together. "But there is more behind your dedication than money."

"It helps ease the itch, my lord." He could tell it was Robert who had spoken, but only because of the pokes in the rib that almost knocked him off his feet.

"Money never hurts, I am sure. Nevertheless I want you

to know that you are taking the first steps in rebuilding Braemoor. We will triumph over this catastrophe. We will."

It was not the right space for such a speech. Did he even believe it himself? No matter, the staff did. They straightened and sincere pleasure replaced the more perfunctory kind. He sent them off with a wave; heartened and more certain than before that they would be back tomorrow.

James made his way around the space they had cleared in the last few hours. He wished he could say he was impressed, but at the rate that they worked, it would be months before they finished clearing the site of debris.

His housekeeper stood with her back to him. Even as he watched she glanced over her shoulder and quickly back at the basket in front of her.

He walked up to stand beside her and still she remained silent. If housekeepers were not supposed to show annoyance, it was equally true that they were not supposed to cry.

"They worked hard today, madame. They made progress. Everyone did. Marfield tells me that the stables and outbuildings suffered no damage and they are running as before. He suggested that we could use the workhorses to move some of the larger debris. There is a salvage company from London that we can commission to direct the work when you have completed the initial survey."

He stopped, well aware that this sort of babbling was more her trait than his.

"The ash and dust irritates the eyes, my lord."

She drew a deep wavering breath as she spoke and looked at him with a wide-eyed determination.

Liar, he thought. The track of tears down her cheeks was evidence enough.

James reached over and pulled a piece of scorched, dirty embroidery from the top of the basket. "I would wager my sister, Mariel, would have been pleased never to see this again." How odd that such a silly thing should survive and recall such memories.

"Was it her first sampler?" Madame cleared her throat and straightened a bit, no longer hovering over the basket as though she feared thievery.

"Her first? I suppose it might have been. Hardly a work of art is it?" He shook his head. "Mariel worked at every little bit of her education, though even she would admit that needlework was never her friend." He looked closer at the fabric. "Does one learn letters first or the various stitches?"

Marguerite shrugged and looked at him with a blend of interest and curiosity. Taking the fabric that he held out to her she examined the list of names. "Jamie?"

"My Christian name is James."

"James I can imagine, my lord. Jamie does not suit you at all."

How could it be possible to say James with a French accent? He bowed to her. "I assure you, madame, that Jamie was an adorable infant and an even more charming young lad."

That did make her laugh, finally.

He nodded at the scrap in her hand with its list of names. "Mariel is my oldest stepsister, Morgan is my brother. Our sister Maddie died at fourteen, and then there is Rhys. He was probably not yet ten when Mariel did this."

She nodded, the hurt gone from her eyes, replaced with a look he could only label as longing. "How good that we started here. For it must be filled with happy memories."

"Not entirely." She did not need to hear about those days and he tried never to think of them himself. Surely he could dredge up some memory that would entertain her.

"I made life torture for my brothers and sisters. After all I am the oldest, the leader, and I lived here for years before they were born. I remember once I convinced them that the marquis, our father, had three wives buried in the cellars and that their mother would soon follow them."

"My lord, how awful."

"Oh yes, and Morgan gave me a bloody nose for it. He is such a loyal sot." Enough sentiment. Enough. She was no longer upset. She was smiling.

He looked away from that encouraging air and up at the old stone wall that had survived the fire. "The top floor was the nursery, below that rooms that no one has used for twenty years, and on the ground level are rooms that we used to house guests."

"Prentice made a drawing of the rooms and their contents. Was that not enterprising of him?" Her good humor faded. "My lord, today I left a list for you. . . ."

"Yes. I have already sent to London for the physician who cares for my father. I am sure I can convince him to examine Prentice."

"Oh thank you, my lord. Thank you so much." If she had been smiling before, she glowed now.

"I can hardly afford to lose any more staff." He moved a step away and reached out to test the strength of the blackened wall as he spoke. "Not when good replacements are so difficult to find."

When she failed to answer, he glanced back. The glow had disappeared and she stared at him with a calculating look that he did not find at all reassuring.

"Would you allow some of the field hands to help with this, my lord? Despite your praise," she said with the faintest echo of sarcasm, "I feel that the work is moving much too slowly. Surely you are anxious to rebuild and the more quickly this work is completed the sooner you can begin to replace what has been lost."

"I appreciate your energy, Madame, and regret that I cannot spare the field hands. They are in the midst of spring planting." He gestured to the pathetic bits and pieces in the basket at hand. "And that is hardly worth a day's work."

"Today, we learned what we are about. We all understand better how to remove the debris without damaging anything hidden beneath." She picked up a broken plate. "I think John ruined this with his shovel."

James took the two pieces. "One of hundreds that are still safe in the west wing. Easy enough to replace." He dropped the pieces into one of the debris baskets that had not yet been taken away.

"There are any number of items that I am not sure are worth keeping. In truth, I feel that only you can make that decision." She handed him a mass of toy soldiers, the lead melted enough to fuse them together. "Did you play with these?"

"I must have, but it is Rhys I recall using them." He looked away from her curious look, determined not to be caught in their sentimental trap again and tossed the mess into the debris basket. "Not worth keeping."

With a businesslike nod, Madame turned the whole of the basket in front of her into the last of the large baskets that held detritus. He saw some blocks, several drawings, two ruined dolls and a framed picture.

He reached over and rescued the framed drawing from the rubble, fully aware of her game and annoyed by it.

"Madame, there are indeed memories here." He looked at her steadily, "Not all of them happy ones. Damn few in fact." With Maddie's fairy drawing tucked under his arm, he made to leave. "Each day, please bring any items you think are of value to the estate office. I will examine them when I have time."

"Here, Jenneth, do sit down." Though they were in the Marfield parlor, Marguerite tended to her friend who looked pale and overset. Marguerite draped a shawl over Jenneth's shoulders and handed her a cup. *"M'amie,* drink this and rest a moment. You should not be scrubbing the floor in your condition."

Jenneth leaned her head against the high back of the chair, "Yes, you're right." She sighed. "But I do so not want to be one of those women who take to their beds for nine months." She looked at Marguerite and raised her eyebrows.

Like the Vicar's wife, Marguerite thought as she nodded. She took not a little delight in the fact that she had been in the area long enough to understand this bit of unspoken gossip. "Jenneth, there is some middle ground between constant bed and scrubbing the floor."

"I promise to be more careful. I did do too much today, I admit it, and will not press so in the future."

Marguerite nodded. She would be content with that promise. Already her friend's color had improved.

"We are a pair, Marguerite. That dust must be dreadful. When you came down the path earlier, you needed no makeup to look the part of an aging crone."

"It is just as well I do not have a glass in my cottage, for I have no doubt you are right. Despite a wash, I expect that I still do. And will for the next few weeks at least. That is to the good, though. Even if the viscount has seen through my disguise, he is not likely to tell the staff, is he? Let them think I am older. It is what I wish. Though I suppose there is no such thing as a beautiful crone, is there?"

They both laughed at the idea.

"Tell me, Jenneth," Marguerite said, focusing on the real reason for her visit. "Has the viscount always had this habit? He makes the slightest compliment, and then does his best to undo it! It is so very annoying to be smiling at him one minute and out of countenance the next."

Jenneth looked away and did not answer.

"Oh please, I do not mean this as gossip. I ask so that I

am able to deal with him in a useful way. I have been distracted by it all morning, but first I had to make sure the night guards knew exactly what they were supposed to do. I definitely had to eat some dinner and praise the chef. I had also to talk to Prentice and find a way to convince him that he will never be replaced and that the under butler is doing well. Which, I might add, is a complete lie. Cludde is worthless, and I shall simply have to do his work until Prentice is recovered and is able to hire more staff, for the viscount has made it clear that he has neither the time nor the inclination for more interviews.

"All that time I wanted nothing more than a few minutes to talk with someone who would be able to help me understand the viscount."

"Marguerite, I am hardly the right person to ask about that family, any of them."

Jenneth Marfield may not be the right person to ask, but she remained the only person Marguerite knew well enough to question. When Simon Marfield had left for a meeting with the viscount it seemed a heaven-sent opportunity to talk.

Now Marguerite saw that Jenneth's sympathetic interest had hardened. "Jenneth, you have only to see how his face softens when he speaks of his brothers and sisters. Then you would appreciate how important they are to him."

"He is responsible for them, Marguerite. There is a vast difference between that and familial affection. I doubt that he is capable of true caring."

The sentence ended the conversation with cruel finality.

Or would have if Marguerite had been willing to accept that judgment. Instead she leaned forward in the chair and spoke very quietly. "Tell me."

Jenneth shrugged. "He has no finer feelings. He is selfish and arrogant. He thinks that everyone is the same as he is, interested only in their own gain or pleasure."

This was so far from her own experience of the viscount that Marguerite sat back and shook her head. "Has your husband told you this?"

Jenneth gave a bitter laugh. "Simon thinks he is the right hand of Saint Michael. As close to an archangel as makes no difference."

"You know otherwise?" Marguerite asked with true caution, not at all certain that she wanted to hear Jenneth's explanation for her ill will.

"When Simon wrote and told the viscount that he needed some time for our wedding, Lord Crandall told him to come home and wait until after the harvest."

"Oh my, I can see where that might cause some bad feeling." Marguerite shifted in her chair, more than a little unsettled.

"That is nothing. When Simon told him that he would resign, Lord Crandall came to town. He called on me at my home and offered me money not to marry his steward. That is exactly what he called him. Not Simon, not Marfield but 'my steward'."

Oh, my lord, how could you? Marguerite thought.

"It was because I was an actress, you see. Lord Crandall had no hope that I would be the kind of wife Simon needed and that would mean that his work would suffer and Braemoor needed his full attention. Braemoor, Braemoor, Braemoor. That is all Lord Crandall cares about."

"And yet you are here, after all, so the viscount must have reconsidered."

Jenneth stared down at her teacup. "He had no choice. I told him exactly what I thought of his offer. I am, after all, an actress and I gave him my theatrical best. But you see, Marguerite, what he said so exactly matched what I most feared. Despair haunted me in those days. I wanted so much to escape what life had become and Simon made that possible."

She looked up at Marguerite. "The viscount saw that weakness and tried to take advantage of it. It is so exactly like his father, using money to achieve his ends, using his power to make life a misery for others."

"Oh Jenneth, that is not wholly true. This very day he sent to London for a physician for Prentice."

"You are being naïve, Marguerite. He called for a physician because Prentice is useful to him. If it were someone else, someone like me, he would no more call for a physician than he would dry your tears."

Now she knew that Jenneth's prejudice was unfair. No, he had not dried her tears, he had gone one step better and ignored them, then teased her into a good humor.

"Is there nothing that he can do to raise your estimation of him?" Marguerite spoke gently. "Surely your husband's high opinion must carry some weight."

Jenneth considered the question and then shook her head ruefully. "Simon is loyal to a fault and generous in the extreme. He is a genius at land management, but where people are concerned he is obviously too inclined to champion those whom no one else can hold in regard."

Marguerite wondered if she referred to herself or the viscount.

"I am being frank with you, Marguerite, because I see that same romantic streak in you and the viscount will see it as well. He will have no qualms about exerting his charms to achieve his own ends, to rebuild Braemoor, to make it grander and wealthier with no thought as to the consequences to your mind or your heart."

Nine

Marguerite wanted to argue with Jenneth. Well, not argue; only convince her that her understanding of Viscount Crandall was unfair.

True, he had been less than gracious to her on more than one occasion, but he had hired her even though she had such limited experience as a housekeeper; and just today he had teased her sadness away. So perhaps the kindest thing to be said about him was that he was difficult to understand.

Marguerite stood at her door, her hand on the latch still carrying on this internal debate when the door to the cottage next to hers opened.

It was the marquis' cottage, and the nurse stood in the doorway, her hand in her pocket.

It was past twilight and Marguerite knew that her black dress against the dark of her doorway made her almost invisible. The nurse, however, was lit from behind. She pulled a bottle from her apron, removed the cork, and took a long swallow. She curtseyed to the empty lane. "Thass for you, my lord. May you sleep the sleep o' the dead."

Marguerite wished for nothing so much as her bed. But the slurring of the words made this a more pressing need than sleep. She spoke without moving from her doorway. "Nurse, that is not the best way to handle the charge of the day."

She so startled the nurse that the woman dropped the bottle and it shattered on the cobbles at the entry. She looked around with a panicked eye and made to step back into the cottage.

Marguerite shrank deeper into her own doorway and spoke again. "Wait!"

The command stopped the woman, her panic even more pronounced.

"Did not the fire convince you that drink is unwise?" Marguerite pressed her lips together to keep from laughing out loud. Instead, she deepened her voice and tried to speak as if she was a vision from the grave. The viscount had said that the nurse believed in all manner of specters.

The woman looked around wildly trying to see the source of the voice, but the deep doorway not only made Marguerite invisible, it also cast her voice in an entirely different direction.

"You must change your ways. Pour your spirits into the ground. Abandon this evil for the good of nursing those in your care. Take the fire as a warning. Take heed."

The woman nodded with jerky agreement and made to close the door.

"Wait!"

The woman stopped again, deeper into the cottage.

"Tell me you will do as is commanded."

"All right. I will. I will." She spoke without slurring one word. Clearly fear made as good a sobering tonic as anything concocted by a medico.

"Very good. Keep your word and I will not return. There will be others watching you."

Nurse slammed the door shut and Marguerite moved closer, intent on peeking through the window of the marquis' cottage to see if the woman would do as bid. She tiptoed carefully, hoping to avoid the glass that had showered the path.

"Brilliant, Madame!"

Mon Dieu! Marguerite clamped her hand to her mouth to keep her scream inside and whirled around. She searched the lane, which at first appeared empty. As she stepped away from the cottage a figure moved. She could make out a form, clearly human, clearly the viscount. She stepped closer to the shape, her hand pressed to her heart, willing it to slow.

"Or at the very least, extremely clever." The viscount waited until she reached where he stood.

"Thank you, my lord." She curtseyed, not entirely sure he meant it as a compliment.

He stood watching her for a long moment. Marguerite prayed that he did not plan to send her packing.

"I suppose it was unconventional." She winced when the viscount whispered, "Suppose?" He did not sound angry, precisely, so she continued her explanation.

"You were the one who told me that she saw spirits at every turn."

"I did?"

"Yes, my lord, during my interview." How could he have forgotten any detail of that conversation? Every aspect of it was firmly planted in her memory. "If the fire did not convince her to put down her drink then no ordinary person would be able to do so."

"Madame Voisson, there is nothing *ordinary* about you." He spoke on a laugh. At least she thought she heard a laugh. Surely he meant *that* as a compliment.

"When she mistook my first words for those of a ghost it seemed the most natural thing to use it to our advantage."

He began to walk away and she moved into step beside him. "Did you wish to see your father?"

"No, I intended to fire the nurse."

"You did not trust me to affect a change?"

"I can see now that I was not patient enough." He bowed

slightly and she decided that this was his version of an apology.

"My lord, I visit your father whenever I return to my own cottage and this evening is the first time I saw any hint of drink. I think the two men who help during the day have a steadying effect on the nurse."

"I have no doubt the marquis keeps all three of them dancing. It is one thing about him that has not changed."

They had come across the rise and through the band of trees. From this point they had an unobstructed view of the ruins. Braemoor appeared truly gothic by night. Even the standing west wing rose dark and inhospitable. How could anyone sleep well there, she wondered. "It makes an impressive ruin, does it not?"

"Oh yes, it does."

"One can easily imagine it destroyed in battle, with noble knights fighting to the bitterest of ends."

"Hardly. Built to intimidate and impress by the first Lord Braedon before Elizabeth. Never once a battleground not even during Cromwell's time."

How must the first Lord Braedon feel to see his monument in ruins? "My lord, are there ghosts at Braemoor?"

The viscount remained quiet for so long that Marguerite decided he had not taken her question as playfully as she intended.

"My brother Morgan used to pray that our sister Maddie would come back as a ghost. It was a vain wish. None of us ever saw her. Prentice insists that there is, or I should say, was, a cold draft in the north tower even on the warmest nights. He is convinced that is the sign of a ghost and always refused to house anyone there. As for me, I have never seen a ghost, or even suspected one until I met you on this hill and tonight heard one disembodied voice coming from your cottage."

She laughed. "So I will become part of Braemoor's

legacy. Oh, I like that very much." She considered that this part of her legacy would be nameless and decided it felt better than no legacy at all. "Where do you suppose homeless ghosts go?"

When he only shrugged, she knew he would not be easily cheered. Had he always been so grave or had it been brought on by his father's illness and Braemoor's ruin?

She cleared her throat and tried again. "If the north tower is gone then the ghost who lives there must find a new place to haunt."

"Oh, I feel certain she will."

They stood in silence. For her part, Marguerite strained her ears and stared hard through the dark, wondering if the ghosts might make themselves known. She had no doubt that the Viscount's thoughts were not as fanciful.

He should say good night and make his way down the hill back to the home that even the ghosts had abandoned. No wonder he wanted to stay right here with Marguerite Voisson and her whimsy for company.

"His recovery from the apoplexy has been very slow, has it not?"

"Yes." Just when he had determined to enjoy her always-active imagination, the crooked set to her cap, and her engaging ways, she must turn practical on him.

"My lord, I know it is painful, but it would be helpful to me if I understood his situation."

"Tell me Madame, exactly how would it be helpful? How could knowing the history of the Braedons help?" She asked so many damn questions and for some reason he answered them.

"My lord, I am possibly the only person on the estate who does not know every detail you care to share and many that you do not. Coming to work here as I did, knowing nothing of the family history does truly put me at a sad disadvantage."

"And you would like me to be the one to tell?" He bit his lip. Laughing at her would either make her angry or encourage her.

"Yes."

"Is that all, Madame? Is that all you have to say? I am amazed."

"My lord, are you trying to distract me from my question?"

"Me? Distract you?" Now he did laugh. "Never, never, never! Let me strip my soul and bare all to you. What a lovely way to spend a spring evening."

"My lord, do not be so dramatic. I simply asked about your father."

Fury rushed through him. Where the laughter had come from he had no idea. She was an unrelenting busybody. "His apoplexy happened more than a year ago. Morgan insists that it had been coming on for months beforehand. The marquis had headaches and temper tantrums and lived much too rich a life, hurrying to town and back even in the worst weather. I had been living away from home for years. When word came of his attack, I came home immediately."

What a miserable winter that had been. The news had found him at Westbourne's hunting box enjoying some very entertaining company, an actress with enough brains to be charming both in and out of bed.

"And your whole life changed in an instant."

She imbued the words with drama. When he looked at her, expecting a smile he saw none, but rather somber, even grave understanding. Ah yes, how selfish of him. She had much the same experience herself.

"Precisely, Madame." He looked away. "For a long while we were sure he lay at death's door. Then we were as certain that he had turned quite mad. He made absurd demands. The physician explained that as you did. Still he remains inclined to violence.

"Not with his fists, but only because he does not have the strength. No, he throws things. If you have visited him you will notice that there is nothing breakable in his apartments and very few items that can be tossed at someone."

How did she do this? Draw more from him than he had ever told anyone? Was it because her attention never wavered? Even now she leaned a little toward him, listening as though spellbound. He could smell the mix of smoke and vanilla on her, the one surely a perfume of some kind, the other the result of her day's work.

"You are to be commended, my lord. In spite of it all, you have kept him here at his home, provided such care as you could find, and not even considered sending him away."

"Oh, please, Madame, do not credit me with better motives than I deserve. I insisted that Morgan and Rhys come here to discuss the possibility. I would not make that decision myself. I was not impartial."

He watched the night watchmen making their rounds. They stopped and spoke to each other before moving in opposite directions.

"In the end we decided that he would be better cared for here. Mrs. Lanning hired those two brutes that are with him and the nurse and he did improve. Braemoor had so many rooms that I could go weeks without seeing him. Now I wonder if we made the right decision. In the end he himself destroyed Braemoor, the thing he values most. Me, I hate the place. If I had been here when the fire started, I would have told them to let it burn."

She had no answer for that. Had he told her more than she wanted to know? Now would she, please God, be so shocked that she would stop asking questions and leave him alone?

"How absurd, my lord. You never would have let it burn." She considered the idea a moment longer. "Perhaps it is as well that you came upon the fire so late. You derive all of the benefit and none of the guilt."

Good God, this woman was half mad herself.

"Please my lord, do not look so amazed for then I must defend myself. Did I not explain it before, that first night when we met on this very spot? Braemoor is nothing more than a building and it can be easily replaced and even improved upon.

"It should serve your comfort first and foremost, should it not? Yes, it housed valuable things and dear memories. You know as well as I do that those things can be replaced. The memories will always be yours and can easily take root in the new Braemoor."

He had no want of the memories. Why could she not understand that? "This is not what I expect to hear from a woman who is prepared to spend weeks sifting through every bit of dirt and dust for God knows what."

"It is one of the things you hired me for, is it not? So I do it even though I know the most valuable artwork is worthless compared to love. I told you that I lost my own home this way when I was a child. It did not take me very long at all to understand that there are losses much worse than wood and wool."

"Is there a point to this morality tale? One that applies to you? Or could it be me that you wish to instruct?"

"My lord, that tone of voice is very discouraging. I have no wish to irritate you. Are you so unwilling to benefit from my experience? Sharing my wisdom is the only thing that makes it worthwhile. Do you not agree? Have you not learned lessons from your experience with your father from which others may someday benefit?"

He watched the guards, willing himself to be distracted by the monotony of their set routine. He had answered her first question and he could see that it would only beget more.

"Madame, let me remind you that you have been hired as a housekeeper not as a chaplain. I have no need of a chaplain and, if I did, I would not ask you to perform a task for which you are wholly unprepared. And let me advise you of one more thing. I can see that you have a disturbing inclination to see others as moved by the same high-minded principles that you are. If one considers meddling and endless optimism high-minded." He paused a moment trying to think of something less complimentary than optimism but gave it up as not worth the effort.

"I have answered your questions in hopes that it will help you care for the marquis and leave me as free as possible to deal with the reconstruction of Braemoor. Is that perfectly clear to you?"

"Yes, my lord." She spoke with a quiet submission so completely out of character that he actually waited to see what she would say next. She remained quiet, pointedly so.

She would not look at him, had even turned slightly away from him. He took her by the shoulders and turned her so that she stood directly in front of him.

In the eternity of the second before she looked up at him, he felt the softness of her shoulders, the pulse in the hollow of her throat where his hand rested. When her eyes met his, he let her go immediately, for he saw a disconcerting openness overlaid with a quickly hidden flash of fear.

He turned sharply and hurried down the hill. The guards approached him and then merely waved when he answered their hail. James kept on walking, not once turning back to look at her.

If she had not been afraid, he would at least admit to himself that he was. It had taken all the strength he had not to pull her closer and end their conversation with a kiss.

Damn it all, why did it feel as though she was the one with the power, with him at her beck and call?

Ten

The sun promised warmth, but it had not yet burned off the morning fog that rose from the fields and entwined in the trees. Marguerite hurried down the track. It was no burden to walk back to her cottage, not on such a morning as this.

It could be that the viscount wished for rain for his fields. And, yes, a light shower might settle the dust that irritated their eyes and throats. But even knowing that, she could not do anything less than thank *le bon Dieu* for the blue sky and growing sunshine.

Where had she left her gloves? She would have to find them. The order had arrived from London with admirable promptness, but there were none to spare. At least she was up early enough that the others would not be kept waiting. Most were still at breakfast and she truly had not been interested in eating herself, for the same reason that she had not slept well and was walking back to her cottage in search of her gloves.

She had spent half the night trying to see the world from his perspective. She understood it better now. He felt trapped here at Braemoor with a father who did nothing but swear at him and never showed any affection.

How awful. Even worse than her own loss. While she barely recalled her father, she did know, always, that he loved her.

She even understood the viscount's anger with her. Had she not insisted that he tell her a history that proved more painful than pleasant?

She hurried down the path and pushed open the door to her cottage. The gloves were not on the shelf near the door. She looked under the few things in the room and even felt beneath the covers. Nowhere. She put her hands in the apron she wore and found the gloves nestled against her hip. How vexing. They had been with her all the time.

She paused by the chair near the fire and leaned on the back of it staring at the cold, empty fireplace.

The true reason for her lost sleep had nothing to do with her presumption.

Just the memory of his hands on her shoulders made her heart hammer. The hard gray of his eyes had softened. His lips fascinated her. Then he had let go, very carefully, very gently, and almost ran. He must have been very angry to leave so abruptly, not to escort her back to her cottage. Had he been angry, or had he been tempted?

After last night, he would be even less likely to answer her questions. She could pretend it did not matter but her heart knew that for a lie. She found him fascinating even when provoked to anger. *Bon Dieu,* if that was so, how would she react if she ever found him in a smiling good humor?

Had he seen into her heart when she raised her face to his? Had he seen that she shared the interest, that she was as attracted to him as she had ever been to any man?

She hurried from the room and stopped short on the doorsill of her cottage. From next door, she could hear shouting and the familiar stream of unintelligible curses the marquis favored.

She stepped quickly between the paths and knocked on the cottage door with as much strength as she could command. No one came to the door. No one called. She knocked again, and then blew on her bruised knuckles.

This wrangling had to stop and she would see that it did. Mrs. Beecher must be made to understand the precarious state of her employment. But how could she approach the subject without admitting that she was last night's ghost? A resounding crash had her reaching for the door handle.

As she hurried into the room, the others turned towards her. The nurse was wringing her hands and the two manservants were trying to get control of the enraged marquis. One had been bested and had moved out of range of the marquis' arm as Marguerite crossed the room. Marguerite paused long enough to hand him her own handkerchief for his bloody nose and moved deeper into the dimly lit space.

The marquis sat at table, despite the other servant's efforts to get him to stand and move away from any potential weapons. Most had already been used. The remains of breakfast lay all around him. A pewter mug had been thrown to the floor as well as plates and cutlery. A puppy that appeared to be the only creature happy with the contretemps was attending to food scraps.

"May I help, my lord?" Marguerite did not know why she addressed the marquis rather than the servants, but it did draw his attention. His glare had her looking around for a suitable shield. She did not need one. His expression softened and the fight went out of him on the instant.

"My darling Gwynie, how glad I am to see you."

He stood up. Though he did not move smoothly, he did have his body under control. He took the stick that served more as his crutch and moved to the chair by the fire.

"Come sit here, my dear. And tell me your plans for the day. You must not leave until I have heard every detail. Has the new gown arrived yet?"

He had done this before, mistaken her for someone else.

He had named her for each of his daughters, Mariel and Maddie, and one or two names she had not recognized.

Gwynie, however, was the name she heard most often. It had first happened during her interview, when she had no idea that it was a name and not some misspoken word. All his other confusions had been brief. She blamed them on poor light and his failing eyesight. This time he seemed to think Gwyneth had come to see him. His good humor after the show of bad temper was unnerving.

The three servants eyed her with bewilderment tinged with suspicion.

She waited until the marquis had seated himself and then walked closer and knelt beside him. If she was very close to him, would he recognize her as Marguerite Voisson, housekeeper? "My lord?"

"Yes, my lady." He spoke in a coy, teasing voice.

Oh dear. He was confused, truly confused, but, given his tantrum, this seemed a bad time to insist on her true identity.

"Let me speak to the servants and I will sit with you."

He nodded, sat back and closed his eyes.

She turned to the three, who watched her with true consternation.

"Clearly he thinks I am Lady Gwyneth. You know this has happened before."

They all spoke at once. The nurse shut up the two men with an elbow punch to one's stomach and a kick to the other's knee. "Not when we been around." She turned to the men. "He always did talk to her paintin' what hanged on the wall across from the foot of his bed. It burned."

"Thank you, Mrs. Beecher. That is very helpful. I would appreciate it if you would clean up a bit and then leave us alone. I am sure that a short break would be welcome. I will do my best to calm him and afterward I would speak with you."

Without waiting for agreement, she returned to the second chair near the fire and settled herself. The marquis still had his eyes closed. Was he napping?

She sat watching him and waited and let her own eyes drift shut.

"Is that fool Crandall giving you trouble?"

"Your son? Giving me trouble? Oh no, my lord."

His voice startled her. Had she fallen asleep? True, her night's rest had been fitful, but this was hardly the place to amend that.

"Why are you so tired?" Before she could make an excuse he spoke on. "You should let others do more of the work. I do not want you so fatigued that you would not welcome me to your bed at night."

How to answer this? Surely it could not be healthy to encourage his misunderstanding.

He began to speak again. They were the words of a lover and Marguerite looked around to be sure that the servants had left. They were alone; still she could not let this continue.

"Please stop, my lord." He was making her blush.

"Always so shy, Gwynie, except in the bedroom."

Marguerite cleared her throat and focused on the one word that caught her interest. Gwynie. "Why do you call me that, my lord?"

"You prefer Gwyneth, but you are still such a child to me. Oh not in your age, so much. More in your attitude toward the world. For you it is sunshine and enchantment. I marvel that we can both be acquainted with the same people and understand them so differently. Like Crandall."

Marguerite straightened.

"Do not get in a lather at the mere mention of his name."

Marguerite made herself relax, wondering why this possibility had not occurred to her. Who better to tell her about the viscount than his father?

"I am not annoyed, sir. I was only this moment thinking of your son myself."

"Put him out of your mind. It is what I try to do. He is a constant reminder of Annabelle. A reminder of my greatest mistake. Eh, how many men can say that? Their first wife was their greatest mistake?

"How do I even know that the music master was the first? He was the last. I was sure of that." He laughed with a vicious pleasure that made Marguerite shiver.

"I should have known when the music playing fool fell injured that it would come to no good end. He bled like a stuck pig and took to bed here for weeks. The horse would throw him right at our gate. And it was our gate that he hit. Could hardly turn him away. And she would play the nurse.

"Not sure if Annabelle being my greatest mistake makes me a fool or lucky. She died not one year after she ran off and I met you. Guess that makes me a lucky fool." He cackled at his joke.

This part of the story she knew for it was common knowledge in the neighborhood and Prentice had told her of it as well.

"Crandall has her eyes, Gwynie. I see her face every time I look at him." He lay back into the wooden high-backed chair that could not possibly be comfortable. "She did me a favor when she ran off to France. She did me an even bigger favor when she died. Wish she had taken the boy with her." He stopped talking and closed his eyes.

Marguerite knew shock beyond words. The viscount's own father wished him gone, wished him dead? Did the viscount realize this? Of course he did. How did he bear it? It explained so much: his anger, his bitterness, his distrust.

Marguerite watched as sleep overtook the marquis. Despite his age and infirmity, she could tell that the viscount drew much of his looks from his father. Lord Crandall's gray eyes might remind his father of the reviled Annabelle, but every other feature was pure Braedon.

The marquis must have been a commanding presence before his illness. As the viscount was now. She cringed at the thought of the two strong wills in constant conflict.

They had so much in common and shared nothing. She treasured the idea of family, she truly did, but perhaps this one was too devoid of love to merit the name.

Oh, if she could give the viscount any one thing it would be his father's love. She would have to pray for it, for only God could heal this kind of break. In the meanwhile, she could at least understand where Lord Crandall's anger and frustration came from.

Marguerite went to the door. Mrs. Beecher sat on a stool outside the cottage, smoking a pipe. Marguerite left the door ajar and spoke quietly.

"He sleeps."

The woman nodded and slipped her pipe into her pocket. She would have gone into the cottage, but Marguerite held up her hand and she waited.

"If we leave the door open, you will hear him if he wakens. I would have a word with you."

The nurse nodded uncertainly.

"Mrs. Beecher, you must know that your continued employment is uncertain at best."

The nurse's cautious expression turned bitter. "I saved his life. You said it yourself."

"Yes, but would the fire have happened if you had been awake?"

She looked surprised.

"There is very little that a housekeeper does not hear."

Mrs. Beecher's shoulders slumped a little. That was as close to an admission as was forthcoming.

Marguerite dragged a second stool from under the eaves and sat down. "Do tell me about your rescue."

With an uncertain nod, the nurse turned to face Marguerite. She fingered the pipe in her pocket but did not pull it out.

"You see, miss, it was the candles. They caught the bed curtains. I saw one on the floor and knew the marquis must have knocked it over when he got up. He was out of bed, you see, standing in front of that picture of his wife, talking to it, taking no notice of the blaze nipping at his night shirt."

The nurse drew a deep breath and shuddered. "At first I thought we was trapped. I could tell the fire had gone too far for me to put it out, though I did throw the water and the chamber pot at it. It made no difference.

"The old man fought me. He refused to leave the picture behind and I could not pull it off the wall. It was too big anyway, as big as a person full grown, not some little paintin' you can carry around like most of the nobs have."

"You mean a miniature?"

She nodded. "Miss, I will tell you the truth. You see I had to knock him out to get him out o' there. I was mort afraid I'd killed him, but there was no blood so I thought maybe not. I carried him downstairs. By that time someone else had raised the alarm and alls I did was take him to the wood where he would be safe from the fire."

Marguerite shook her head. "Do you not understand that what you did was everything brave and good?"

The woman's laugh came out as a snort. "What would my life have been worth if I had left him behind?"

"Not much, I suppose. But you would have survived more surely if you had come out alone. Mrs. Beecher, you were smart enough to think clearly in difficult circumstances. Many would have been in a blind panic and thought of nothing save their own lives."

Mrs. Beecher's eyes narrowed in consideration and she stopped fingering the pipe in her pocket. "I saw a fire once. No one deserves to die like that."

"Exactly. For I have seen one as well and I tell you that you behaved in an admirably heroic manner."

The nurse nodded with a little smile this time.

"Having risked your own life to save your patient's, it would be most unfortunate if your later behavior would cost you employment for which you are so ideally suited." She paused and decided to address the practical. "I see that you smoke a pipe."

The woman nodded, her gaze faltering. Honesty did not come naturally.

"I have no objection to that, Mrs. Beecher." She waited until the nurse looked up at her again. "There is no flask in your pocket, is there?"

At this Beecher blanched slightly and shook her head with urgent frankness. "No, I gave that up."

Yes, I know, Marguerite thought, *you gave it up last night.* "And will your abstinence last?"

She nodded with the same urgency and Marguerite let herself be convinced. She could not spend all day questioning the woman even if Lord Crandall had made this another of her responsibilities.

The woman seemed sincere in her commitment to abandon drink. What Marguerite had to decide was whether it was worth her job and the marquis' health to accept her pledge. How could she insure her cooperation?

"Mrs. Beecher, what would make your work easier, more comfortable, if drink is denied you?"

The woman gave her a blank look.

Marguerite tried again, pleased that money was not the first thing that came into the nurse's mind. "Tell me what the demands of your position are."

"I do everything for him."

Marguerite nodded, sure that she did not want to hear every mean detail. "What of his valet?"

"He left as soon as he could tell the old man would never

go to London again. Why would he stay here with a man who did little more than throw things and yell?"

Marguerite wondered if the valet had been related to the recently departed housekeeper. Loyalty was clearly not one of their virtues. "What are your hours?"

"All the day and night. T'others get to go out in the evening once the marquis is put to bed. They get time away. Me, I only get one day a week and that got put off 'cause of the fire. And since we moved from the big house, I clean too."

"That does seem unfair." She looked back into the cottage. It seemed clean enough, though not as clean as Marfield's. It was certainly better furnished, crammed full actually, with pieces rescued from Braemoor.

"I can arrange for someone to clean and someone to come in the evenings for a time, perhaps after tea. Do you think that will give you a more comfortable working situation?"

"Yes, ma'am." She looked very suspicious, not quite able to bring herself to ask why anyone should care.

Marguerite chose not to explain that if she was the one who came every evening, she would be able to maintain a daily confidence that Mrs. Beecher did the work and avoided drink. She did not have to explain her generosity. It would be all the more effective that way.

Eleven

Madame Voisson spoke with far less volubility today. Even if he opened the window, James did not think he would be able to hear what she said. He continued watching, though, until the servants clustered around her nodded and made their way to the work areas she pointed out.

He walked away from the window, but he could still see her as she looked that night, wearing a dark blue dress and frilly cap wholly unsuitable to a housekeeper, her eyes as blue as her dress and sharing with him her words as well as her interest, her warmth, her caring. The vision had plagued him for days.

What did he think he was doing to have touched her that way?

He laughed. It came out a dark, villainous sound that bothered him even more than the memory. At first he might have been thinking about his responsibilities and the need to convince her. One moment later all he could think about was pulling her tight against him, kissing her, tasting her laughter.

Her sweetly curious look had been almost all the invitation he needed. The look of fear that followed as quickly had stopped him. Did she feel the same explosive possibilities that he did?

One thing he knew above all else. It would be best to

never test the answer to that question, or any of the others running riot through his head.

He kept his eyes closed a moment longer and made himself concentrate on the needs of the day: letters to several architects, a letter to Christie's to see who they would recommend to restore paintings, and a letter to his man of business.

The sounds of the nursery reached him, distracting him from his mental list. Some childhood song that made him smile, reminded him of Maddie and Morgan dancing to Mariel's playing. He roused himself and followed the sound to the window.

Indeed, his very own scavengers were singing, still working but singing as they did. At a pause in the rhyme someone began a more rousing drinking song. The rest laughed long and hard before joining in the chorus.

A long echoing *kerchunk* brought immediate silence. He could feel Madame wince even as she hurried over.

James was about to leave her to handle the discipline, but Robert's excitement was so obvious that he pushed the window open so as not to miss a word. This eavesdropping could become a very bad habit. He could not resist.

"I was careful, ma'am, I was. Look, though, there is something very big down there."

Madame peered over his shoulder and looked back at the group with a conspiratorial grin. "It is big. And it appears to be in one piece."

The workers moved closer and she directed two of the others to help Robert clear away the debris. Whatever he had uncovered lay buried beneath some charred pieces of wood and a few good-sized pieces of stone.

James had a better view than most of the workers and could see clearly as Robert hauled it to the surface. It was a chest. Robert grunted as he lifted it up and out of the ground, attesting to its weight. He placed it on the broken wall that held the usual two or three charred items that were certainly worthless.

Madame's voice called over the babble of the others. "Of course we will open it."

She gestured to Robert again. "You found it. You may open it."

The way she said it made it a reward rather than a task, even better than a bonus. He watched Robert swell with pride as a smattering of applause acknowledged the honor. It made James laugh. She would have been a wonder in the army.

"Can you see how to open it, Robert?"

Hurry up, my boy, he thought, *or she will wrest it from you.*

Robert nodded nervously and madame held up her hand for attention before he began.

"You must prepare yourselves. This may be nothing of import or it may be in ruins."

Open the box! James almost shouted from the window. Robert took a hammer and gave the lock a great whack. He missed it, putting a healthy dent in the chest itself.

James could not tell if the chest was leather or wood. If he went down it would be easier to see what material it was made of.

Another whack and the lock fell open. Automatically Robert stepped back and Madame Voisson moved forward. She wore gloves, but could not work the broken latch. With a look, she invited Robert to open it with her. They each grasped an edge of the lid and lifted it so that it fell back, detached from the box itself and fell to the ground.

The crowd pressed closer, looked inside and stared. They did not move for so long that James wondered if they had been turned to stone. Then his housekeeper abandoned all semblance of lady-like behavior, turned to look up at him and shouted, *"Mon Dieu,* my lord, come down at once!"

Of course that very command drew the attention of everyone within hearing distance and before James had joined the group there were at least a dozen others crowded round.

They all stepped back as he approached the chest. His housekeeper stayed in place, barely able to contain her excitement. She stepped back with a sweeping gesture that would have done any actress credit.

The chest was filled with jewels. Brilliant in color against the undamaged white velvet lining, any London jeweler would have acknowledged this collection as the best of his inventory. A diamond parure spilled from one box. The necklace, bracelet, and brooch mixed with the rubies, garnets, and sapphires of the other pieces in a surfeit of glittering color. He saw a gold chain with a cross pendant, several cameos, and other necklaces of amethyst and emeralds. Most lay without protection having fallen from their boxes, some tangled in an obscenely long rope of pearls.

Where did they come from? His stepmother had shared a suite with his father in the south wing. Besides, her jewelry was in London. This wing had housed the nursery and some guest rooms. All at once, a memory surfaced. He remembered what suite lay between the two floors.

He looked at his housekeeper, who could not contain her grin. "I think I have earned my first month's pay already, my lord. Perhaps even my first year's."

He wished he could share her pleasure. Indeed to some extent he did. But as much heartache as wealth lay before them. This collection had belonged to his own mother. Her suite had been in this wing until she ran away.

With a nod, he turned to Robert. "Thank you for your care. These belonged to my mother. The marquis will be pleased to find out that they have survived."

Robert nodded. No grin from him, more like a dazed shock in his eyes.

Madame Voisson stepped forward and addressed the others. "I think we have done a good morning's work. Now we will take time to change, wash and prepare for dinner. Be assured that there is much yet to be done."

No one objected. They turned and trooped into the house, the excitement in their voices guaranteeing that news of the discovery would spread like wildfire.

Here was a new cause for worry. James could think of no way to keep the find secret. Privacy was as rare as comfort at Braemoor, especially now that they all lived so close together.

Robert moved away slowly and turned back at the last moment.

"My lord, would you like me to carry the chest inside for you?"

Hard to let your discovery go, eh boy? James nodded and he and Madame Voisson followed as Robert carried the heavy chest into the estate office. He put it carefully on the desk and, with one last lingering glance, left the room.

Madame stood at the doorway. "We will continue the search later this afternoon, my lord."

He nodded. They would not stop now. A discovery like this would inspire them for days.

She looked at the box for another long moment. "Though I expect that we are not likely to find anything else as grand as this."

He shook his head, distracted by memories, not of the jewels, but of his mother.

She stepped away from the doorway, still holding the door open as though she was about to leave. "My lord?"

He only half heard her. She moved a step closer. Leaving the door ajar. "My lord, I am very much afraid that this discovery will cause any number of problems."

"Entirely possible." *Be practical, James,* he urged himself, "I can think of several myself."

"Should I have allowed Robert to open the box?"

"Madame, who could have known that there would be a fortune inside? It is exactly what I would have done. I can hardly fault you then, can I?"

She grinned. "It is like something from a novel, is it not?"

He nodded, "And I am not sure we have any control over how the next chapter will read."

"For one, I suppose we can expect more of the curious from the village once news of this find is made known." She walked back to the door and closed it quietly. "I must tell Harold. I have asked him to handle visitors. I know it is the housekeeper's responsibility and not the hall porter's, but I am so rarely dressed for callers and I had to find something for him to do."

"It's close enough to his actual work," James agreed. "Hopefully all the visitors will see is our people hard at work with no time for distractions. Is that understood?"

"Of course, my lord. One can hardly put the jewels on display."

Her eyes lingered on the tightly fitted lid. Did she hope for one look before they were put away? He hid his surprise when she did not ask to see them. She went on discussing the topic at hand. "I suppose it is too much to hope that Robert can keep this news to himself."

"Oh please, Madame, what we eat for dinner is news in the village. This will fuel gossip for weeks. Robert will be rewarded with more beer than he can handle." He could easily envision the audience in the taproom encouraging the telling. "And within two days his effort will have grown to a feat beyond all recognition."

"Mais bien sûr." She untied her smock and took it off, draping it on the back of the chair near the desk. "In no time, I shall be the villain. He will tell everyone that he refused to stop searching despite my orders and that he had to insist the box be opened."

What an imagination she had.

She sat without invitation and did not seem to notice the puff of dust that rose from her skirts "Do you think this will encourage looters?" She brought her hands together and leaned forward in earnest concern.

He shook his head. "No. There are too many people around during the day and we have already posted night guards."

"A treasure like this is so tempting." She sat back in her chair and stared for a long moment at the box, as though she could see through the leather to the glittery contents. He saw more concern than envy in her eyes. "It could be that I am searching for worries. It is one thing to consider such a theft, another entirely to put together a plan. One that will work. It is more difficult than you would imagine."

James sat in his chair opposite her and tapped the blotter with a letter opener. "You speak from experience?"

Madame nodded as though every schoolroom taught lessons in larceny.

He dropped the letter opener. Good God, who had he hired? But what true thief would admit to the crime? She did not elaborate and finally he realized that she would not unless he pressed her. "Explain that, madame."

"I suppose I must if I ever have any hope of winning your trust."

She looked down at her hands for a long moment and when she raised her eyes to his, they were sad. He had never seen her so wrapped in melancholy and he was sorry he had asked.

"You see, in France, when it was only me and Miss Morton, well, we had very little money, hardly enough for food. Life was," she paused, ". . . life was difficult."

She stopped a moment as though admitting that life was difficult violated some personal code.

"With such a need for money I began to consider ways of making my own fortune."

Her tone of voice had changed, becoming more of story-teller rather than one making a confession. She smiled a little and the dejection faded. He allowed it, still wondering at the pain she so carefully tamped down.

"Oh, I had wonderful ideas. My lord, they were magnificent, I assure you, and I could never determine how to put most of them into practice."

"And those ideas were?" Did he need to know? Not at all, but he was damn curious at what her young mind had conjured.

She warmed to the discussion and leaned forward still further, almost rising from her seat. *"Bien,* you see, one of the men in the village had a marvelous wine cellar, wines stolen from the people he arrested or those who ran from the riots. He himself did not drink them, preferring the *vin ordinaire.* I thought if we could steal some of the wine, we could sell it and, *voilà,* have money for food. The windows into the cellars were very small, but I was very small as well. And, yes, there were rats. That was nothing. By then I had named the rats who lived with us and was not at all discommoded by them."

He looked away for a moment, ran his tongue around his mouth, and did everything he could to keep from laughing out loud. "You named the rats? Madame, I do not believe half of what you say. Surely you are as guilty of exaggeration as Robert will be."

"Perhaps," she conceded, "but it made you laugh, did it not?"

"Almost." He smiled back at her. *And you too,* he thought. "Tell me, madame, why did this plan not work?"

"It did work! Very well. I would hardly talk of my failures. But we had to stop, for it would not have been wise to steal so much that the *imbécile* would realize the theft."

"And exactly where are these skills addressed in your references?"

She stood up and walked toward the window.

"Alas, my lord, there is no one alive in England who knew me as a child. It is just as well, is it not?" She walked back to the opposite side of the desk and looked at him with earnest entreaty. "And, my lord, my ways were brought on by only the greatest need. What else is a child to do when everything is taken?"

He nodded, for this he could understand from his own experience.

With his agreement, she relaxed. "Miss Morton always insisted that we should count our blessings. I understand now that those years taught me to rely on myself and have faith that life would get better. And I do not want you to think that it was all difficult. Being without a home and a familiar routine can make for great adventures."

"And this supposed confidence is shared with me in hopes that I will," he paused choosing his words carefully, "have more faith in your ability to ferret out such rascals?"

"Exactly."

"I ask you, Madame, how am I to know that you are not going to use your very fertile imagination to devise a plan to steal from me?"

"Mais, my lord, that is why I hope you can bring yourself to trust me, in this at least. Have I not this very hour turned over to you a chest of riches the likes of which I have never seen before?"

"Indeed, but it would have been difficult to steal something from under the envious eyes of Robert and the rest of the staff."

"Pickpockets perform amazing feats, my lord."

"You know this first hand?" He stepped around the desk, checking that the top was firmly fixed on the chest.

"Oh no, my lord." Madame wrinkled her nose. "To pick

a pocket you must touch a person in much too intimate a way. Miss Morton would not have approved."

"But she approved of your thievery?"

"Oh, no, she never knew. I did always try to consider what she would think of my plans. *Hélas!* It is why so many never happened. She would definitely not have approved of my plan to go to the brothel to steal while the customers were occupied. It would have been so easy to do." She shrugged away the sacrificed opportunity.

"Good God, what were you thinking about? Surely you knew what would have happened if you had been caught in such a place? A ten-year-old virgin would have been a very valuable property."

"I planned to dress as a boy."

He shook his head. "Madame, need I remind you that your skill at disguise is not nearly as effective as your story-telling ability?"

He raised a hand to his forehead. Here he was starting a headache over something that had *not* happened a dozen or more years ago.

Madame stood up. "Oh please, I would not see you upset over such ancient events. You must remember, we found our way to England and have lived a very respectable life. Indeed, I am happy, happier than I can say, to have left that life behind. This is where I am meant to be. Here at Braemoor. I feel it in my heart and my mind."

He opted not to answer, amazed that anyone with her background could be so sure, so content, even happy with this lot and place in life. He stared at his blotter, his lips pursed, finally looking up and giving in to a smile.

"No matter how you came here or why, today you have returned to the family gems that we had long thought stolen."

She nodded and accepted his lead, moving toward the door. She paused there and turned back to look at him. He might be finished. She was not. *Now she will ask to see the diamonds.*

"You thought the gems were taken by Lady Annabelle when she ran away?"

"Yes."

His brevity was not discouragement enough. She walked back to the chair across from the desk, but did not sit down. Resting her hands on the back of the chair, she spoke with earnest appeal. "I can only hope that this one innocence eases your heartache."

"You said yourself that possessions have little meaning. My mother's behavior was no better than a slut in the stews. The only happiness I derive from the recovery of these is that she lived her last year as poor as the whore of a music master could be."

A couple of startled blinks were the only response to his vehemence.

"It could be, my lord, that she knew the wrong she committed, knew it would hurt and felt she deserved the humility of poverty."

"It could be that she could not handle the weight of this chest."

Marguerite gave a slight nod. "It is something I know little of and time has embellished the story beyond all recognition."

"Has it? It is not a happy tale, only one more grim detail of Braedon history."

She stepped away from the chair, and turned yet again when she had reached the door. "You said that marquis would be pleased to hear that jewels had been recovered. Would you prefer to tell him yourself, or shall I?"

Twelve

"Neither one of us shall tell him, Madame. Even if the marquis were in his right mind, this discovery would bring him little pleasure. I lied to Robert when I said the marquis would be happy to hear of their recovery. I lied to curb gossip. And I trust," he paused so that she would fully appreciate his use of the word, "that you will respect my wishes."

"But of course." She looked offended that he felt the need to remind her. "Indeed I do understand that the memories awakened by this discovery are not happy ones."

He opened the ledger in front of him, as though it was work in progress. "If I keep on this way, Madame, I may well tease you into another argument as unpleasant as last night's. Then you will resign. And I have no intention of interviewing another housekeeper this week."

She had reached the door when he could stand it no longer. "Madame?"

She turned back towards him with an expression of long suffering as much as saying: Have you not dismissed me?

"Would you like to see the jewels before they are put away?"

Why had he done that? Because her delight at the invitation was such a joy to watch. Because looking at them with someone else in the room would ease his own recollections.

She hurried back to the desk, waiting with every appearance of patience while he removed the tight-fitting lid.

The old trunk had two leather straps ending in buckles. The buckles remained though the straps had been burned away. Robert had broken off the lock with his shovel.

James lifted the top and put it aside. She took a step closer and stared into the chest. She made to lift a piece out and looked at him with a wordless request for permission.

He nodded.

She touched one piece, then another and finally decided on an emerald necklace.

He watched as she laid it carefully on the desk, and straightened each of the dangling stones, moving it into the circle it would be when around a woman's neck.

"My mother wore those only on the grandest occasions. I thought she looked as golden as a queen. Even the marquis admired her. He wore his pride like a medal. She was a beautiful woman." Not kind, and as selfish as a hungry dog, but very beautiful.

He reached into the chest and drew out the rope of pearls. "These were her favorite." He looked at Marguerite. "I recall her telling me once that wearing pearls gave them life and made them last longer." He raised them from the box completely. "They have been without such warmth for too long. Put them on."

When she looked doubtful he teased, "Purely in the interest of their further preservation."

She leaned closer to him, bending her head. He could smell dust and even smoke, but wafting above that, he recognized the far more appealing vanilla scent. It stirred his memory of last night and a hunger that he could not, would not satisfy.

The column of her neck looked delicate, too delicate to bear the weight of the pearls. He settled them on her, careful not to touch the sweet curve of her skin. Tendrils of hair had escaped her cap and he brushed them aside lest they become tangled in the pearls. Was that shiver from him or her?

She looked up at him, her face aglow with a very womanly enjoyment. With both hands she took the strand and looped it around her neck again. The pearls fell almost to her waist in a double coil.

James could easily see these pearls draped over Marguerite Voisson, the pearls and nothing else.

The door creaked opened with its usual noisy certainty and they both jumped.

Morgan Braedon walked into the room, stopped suddenly, his grin changing abruptly to doubt.

What is he embarrassed about, James wondered. The speculation was eclipsed by the pure pleasure of seeing his brother. "Morgan! What brings you here?" He stepped from behind the desk and shook his brother's hand, clapping him on the shoulder at the same time.

"The place burns down and you wonder why I am come?" Morgan asked with genuine astonishment, and James laughed.

"Oh, the fire." James spoke with an absurd distraction that was all Madame Voisson's fault. "You know there are entire minutes that I am able to put that from my mind."

Morgan glanced at Madame and back at James. "Yes, brother, and I am sorry to interrupt. I could leave if you prefer."

Morgan walked towards Madame with a familiarity that should have been a warning. James missed it completely and merely said, "Madame Marguerite Voisson, this is my brother Lord Morgan Braedon."

Madame curtseyed, giving him a quick look from downcast eyes. More coquette than servant, but still demure.

"And has he bored you yet, Madame?"

"Oh, no, I am very happy here."

Morgan laughed. "You mean to tell me that you enjoy the attentions of a morose, laconic autocrat?" He glanced back at James.

"Attentions, my lord?" Madame looked at James. "You do understand, sir, that I am the housekeeper?" She spoke without the slightest edge to her voice, more like a bit of confusion, as though she were having trouble with the language.

Morgan's laugh faded, and his smile grew cautious. He turned to his brother. "James, I fear you go too far."

Madame looked offended at the same moment that James realized exactly what Morgan had surmised. "Morgan," James raised a cautioning hand, "You are making a mistake here."

Madame's eyes widened and she looked at James. "He thinks that you and I—that we. . . ."

James nodded. "I do believe so. I am so sorry. He can be a complete fool without any effort. It comes quite naturally." Never mind that similar visions had been infiltrating his own thoughts lately.

Madame laughed out loud. Not one of those ladylike titters, but a sincere laugh, more merry than musical, that brought tears to her eyes and seemed hard to control.

James laughed too. Not quite as heartily, wondering exactly why Marguerite thought the idea so hilarious. Surely this attraction could not be one-sided.

Morgan looked from one to the other.

James controlled his mirth and shook his head. "Morgan, you idiot, Madame Voisson is Braemoor's housekeeper and nothing more."

"Look at my clothes, my lord. What woman bent on seduction would wear something as awful as this?"

Morgan's expression turned sheepish and then defensive. "One hardly notices the dress for the pearls around your neck."

Madame removed them with a promptness that put their ownership exactly where it belonged. She schooled her features into a practical, blank gaze and moved to cross the room, very much a housekeeper if not a mere servant.

"Ah yes," Morgan looked thoroughly abashed. "I see now that I was completely mistaken."

Morgan turned to James who was enjoying every moment of his brother's discomfiture. James held out his hands. "I will say one more time and trust that your hearing has improved. Madame Voisson is indeed the housekeeper."

This time Morgan acknowledged the introduction with a more than gracious bow.

"She has, in a remarkably short period of time managed to organize the staff, make this wing a tolerable place to live, and still finds time to interfere in almost every part of my life."

"I am used to this." Madame turned to Morgan, her housekeeper persona gone for the moment. "The way he compliments and then insults. Does he do this to you as well?"

Morgan nodded, though she did not wait for his answer.

"And, yes, I admit that I meddle in his life. But always and only with the aim of his comfort. Is that not the role of any competent housekeeper?"

James watched Morgan, very interested in how he would respond to Madame's unique view of her role at Braemoor.

"So," Morgan began, turning his full attention toward him, "What happened to Mrs. Lanning?"

Before he could answer Madame Voisson spoke. She really had no notion of how a servant should behave. "My lord, I can see you have a great deal to discuss with your brother. I will come back later to report on the rest of the day's discoveries."

James nodded. She had already left the room.

"Exactly who is in charge here?" Morgan watched his brother with singular interest.

"I am, of course. It is all a ruse on my part. I merely allow Madame to believe she is the one giving the orders."

Morgan laughed as James knew he would. "I suspect that she and Christiana would get along famously."

"And how is your lovely, and almost forgotten, fiancée?"

"I did not forget her for a moment." Morgan moved over to the desk and the leather chest. "Christiana is engaged in the constant and very irritating battle of wills with her mother over various wedding details."

"And you still wish to go through with it, Morgan? I know that I presented marriage as an ultimatum when you were here last spring. I was half crazy myself to demand something so ludicrous."

If Morgan was surprised by his apology, he was generous enough not to show it. "James, those were difficult times." Morgan gestured toward the window. "Though it does not look much better now."

James shrugged. "I suppose a man can adjust to anything in time and I was speaking the truth when I said that madame has worked wonders. It began the day of the interview. But before I tell you of her first meeting with the marquis, I want your word that you no longer feel forced to make this match."

Morgan laughed out loud. "No, I do not. And if bickering between mother and daughter is a test of my good humor, I can only be grateful that I am spared the role of mediator. Christiana protects me quite nobly. In any case, I have only to dance with her, or catch her eye to know that we are made for each other."

"Revoltingly romantic, Morgan."

"Yes, it is, is it not?"

James came around to the chair behind the desk, but did not sit down.

Morgan drummed his fingers on the top of the chest. "Tell me, James, how is it that Madame Voisson is your housekeeper?"

James explained about Mrs. Lanning and their urgent need. Morgan listened with admirable concentration and appropriate ire at the Lannings' disloyalty.

"Madame is obviously French and of good birth. She is doing the work?"

James nodded. "In her own unique way she is extremely competent."

"Is that a compliment?"

"Most of the time." Was that not the third time he had praised her? Why did Morgan find it so hard to believe?

"And what of Monsieur Voisson?"

James's laugh was half derision. "I am convinced that there is no Monsieur Voisson. There never has been."

"It is a convenient title then?"

"Madame uses the truth as a convenience. And lies whenever it meets her needs."

Morgan looked nonplussed by this. "As long as you can tell the difference."

"Most of the time." James thought back to her story of wine thievery and smiled.

"Well, James, she makes you laugh. I have not heard you laugh like that in months, if not years. And it was a welcome sound, even if it was at my expense." Morgan spoke with convincing sincerity. "I tell you, seeing you two like that was a damn compromising picture. You both looked as though you had discovered a hidden treasure."

"Open the box, Morgan."

Morgan did and was more than distracted when he saw the contents. "By all the gods of greed, you did find a treasure. What in Hades is this?"

"Oh, do I have stories to tell."

Morgan looked at him, still stunned by the fortune before him. "Do begin, my brother!"

"You do not wish to change first?"

"This is hardly the drawing room and I find myself driven with curiosity."

"In that case, we will make ourselves comfortable."

James walked over to one of the cabinets, opened it, and pulled out a bottle and two of the four glasses. He poured a generous tot for both of them. He handed one to his brother, and gestured for him to sit down. Morgan put the top back on the chest and with a last lingering look, moved toward the chair.

"This is a cursed unpleasant room, James. Are you doing penance for some wrong?"

James shook his head. "It was the estate office. Marfield kindly gave it up for my use."

"Which does not precisely answer my question. Why are you still living in this ruin? Where is father? Have you heard from Rhys?"

James walked back behind the desk and sat in his chair. He raised his glass and after a fortifying swallow, began to explain.

Marguerite hurried down the hall, moving away from that interview as quickly as possible. Later, much later, she would think about the brush of his fingers on her neck and the echo it brought of his hands on her shoulders.

She must arrange for a room that would suit Lord Morgan, talk to the chef about the week's menus, discuss her dissatisfaction with the laundering of the sheets, find out exactly what the garden and succession houses were producing and give thought to finding other accommodations for Viscount Crandall.

This place was worse than uncomfortable. Even the warmth of spring could not penetrate the walls. Come winter, the viscount would be miserable in his office. And the marquis needed accommodation better suited to a man of his rank. She would not have it said that Braemoor treated him as less than his title deserved.

After arranging for Lord Morgan's room, she would search out Marfield and see if Prentice felt well enough for a conversation. Surely one of them could tell her if the dower house could be made habitable. It had been in her mind since Jenneth had told her that Marfield had insisted it could be made livable "in a trice."

Here her command of English failed her. Exactly what was a trice?

As she reached the top of the stone steps that led to the cavernous kitchen she could hear the excited conversation below. What had them so animated? Oh, yes, the discovery of the jewels. She had almost forgotten.

She paused on the first tread, even though they would not begin to eat until she had taken her seat. She heard Robert's excited voice and knew the conversation would fade as soon as she joined them. It was no burden for them to wait a moment more for her.

She looked back down the hall towards the office. The door was closed and much too thick for her to be able to hear any discussion between Lord Crandall and his brother. Not that she needed to. The most interesting element of that conversation had taken place within her hearing.

Lord Morgan's blunder rose to the forefront of her consideration, supplanting all her true responsibilities.

His notion that she and Lord Crandall were lovers had made her laugh then, but not now. As she moved very slowly down the stone steps, she did her best to allow herself to be distracted by the smell of simmering onion soup.

She closed her eyes and did something rare. She lied to herself. With pure physical effort, she insisted that she did not long for his touch, much less his kiss, much less his love.

Thirteen

"In a trice, madame?" Marfield swept off his cap and returned her greeting. "It means quickly, or in an instant."

"*Très bien.* That is wonderful. Just as I hoped. Mrs. Marfield told me that you offered to repair the dower house for her and said that it could be done 'in a trice.'"

"Yes it can, madame, but please, I never suggested that Mrs. Marfield and I move into the dower house. No, it was Lord Crandall's idea."

"Was it? It sounds very generous." Especially when you considered that it came from a man who had done his best to stop their marriage.

"Most certainly. Lord Crandall insisted that no one was using it, nor would anyone for his lifetime and we were welcome to it. You must realize, as I told him, that it would be beyond presumption for us to take up such a residence."

Marguerite tried not to be annoyed by his sensibilities. It was a house and he had needed one. There were times when position took second place to need and availability. After all, the marquis was currently living in a cottage. "I thought you offered it to your wife, at least she spoke to me of it once."

"Yes, I did. Lord Crandall convinced me that we would be seen as caretakers and not interlopers. So I did make the offer. I hoped it might soften her dislike of coming here."

This could prove interesting. Marguerite waited and hoped for more of their story.

"In the end," he continued, "Jenneth preferred the cottage and when Lord Crandall suggested we incorporate the second cottage into ours, well, that was ideal."

Given their prospects for a family. Yes, she could understand that. She wanted to know how he and his wife met, why he thought she hated the idea of leaving London when Jenneth had told her that Marfield's proposal had been "a gift." Had her dislike of Lord Crandall lessened her pleasure at leaving Town?

Despite her curiosity, Marguerite had more pressing questions, and truly, she could not see Mr. Marfield as the kind of man who would freely discuss his courtship. And not only because he was conscious of his place and hers. "I am wondering, sir, if you would give me an hour this afternoon, before we lose the light, to show me the dower house and describe to me what is wanting to make it habitable?"

Marfield nodded slowly and smiled. "Are you considering moving the household there?"

"Yes, though it is little more than a hope, you understand." She waited for his nod. "There are many questions to be answered first."

"The dower house has a suite of rooms on the first floor that would be appropriate for Lord Crandall." Marfield spoke with enthusiasm. "I could easily arrange the remaining rooms into a suite for the marquis."

"The stairs could prove to be difficult for him. Is there space on the ground floor that could be converted to his use?"

"Why, yes I think so." He paused considering. "If I recall correctly, one of the dowagers had the north dependency converted into a suite when the stairs became too much for her. It may be that it was never restored to its original use. And if they had separate floors, his lordship and the marquis would be guaranteed the privacy they so value."

Marguerite nodded her approval. "Well put, Mr. Marfield." It was hard to imagine the viscount and his father living together in a place smaller than Braemoor with its dozens of rooms.

An hour later they met at the front entrance to the relatively new Georgian mansion. Less than two hours after that, they were standing again at the entrance, grateful for the fresh air after the offending mold and gloom. The fading light took the warmth of the day with it, but they stayed a moment at the foot of the steps, discussing what seemed to her to be a formidable list of repairs that were the minimum necessary for the family to live in any more comfort than they were at the moment.

"The rats are easily ousted." Marfield said. "The barn cats would make short work of them. I'm afraid the damage to the wainscoting will take real skill to repair."

"Yes, I can see that is true, Mr. Marfield, but a perfectly appointed dining room is not essential to the family's ease. A fireplace that draws properly is."

"Madame, it can be done quickly. However, it will mean taking a number of the laborers from the salvage work you are doing. The mason, certainly, and I think the roofer is working on the team with the under butler." He paused and his excitement faded. "Do you think that you might consult Lord Crandall first?"

"Yes, I suppose I should." She thought about it a moment. "Why do I have the feeling that he will see it as an unnecessary move?"

"The truth is, Madame, that eventually Braemoor must be abandoned. Once an architect is chosen, it will be only a matter of time before he completes his plans. It will surely mean that the whole house, even the part in working order, will be gutted for the new design."

"Yes, of course, you are absolutely right. And if I tell Lord Crandall that more of the staff will be returned to full employment it will have the ring of good stewardship even if the family is our first priority."

"I would call it mutually beneficial."

"Oh yes, exactly!"

They were smiling at each other like the schemers they were, when they heard footsteps. Turning, they found Lord Morgan Braedon walking toward them wearing riding clothes and still carrying his crop. He waved in greeting and came closer. He bowed to Marguerite and exchanged pleasantries before turning to the land agent.

"Marfield! I have been down to your drainage project. It looks as though it will solve that problem admirably."

"Thank you, my lord."

"Where did you come upon the concept? There is a field on my property in Wales that would be wonderfully arable if I could only drain it better."

"I read of the technique in a pamphlet I brought back from London several years ago. If you would like, my lord, I could pass it on to you."

"Yes, shall I come by your cottage? I would like a word with Madame Voisson and then I will see if my father is receiving visitors. He is staying in one of the cottages near you, is he not?"

"Yes, my lord. Very well." With a brief nod of farewell, Marfield hurried down the path toward home.

Morgan turned to Marguerite with a smile, all rueful charm. He bowed to her. "Once again, Madame, I must apologize for my earlier misapprehension."

Marguerite curtseyed formally to him, as if they were in a drawing room. "Thank you, my lord, it was a mistake that will, I trust, go no further than the three of us and, as such, is hardly worth concern."

"It is not very often that I hear James sing the praises of anyone as wholeheartedly as he endorses you."

They had talked about her after she left. She tamped

down her curiosity since she could think of no way to draw more from him.

The front door stood open still and he walked up the steps, waiting at the door for her to join him. "Tell me, are you thinking of opening the house up?"

Marguerite nodded. "Now that Mr. Marfield has convinced me that repairs can be made in a trice."

He stepped inside. She followed him. He looked around the entry hall, the details barely visible in the half-light. "I am completely on your side in the effort. This has to be better than that office James is using, which is like a mausoleum. And he can never get away from the smell of the ash and rot."

"Exactly so, my lord. It is as though he is trying to punish himself for not being able to foretell the fire. Mr. Marfield and I have devised several arguments that I hope will convince your brother that opening the house will go a long way to reestablish some sense of the regular routine for the staff."

"That is an excellent notion." He spoke with a note of surprise in his voice as though he had not expected such insight from her. "He has an overdeveloped sense of responsibility."

"Yes, and I have wondered if he has been that way forever? I suppose so. He is the oldest and the heir and must always feel the burden." He might see this as presumption, but she would risk his set down.

"James more than most. He seemed to always feel the need to prove himself a Braedon. He excelled at his school work, learned all about estate management."

He stepped toward the door, looking out to the fields as though they were proof of his brother's good education.

"By the time I was old enough to understand the undercurrents, he had long since given up trying to win the marquis' approval, much less a word of praise. Father thought sending him to school was banishment. James considered it an escape."

He looked at her, a speculative gleam in his eye. "Are there any other family secrets you wish to know? You do have a way of hanging on my every word."

"Please, do not ever think I am a gossip. It is as I have told Lord Crandall. There is not a person here who knows less about the Braedons than I do. And I can hardly ask the staff. Nonetheless, a little knowledge does seem essential to my work."

"And what has James told you?"

"Only the barest of the family history. Of his mother and yours."

"For James even that is close to sharing a confidence."

"Yes, yes, I know that."

He added nothing more, but stepped back into the entry hall. Using his crop, he pushed open the door to the room nearest the doorway. He did not go in.

"After our grandmother died, my younger brother Rhys and I used to play hide and seek in there, all over this floor. Not upstairs though. Ghosts lived there."

Marguerite had been upstairs. She could believe that a child might look for an excuse to avoid the dark paneled rooms with the heavy drapes that covered the windows.

"I used to hide under the holland covers. If I could keep from moving, Rhys would look for hours before he ever found me. It was torture, staying still for so long."

"Did Lord Crandall play with you?" Marguerite did not have to pretend fascination.

"Never. He was too old by half. I do recall once that Rhys could not work his way out of the nook he had hidden in. And I ran to get James. I knew I could rely on his help and he would not give us a tongue-lashing. He came readily and managed to pry Rhys loose."

He pulled the door shut. It would not stay latched and with a shrug he left it slightly ajar.

"It was so very funny." Lord Morgan shook his head, the memory drawing amusement to his eyes. "At first James insisted that there was no way out, that Rhys was trapped forever. And suddenly Rhys was free. He was furious with James for frightening him so badly. The next few minutes were all flying fists and kicks, Rhys angry, and James trying to protect himself."

"You were not able to stop them?"

"Madame Voisson," he pretended dismay, "Of course not. I stayed on the other side of the room and watched. For it is always the peacemaker who bears the worst of the injury." He paused, "You have no brothers, do you?"

He nodded, assured of his insight, when she shook her head.

"We had great fun until the steward, the one before Simon Marfield, came to investigate the open door and the noise. He had not one jot of humor and he led us all to our father without a moment for explanation."

Morgan moved to the front door and Marguerite followed him outside again.

"James took the blame, insisted that Rhys and I were innocent and we were scared enough of the whip to let James take the beating. He can be overbearing and as autocratic as father, but there were times when I swear he appeared from nowhere. Always around to rescue us, stand up for us, show us how to get on."

One more piece in the puzzle of the viscount's relationship with his family fit into place. She locked the door, wondering if the viscount would recall this story. What memories of his were stored here?

"Madame, that is all the family history you will have from me. I am on my way to see my father and James tells me that you have been instrumental in achieving a new level of communication with him."

Marguerite nodded and decided to accompany him. As they moved down the path, he offered her his arm and matched his stride to hers. He might not be as tall as his brother or have nearly as imposing a presence. He was, however, far more charming.

"You are engaged, Lord Morgan?"

"Yes, I am. Miss Lambert and I hope to be married later this spring."

"Has your *fiancée* met your father?"

"Not yet. That is part of the reason for my visit. If father seems healthy enough, if his mind is sound enough, I expect I will bring Christiana and her family here for a visit before the wedding. It is unlikely he will be well enough to attend the ceremony itself."

The marquis' blessing seemed to be important to his second son.

When they arrived at the cottage, Marguerite would have left him at the door, but Mrs. Beecher stopped her, urging her inside. "He be that upset that you've not been here today."

Marguerite closed her eyes and prayed. *Please, let Lord Morgan understand this sham.* Before she stepped over the threshold she turned to him. "My lord, the marquis is improving, truly he is, however there are times when he mistakes me for your mother. When I assume the role, it seems to calm him, though I do have mixed feelings about the charade."

Morgan did not respond with more than a nod and let her enter ahead of him.

The marquis sat near the fire, as he usually did at this hour. He did not look up until Marguerite settled in the chair near him. When he did, his whole expression shifted from fatigue to delight. "My dear, how are you? Where have you been? What discoveries did you make today?"

"My lord, what a wondrous day! Do you think that it will ever rain again? I had heard that Sussex has the rainiest springs. I think it is a lie you tell to keep this beauty all to yourself." She detailed briefly the trivia of her day, anxious that he not be too tired to talk with his son. And she completely avoided mention of the long lost jewels, exactly as the viscount had asked.

She answered two or three questions that showed his mind still somewhat disordered: What were the girls wearing to the assembly? When would Mrs. Lanning be back from her most recent confinement?

She stood up and stepped closer to him. "My lord, your son, Morgan, has come to visit."

The marquis looked pleased and scanned the room. His rheumy eyes could not make out anything beyond the light cast by the fire.

Morgan came forward cautiously. When had he last seen his father, Marguerite wondered. He looked uncertain. When he stepped into the light the marquis finally saw him and the two stood staring, sizing each other up. The marquis looked at her and nodded.

"He's the good one." He turned to Lord Morgan. "Come here, boy, sit down, before I break my leg looking up at you."

Morgan looked at Marguerite before he came closer. He took the chair Marguerite had vacated and jumped up like a shot when his father railed, "You would sit while your mother stands! If I had a crop, I would beat you!"

He looked at Marguerite and she sighed an apology. He needed no more explanation but turned to his father, using his charm like a weapon. "I would never slight my mother or you, sir. I thought that she had left the room."

Marguerite walked forward with her shawl wrapped

around her shoulders. "Indeed, with your permission, I am gone, my lord. I must close the house for the night."

"Come back."

"I will, my lord, but not until tomorrow."

Lord Morgan escorted her to the door and stepped outside with her. "I assume he meant neck when he misspoke leg?"

"Yes, it is not an uncommon effect of apoplexy."

He nodded. "And mistaking you for my mother. Is that common?"

She shook her head. "Not that I ever observed before, though my experience is very limited. In the early days he mistook me for one or the other of your sisters as well. Over time I have become Lady Gwyneth alone." She turned and looked at him. "You do appreciate, my lord, that I have done my best not to further his misunderstanding. There seems to be no way I can convince him that I am not his Gwyneth."

"What harm can it do? And if it makes him happier and easier to manage. . . ."

"Could we say that it is mutually beneficial?" How useful a term that could prove to be.

"Yes, yes, I think so. I hope so." He looked down at the path and back at her. "When I first saw you in that awful room James uses for an office, with that generous length of pearls around your neck, I wondered what god of mischief had sent you to Braemoor. Now, madame, seeing how seriously you take your work, your care for my father, and watching you make James laugh, well, I suspect it is a more caring god than a mischievous one that has brought you to us." He took her hand and bowed over it. "Thank you for all you have done to ease our burden. May the gods bless you for caring so much."

It was so charmingly said that Marguerite felt the sting of tears and could do no more than nod. As she walked down the path she heard laughter from the cottage. Lord Morgan was teasing his father out of his imperious mood.

Her tears disappeared and a great burst of happiness took their place. This felt so like home. She had finally found one in this place, with these people. Indeed, God had blessed her.

And she felt hope for this family. The marquis could feel affection, did feel it for his second son.

Lord Morgan had a way with words, truly he did. Had he learned that charm as a way around a difficult parent? If he had, then the viscount had perfected the opposite: a cool aloofness that made most people avoid him, or at the very least avoid confronting him.

Lord Morgan's smile alone guaranteed that he would never be without a partner on the dance floor or anywhere else.

Viscount Crandall would never be lonely either, but it had nothing to do with charm. His arrogance worked like an armor that few could penetrate. His quiet watchful strength made him a man of mystery. It was an aura to which she was far more susceptible.

Fourteen

The new moon had grown in size and gave precious more light. Standing on the hillside between the cottage and Braemoor, James watched his housekeeper hurry along the path. The spring in her step belied the long day she must have had. Exactly what had she and Morgan been talking about?

As she came within earshot, he stopped her. "When do you ever consider your day's work done, madame?"

She came up short though she did not seem surprised to see him. She answered as if being questioned in the dark, on a hillside, were the most normal thing in the world.

"Good evening, Lord Crandall."

She sounded so cheerful, as though Morgan had charmed the stars for her.

"I have only this moment left your brother visiting with your father. He has made me feel so welcome."

She lowered the shawl from her head and settled it around her shoulders. Her cap was askew as usual.

"Lord Morgan told me of his childhood adventures and how you always seemed to know his every mischief." She stepped closer, lowering her voice to speak confidingly. "And at this very moment when you called to me, I realized your secret."

She spoke again before he could decide whether to ask for her insight. "This has been a particular retreat of yours forever, has it not?"

"I used to climb that tree." *She had determined that in a matter of weeks when it had been his secret for a lifetime. Amazing.*

"That one with the large knot at the base." He pointed toward the grove of trees behind them.

She moved beyond him to identify the tree, walked over to it and touched the bark as though it were special. Looking up she considered the branches. He would not have been surprised to see her begin the climb.

"It looks like a wonderful hiding place." She turned back to him, her eyes brimming with mischief. "This rise is as much yours as any bedroom, is it not?"

He shrugged. "Ever since I was a child."

The turn of her lips grew to a grin and she bent her head with that expression that invited his confidence.

"I used it until I went away to school. I could see, and not be seen."

"Ah yes, that aspect of it does not surprise me at all." She moved closer still, a little impertinent, a little daring.

He wondered if she and Morgan had been sampling champagne.

"What did you think about as you watched the world from your hiding place?"

"Oh, any number of things. Whether hiding a frog in the governess' bed was too predictable. How to convince the groom to let me ride the newest stallion." He turned from her eager expression and for a moment was lost in less pleasant memories. Why his father so favored a whip. Why he could not bear his stepmother's sympathy.

She touched his arm and he pulled himself back from self-pity. He would have covered her hand with his own, but the moment she had his attention, she pulled her hand away. Her eyes held his, almost as warm as her touch.

"I can guess that you came up with something far more clever than a frog and would also have known that meat pies rather than arrogance would have more readily won over the groom."

"Apple tarts. He had a terrible weakness for sweets."

He welcomed sharing the memory with her and watched the light dance in her eyes for a moment.

"Oh, my lord, your brother has filled my head with such stories today. He told me that you. . . ."

"He did tell you he was engaged?"

"But of course." Her good humor faded. "He is to marry Miss Lambert. He hopes to bring her to meet your father before they are married."

"It appears that you are well on your way to knowing as much of the family gossip as anyone else on the staff." He knew he was being churlish. Charm was Morgan's specialty, not his. "If you want more stories either true or false, talk to Morgan."

Embarrassment replaced the light in her eyes. "My lord, I do beg pardon." She began to back up. "I will find another path. I would hate to ruin the retreat that you have here."

She curtseyed and began to walk away.

"Madame, I am no longer ten years old and entirely capable of finding privacy whenever I may need it."

"To be sure."

He could not mistake the frost in her voice.

She turned to face him once again. "Will you be seeing Lord Morgan after he has finished talking with your father?"

Their small enchantment had ended and it was all his doing. "Morgan and I are to settle into cards after he has seen the marquis."

"I am about to invade the kitchen. I missed supper and had hoped to make a meal for myself. Would you like me to arrange a tray for you and your brother?" The way she asked made it sound as though she was prepared for insult.

"You are always thoughtful, Madame." That felt like

groveling. He hoped she saw it that way. "The under butler has already arranged a supper for us."

"Very well." She stood looking at the ruin and finally glanced back at him. "I suppose I shall go." She made another curtsey as though to leave.

"I suppose you shall." He whispered it and saw her hesitate.

"You make it so difficult, my lord," She spoke with exasperation when he would have preferred amusement. "It may be that you are able to find privacy when you need it, and are not quite as practiced at asking for company."

"It may be, madame, that it is not lack of skill but lack of interest that keeps me from asking for company."

"Oh, my lord, you have mastered the veiled slight, truly you have." She laughed as she walked back toward him.

One of the things he liked most about Marguerite Voisson was how rarely she took offense at his insults. And she did not disappoint him this time.

"I have no doubt that you are capable of always making your wants known, my lord. And in this case I can see that you long for company and will not ask for it directly."

He would not admit to anyone, and barely to himself, that the only company he wanted stood before him. Walking back to his climbing tree, he fingered the bark, keeping his back to her. "Why did you miss supper this evening?"

"I had a meeting with Mr. Marfield."

He turned back to look at her and relaxed as he watched the familiar way his housekeeper had of settling into a conversation. Even though there was no place to sit, she folded her hands carefully and leaned forward ever so slightly.

"You were with Marfield?"

"I do remember that you asked me not to interrupt Mr. Marfield in his work, and I did wait until he had a free moment."

"And you discussed the spring plantings?" He meant it as a tease. He suspected it sounded more like criticism.

"No." The single word became a long syllable and filled with as much sarcasm as his had been. She took two steps toward him and brought her hands together in a gesture that usually accompanied entreaty, or guilt.

"We discussed the possibility of moving the household to the dower house. He feels that it can be made habitable in a trice and an agreeable place to live without great inconvenience."

"In a trice, Madame?"

"Yes, indeed, it is a phrase I learned only today."

"And how quickly is this 'trice' to be?" She spoke with such solemnity that he gave up trying to tease her. This meeting with Marfield had been worth missing supper for, he reminded himself.

"Mr. Marfield thinks the renovation can be completed within two weeks."

"And will it take priority over the salvage efforts?"

"Oh no, my lord. At first he will only need to take a few of the staff from the work we are doing there. By the time he needs more hands we will be finished with our work in the ruins.

"Please, my lord, preparing the dower house and moving there will bring so many of the servants back to work fully and to the tasks they are used to."

She spoke the last as from a practiced script. Had she and Marfield rehearsed this? Whose side was Marfield on? "And precisely when were you and Marfield going to include me in this decision?"

"Why, we decided that I should speak to you about it tomorrow at our usual meeting."

"I see." Why did he feel annoyance at their managing ways? "I am settled in the west wing of Braemoor. I have no desire to move to the dower house."

"Very well." She accepted his inflexibility with a shrug. "We can move the marquis to the dower house. And if you wish to have the staff service both places I am sure they will do their best to accommodate you."

James shook his head, exasperation giving way to amusement. "I give up! I know when I am bested. You are nothing more than a managing little baggage."

"Why, thank you, my lord. Does that mean that you agree to the move?"

"It means that I will think about it. Go find your supper." God help him, he had to maintain at least the illusion of control here. Much more of this and her very presence could prove addictive.

"I will leave."

He nodded.

"If that is what you wish."

When had this passed from business to coquetry? Did Marguerite even know that she was flirting and had been for the last few minutes, the warmth of her expression tempered with a bit of petulance.

"Damnation, woman, you play with fire." He took her by the shoulders and turned her to face down the hill. He did not let her go at once. "I do not want you to faint from lack of food." Would she believe that? If they stayed out here together much longer he would want to act on that impulse that had tantalized him since she stood next to him draped in pearls.

"I appreciate your concern, my lord." She did not step away from his touch, or turn to face him but she did lean back ever so slightly.

He let her go and she turned toward him again. Her eyes were warm, her expression inviting.

"My concern is purely selfish, Marguerite. You have become essential to my household."

"I should hope so, my lord. Since Braemoor has no mistress, I am the one who must see to your ease."

She spoke with sincerity. He could see that in the dark blue eyes and the sweet curve of her mouth. "Exactly what do you mean by that?" he drawled, giving in to the temptation that had dogged him for so long, deciding that he would take whatever she would give. Did she even know herself how far she would go?

He stepped closer to her, "Let me assure you that I have lost two mothers and have no wish for a third."

"Of course not, my lord, and I would never presume to think of myself in that way. I do so long to give you another kind of comfort."

She fixed her eyes on his for a moment and finally lowered them and stared at his cravat, but she did not step away. He knew then that the temptation was not one-sided.

"We have nothing in common, my lord." She spoke with conviction, as though it were her best line of defense, sparing him a quick glance before adding, "If you will excuse the impertinence of comparing my life to yours."

Marguerite Voisson serious and solemn was almost as tempting as she was when she laughed. He was, however, enough of a gentleman, he reminded himself, to follow her lead. He kept his hands at his side and watched the top of her head, and her silly cap.

"Madame, I have assumed from the beginning of our acquaintance that you are the child of aristocracy."

"Miss Morton would always say I may have been the child of the nobility but I was not its heiress." She looked up at his face and he waited while she searched his eyes and shook her head. "I can see that this work is my true calling. I am of a different class now and will be content."

"You are a liar, my dear girl, but such a sweet one."

She looked down again.

"You think we have nothing in common? You are wrong."

With a gentle finger under her chin, he tilted her face up so he could see hers.

"We favor the same hillside, lit by the moon and the stars." When he spoke again it was in her language. "We both speak French. We both take our responsibilities seriously. We care about Braemoor and rebuilding it."

She closed her eyes but not before he saw the sheen of tears.

"We both have endured a loneliness that comes from too little love and scant affection. We both want so much more."

What was it about the French language that made love, *l'amour*, so hard to resist, so intoxicating? He let go of her chin and she opened her eyes again. They stood facing each other. He waited for a sign from her, his longing so powerful that it took all his control not to take the choice from her.

When her decision came, a step back, he was bereft. In that gesture she denied them both such pleasure. She turned her head and with her back to Braemoor she spoke in English and very softly. "You make it very difficult, my lord."

"Then why not let it happen? I can sweep you close, press my mouth to yours and we can both forget everything save each other."

She mumbled a few words, French and blasphemous. "Do you not see that it would change everything?" Her words tumbled out in an angry spate, a kind of anger he had never heard from her before. "It would make me not much better than what your brother suggested and name you less than a gentleman."

He could debate the issue with her, but it would be even less gentlemanly than a kiss.

"Leave. Go to your solitary supper." He could not help the edge in his voice. It came from anger and frustration. "I am not accustomed to the noble gesture. If you wish, we can stand here together, but I will not speak for my continued restraint."

She spoke once more and hurried away without even her usual curtsey. Her last words stayed with him. "It would be a moment of pleasure, my lord. One that would take the pleasure from all the moments to come."

Fifteen

Marguerite watched the faint glow brighten in the eastern sky. It would be dawn soon. For long, lonely hours she had been awake, snug in her bed, but so confused in her heart that she'd abandoned the thought of sleep hours ago.

Pushing herself up, she adjusted the pillows and pulled the worn blue comforter up under her chin. With effort she considered the business of the day, though her thoughts never stayed there for long. The birds began to sing and she knew she should rise. Now, of course, drowsiness would weigh her down and dreams overtake her.

He would hold her again. She could feel the delight of the moment she recalled his expression as he searched her eyes, the feeling of his hands on her shoulders, the touch of his finger on her chin.

In her dream when he waited for that sign from her, she would say yes. Or only nod. Or perhaps she would kiss him first, before he was ready, before he could armor himself against feeling. He would be as open to the passion, to the wanting as she was. Neither of them would be in control and they would feel all that they had tried to deny.

The cock crowed, as it did every morning, and Marguerite started up from her half sleep. She jumped from bed and began dressing with angry haste spurred by the chill in the air. She would be late and how many times had she berated others for tardiness?

As she fastened her shoes and reached for her cap, the reality of last night eclipsed her dreams. As haunting by dawn's light was the reality of the kiss that had not been. The kiss she wanted so badly she could weep.

Wisdom dictated refusal. *Hélas,* good judgment was no consolation. It left her alone and lonely with each one of those sweet intimacies haunting her.

He had let her say no. He had accepted her refusal and not pressed her for more. Why?

She jammed the pin through the cap and into the knot of hair. He had not pressed her because he was afraid of what his own reaction would be.

Pulling the cottage door closed, she hurried up the path, still not focused on her work.

The whole day passed that way. She was so distracted that she told Robert to throw away the fine piece of marble that had escaped damage. Later she put into the basket a dirty, smoke-ruined piece of bed-hanging that was not even a worthy dust cloth.

She would see him in a few hours. Should she stand or sit? Where should she look? What should she say? By dinnertime nerves made her irritable, such an unusual state that the chef asked if she felt unwell.

And it was all for nothing. She spent twenty miserable minutes waiting for Lord Crandall in his office before the under butler stepped into the room.

"Madame, I am so sorry not to have remembered. I should have told you sooner. Lord Crandall has gone to London with his brother. He left early this morning."

She wanted to yell at him. *"Why did you wait so long to tell me, you incompetent excuse for a servant!"* Instead, she exerted all her self-control and thanked him before sending him away.

She looked around the empty room. Dust motes danced

in a shaft of sunlight, settling on the basket she had set on the desk awaiting the viscount's attention.

She watched the aimless shift of dust. She existed for his convenience. He could come and go at will. He need never give her wants a thought. She was left alone to deal with her confusion. He would ignore his. London was perfect for that kind of escape. The coward. She sank into the chair and looked at his empty one. One kiss would have made all the difference. Tears trickled down her cheeks and she gave in to the regret and cried.

Ten days later and her feelings had eased. Hard work led to exhaustion and the discoveries they had made were so rewarding that now she stood in his office all impatience.

Hurry home! Please! I have such treasures to share.

She had found them by pushing the staff to work the same long hours she did in order to hurry the renovation of the dower house and finish the salvage work too. The under butler had complained, but he complained about almost everything. But when one of the housemaids nodded asleep over dinner, Marguerite decided she could not expect everyone to work with the same intensity that she did.

They did not have her incentive. They could fall asleep easily. She needed the hard work to sleep at all and still she dreamed of him, whispering to her in French.

There had been no dreams last night and she felt the worst had passed. If he could pretend not to care, so could she. It was the wisest course of action after all. She had work to do here and it would be a sin to endanger it when truly it was work that God meant for her to do.

She put the last basket on the floor with the other three and checked to be certain that the two carefully wrapped packages were still on his desk. To her mind, they were as great a discovery as the jewel chest.

She looked around the room. It had not been his long enough to hold any of his essence. Not like his bedroom. That room, tucked away at the top of the west wing had been his since he had moved from the school room.

In the last few days she had spent hours there and now knew a good bit more about him. She discovered the books he favored: Voltaire was by his bed at the moment, the number of pillows he used: four, and the color of his dressing gown: the same gray as his eyes.

The office had none of that aura. He used what Marfield had left behind or what she had put in place. Marguerite walked around the desk to the chair she had found for him and sat in it.

It fit him perfectly and her not at all. Still she did not get up. Instead she leaned back as he often did and raised her hand to her head in one of his more familiar gestures. Hopefully, his headaches had eased in London.

The door swung open and the viscount strode into the room. He had changed from his traveling clothes, his hair still damp from whatever toilette he had made. His eyes shone. He did look tired, which, she told herself, is exactly what one would expect after a day's travel.

She refused to contemplate the city entertainments that might have kept him from bed until dawn. Or, as a little imp teased, *in* bed until dawn.

"Just as I thought." He walked towards the desk, shaking his head. "I leave for a sennight and when I return even the pretence that I am in charge has been overthrown."

"Not at all, my lord. Sitting in your chair was very much like a magic spell." Marguerite stood up, not as gracefully as she would have liked, for a slight jump was necessary for her feet to reach the floor. "I knew that as soon as I took your seat you would walk through the door. And *voilà,* it happened as I wished."

Bien, she thought, *it is very much as before. He makes a sarcastic remark and I parry it.*

When she moved to her chair, she stepped around the side of the desk farthest from him. The viscount moved to his seat. It struck her as much like a dance. In this case though, each one of them was careful to choose steps that would not bring them close together.

He sat down, stretched, and almost groaned aloud. "I wish I could say that this place is a welcome sight, but that would be a lie. Let me ask, rather, how Braemoor has managed."

"As well as can be expected, my lord."

"Oh, Madame, you do yourself a disservice." He laughed but he was not amused. "I come home to find the salvage complete, my bedroom empty, and the dower house looking much like an ant hill, so frantic is the activity."

"That sounds like praise, my lord. I expect it is not."

"Correct me, if I am wrong. I thought that when I left for Town, I was still considering the option of moving to the dower house. I had no idea that I had completely committed to it."

"The decision is still yours to make, my lord." Marguerite gripped her fingers tightly together. "The staff has worked long, hard hours to have it ready for you."

"I understand exactly what you are saying: Why would any fool continue to live in this cold and damp? You are convinced that you are acting with my health and best interests in mind. That is why my furnishings have disappeared. I suspect I have only to visit the dower house to find everything from my bed to the candle holder that usually sits next to it."

He stood up and walked to the window and then turned his back to it. The sunlight framed him, leaving his face in shadows. She did not need to see his eyes to know he was annoyed.

"I suppose it will only take one night for me to thank you for your presumption. I will not mean it as a compliment. And I warn you, Madame, that each time you presume on our odd situation here, you endanger your employment."

"Yes, my lord." She answered automatically wondering to which aspect of their "odd situation" he referred. This did not see the best time to ask.

He walked away from the window and back to his desk, where his eyes fell on the neatly folded packages. He ignored them and leaned over to pick up one of the baskets and put it on the blotter. He did no more than glance at the contents before setting it aside.

"I have brought a guest back from Town, but no guest room will be needed."

She held his gaze despite the distinct flash of cold that gripped her. What kind of guest had he brought back that would not need a room? A woman to entertain him because she had not been willing? She glanced away. Well, she thought with a small sharp sigh. Well.

"Graely is not precisely a houseguest. He is an architect. He will take up residence at the inn in the village. Most of his time will be spent here, however. He will take his meals here and will require a room, more as an office than a place to sleep."

Marguerite looked down at her hands. The architect had come that was all. In truth, he could bring a dozen trollops home with him if he wished. She would surely leave her post, not from hurt any more than from the insult to her own good morals. Any housekeeper would feel compelled to do the same. This time it was only the architect.

The silence between them lengthened. She looked up and found him considering her with some uncertainty.

"Are you well, Madame Voisson? You look tired."

"I am well, thank you."

"And why are you so quiet?"

"We have all worked long hours of late. If I am tired and quiet it is because of that, not anything that you did."

"How could it be? I have been in London for the last ten days."

"Exactly." She gave him an agreeable nod and added to herself, *you insensitive oaf.* "As for a room for the architect's needs, my lord, there is a large space here in the west wing. It has a fireplace. I think it served as a drawingroom before. It could accommodate anything that Mr. Graely might need in the way of a work table or office."

"See to it. I want him to be able to start work at once with all his needs met."

She nodded. She would have stood but he gestured to the desk and the baskets on the floor. "Is this the last of the items recovered?"

"Yes, yes it is."

"And are there wonders for me to behold?"

"You jest, my lord." Or did he think to cheer her up with his pretense of interest? "These have always meant more to me than they have to you, however, we have made some new discoveries."

"More paintings?"

"No, I am sorry. Most of the paintings are unsalvageable. What we found does not have the monetary value of the jewels. Indeed, they have a merit all their own." She cringed at her pedantic tone. Where had her excitement gone? Three days ago the discovery of these books had thrilled her.

She cleared her throat and continued, leaning forward, her hands on the edge of the desk. "Sir, these books have value that a jeweler could never compete with."

"How intriguing, Madame." The viscount was freeing the books from their protective linen covering. He spoke as he worked. "Surely you exaggerate. I can think of any number of people who would value a rope of pearls more than any book, even the original letters of St. Paul."

"Oh, but of course, my lord. Even I enjoy beautiful jewelry. These books are a treasure of the heart."

"How very sentimental."

The familiar cynicism actually made her feel better. He finished unwrapping the first package and found two books.

Marguerite stood up and held her hands over heart, all the excitement of her first discovery with her again.

The books were of different sizes and they were dirty, the leather bindings scratched and torn. A frayed and scorched ribbon, which had once been deep green, held them together.

"I suppose this is like an oyster shell." Untying the ribbon, he pulled it away from the volumes. He looked at her. "When I open this book, will I find a pearl of great price?"

"I think so. For surely this piece of family history is as much of a fortune to your family as any gemstone."

He opened to the first page and read for no more than a moment. Slapping the book shut, he looked at her. His good humor disappeared and his eyes narrowed slightly. "What are these?"

"Please read more."

"Madame Voisson." He made her name a command and anger blazed in his eyes.

"It will not bite you, my lord. These books and the other package are Lady Gwyneth's personal journals. We found them on the last day of our work in the north wing, near the rooms where the fire started. It is beyond anything amazing that they survived the flames."

The viscount looked at the books, picked up the first one again and turned it over in his hands.

"Opening this, reading it, will bring your whole family closer. It will remind you of happier times, of a stepmother who loved you. I so envy you this gift of your past. I would give anything to have a reminder of my life before England."

"You've read them?" he asked, even as he opened the book to a middle page.

"Only the first page of each volume to determine what they were. There are dates so I put the four in order before I wrapped them in the linen."

With no more than a nod in reply, he closed the book and replaced it on the stack.

"I want you to listen to me very carefully."

He was waiting, so she answered, "But, of course."

"Burn them."

He said the two words again. Marguerite could only shake her head in denial.

"Take them with you, Madame. Take them to the biggest fire you can find and burn them." His expression did not soften at all. "If there was a fire here," he nodded at the cold fireplace, "I would do it myself. Since there is not one in here and I am expecting both Marfield and the architect at any moment, I ask you, indeed, I order you to do it." He spoke with cold determination.

"My lord, you have barely glanced at even one page. How can you tell me to burn them? This is all that is left of Lady Gwyneth except what you cherish in your memory. Her portrait is lost, her favorite porcelain, all her efforts to make Braemoor a home. Everything gone, save these."

He raised a hand and rubbed his brow.

"Please, my lord, would you reconsider?"

"No, God damn it, I will not." He stood up and took the top most volume and threw it against the wall. It fell to the floor in two pieces.

Shock held her speechless.

"When will you understand that I do not want one reminder of my childhood or my stepmother, much less my own mother. Madame, I am moving to the dower house. But this, this is not a battle that you are going to win."

Marguerite stood up, gathered the fragments and reached

over to rescue the other volumes. "This is not a contest of wills, my lord. It is not that I can be right once and then it is your turn."

He laughed and it sounded as though he were truly amused. "Madame, in a normal household, I would be right all the time." He picked up the piece of linen and tossed it to her. "Use this to nurse the flames."

It was an immeasurable relief when Marfield knocked on the door. Marguerite left without a farewell.

She did her best to hold back her upset as she hurried down the path to her cottage. Thankfully she met no one along the way for she would have been hard pressed to be civil. In the privacy of her cottage the quiet stream of tears became sobs.

Her tears did nothing to ease the vicious ache in her heart. She was misguided beyond all reason to think that he would care about these books or her opinion.

Sinking into her chair, she cradled the books to her breast. What had happened to the *rapprochement* they had shared or had it been no more than wishful thinking on her part? Even if the closeness had been real, it had now disappeared. He was as he had been in the beginning, a law unto himself.

She must burn the journals. Running her hands over the covers, imitating his gesture, she tried to feel the words inside. Did he not understand that these were spared ruin because they were meant to be shared, saved, honored?

Even if they contained no more than a ritual account of the day's activities, a listing of costs and expenses of harvests and menus, they would still be worth keeping.

Marguerite looked up at the soot-darkened ceiling. As she watched, the light faded and she glanced toward the back window. The blue sky of the last month paled as rain clouds dimmed the daylight. The breeze that had pushed her along the path would be a wind before long. She breathed a prayer of thanks. Even one day of rain before today would have ruined these books. How could he not see that she had found them for a reason?

Realization broke through the anger, fed by a dose of rebellion. *Perhaps they were not meant for him at all.* Was she not the one who so wished to learn more of the Braedons?

He had insisted she burn them. He had not told her when. He had told her he did not want to read them. He had not said that she could not.

Still clasping the books close to her heart, she bowed her head over them. Without waiting for an answer to her prayer, she opened to the first page and began to read.

Sixteen

The damned headache made it impossible to concentrate on the architect's words. James reached for his glass and set it down again without drinking. He deserved every painful thump. He had been determined to put distance between himself and Marguerite Voisson. Determined to see that she stayed in her place as housekeeper. And at the first test of that resolution he had failed.

He had agreed to move to the dower house. She had convinced him and he had agreed with only a token protest. Had that been enough? No. With her it never was. No wonder he had lost his temper and no wonder she had left in tears. He had his distance. And he would be glad of it, as soon as his headache went away.

". . . I have no doubt that you can bear the expense, my lord," the architect spoke with a certainty that James did not share.

"Graely, the war is going to make any kind of construction difficult. You know as well as I do that the only reason you were available on such short notice is because there is precious little building going on these days."

"Yes, my lord, you are right. However, that same fact will work to your advantage as well. All those who specialize in such work are eager for employment. And with my name on the design they will be available whenever you require them."

James murmured agreement, glanced at Marfield and bit back a smile at Simon's expression.

"If you will excuse me, my lord, before the light is gone, I would like to walk and survey the building and make a few preliminary determinations based on my observations."

"Whatever best inspires you, Graely. We will meet again when you have completed your survey."

"As you wish, my lord." Graely stood up, bowed to the viscount. Marfield stood and Graely gave him the briefest of nods.

As the door groaned shut, James gave in to the laughter. "He does have supreme confidence, does he not? Morgan warned me."

Marfield resumed his seat. "He wonders what I am doing here."

"And so do you?" James squinted against the pain. "As far as Graely is concerned you are here because I want you here. Between you and me, I want you here because I value your opinion and your practical eye. You devised that drainage system you are finishing. You built the scaffold to support the north wing. You have the talent if not the education to grasp whatever Graely has in mind."

"Thank you, my lord."

Marfield tried hard to hide his pleasure at the compliment, but James could see it in his eyes if not the curve of his mouth. James rubbed at his temple. The headache eased a bit.

"You heard me say that this is a rotten time to be building and the costs are a large part of that. Men and goods might be available 'as I require' but they will cost more than anyone except the Prince of Wales would be willing to spend."

Marfield nodded. "It took me months to get the costs of the drainage tiles down to a reasonable price."

"Exactly. Still, you managed it. I am counting on your common sense in this. Graely has a reputation for excellence, along with a penchant for extravagance. I want your very practical suggestions on whatever design Graely concocts."

"As you wish, my lord, only I am not sure Graely will listen to me without feeling it an insult."

"Oh yes he will. Or he will be let go. The new Braemoor will take as many minds as hands. If he does not understand that, he can be replaced." James stood up. "You wanted to show me the dower house." Some air might banish the last of his headache.

"I do believe rain is in the offing." Marfield rose from his chair and moved to the door.

"Then we had best move quickly."

The rising wind encouraged them to move at a brisk pace. James looked down the path towards the cottages. He saw no sign of life. "I would have thought Madame Voisson would be the one to give me this introductory tour."

"She told me that she would be busy packaging the last of the items that have been reclaimed." Marfield clamped his hand to his hat to hold it on. "She has taken a special interest in them. Most will be stored in the old stable once she decides which items should be cleaned here and what ones must needs be sent to London."

"She has the expertise for that kind of decision?" Miss Morton must have been an amazing woman. He tried to picture her lecturing her young charge. Marguerite at ten, thin as a wraith, filled with energy she could barely contain. Her hair a long black tangle when it was not in plaits. And her eyes: brimming with mischief as she pretended to listen. All the while using that imagination to devise amazing plans for winning a fortune. Making her sit still long enough to learn must have been a true test of wills.

"Madame does know a great deal about art. Being French might account for that. She has also been talking to the marquis about the paintings."

"And she acts on his ravings? That has the sound of disaster in the making."

"He is not raving, my lord. It seems that most of the time he recalls the past better than the present and is able to direct Madame Voisson to the value and age of almost every piece she has asked him about."

"Is he that much recovered?"

"I do believe so. I have seen him walking the path with madame almost every afternoon before tea. He still uses his cane, but he speaks with an eagerness that is encouraging."

"Her one month probation is long over. But it is not too late to release her." The idea burst full-blown into his head.

"You would dismiss her?" Marfield stopped short, ignoring the first drops of rain.

It would remove temptation. Effective, if cowardly. The heavier splats followed the first drops and James gestured to the dower house with a nod. Marfield fell into step beside him as James tested his rationale aloud. "She is so curious, so enthusiastic."

"And for those reasons you would send her on her way?"

Marfield sounded doubtful. James had to agree that when said aloud they seemed more assets than shortcomings. He could hardly tell Marfield that he was thinking about letting her go because it was the easiest way to stop fantasizing about her. It was one thing to imagine her ten years old and a child, another entirely to compare her to every other woman as he had in London. He would see Henriette and imagine Marguerite in the same déshabille. He had danced with Christiana Lambert and knew that Marguerite would shine even in that glittering crowd.

They climbed the short flight of stone steps and were inside the door just as the rain began a steady rhythm.

The entry hall smelled like spring and was lit by a magnificent chandelier. Despite the hour, candles glowed a welcome and reflected brightly off the black and white marble squares that covered the floor from the front entrance, down the length of the hall, to the elegant pair of doors at the back of the house.

"The house has a four-room plan, my lord. At least that is how it was originally built. There are two rooms on the ground floor on either side of this hallway."

Marfield opened the door to their left and stepped back so that James could enter first. It was a salon and looked very masculine for a dower house, usually a woman's domain.

The walls were painted a deep green, and though the bookshelves were largely empty, a fire warmed the room and the two wing chairs facing it made it very welcoming.

Two doors led from the salon and he went through one into a good-sized dining room at the back of the house. This room had a large bow window with a table nestled there, the perfect spot for a solitary breakfast.

"There are two ground floor dependencies, my lord, one on each side of the house. The one on the north side was long ago converted into a suite of rooms and has been outfitted for the marquis. Your rooms are upstairs on the south side of the house."

So we are as far from each other as it is possible to be in a house this size. James walked across the hall, noticing for the first time the vase of flowers on the hall table. That must account for the smell of spring. He looked out the doors onto a very elegant stone terrace that led down to gardens he had never seen before. The garden was filled with plantings. It must be the kind of garden that held warmth and invited the sun, a lovely place for a lady to walk in winter.

"The marquis' suite has been located on the ground floor so that he has easier access to the garden."

Did she think of everything? For he knew whose work

this was. She had put all of her longing for a home into this doll-sized house. What would she do with the plans for Braemoor?

Marfield opened another door and stood aside again, this time his grin had James prepared for a surprise.

"A billiard room? Which dowager played billiards?"

"Madame thought of it. She insisted on bringing as much from the west wing here as would fit. And the billiard room was untouched by the fire. Madame insists that everything was spared for a reason."

He'd heard the argument himself. "And the staff did all this in two weeks?"

"As you said yourself, my lord, she is very enthusiastic. And it can be contagious."

"Yes, I can see that even you are ensnared."

"My wife and I count her as a friend, my lord."

Marfield was blushing. That James understood. His wife might call Marguerite a friend, but he doubted there was a man alive who would look on her in such a dispassionate way.

"My lord, on the day we met, Madame Voisson told me that she had been in England for so long that no one would think her born in France."

James laughed out loud. Marfield nodded.

"Exactly so, my lord. And it has nothing to do with her accent, my lord, for it is barely noticeable unless she is excited."

"Which is a near constant state." James spoke without thinking, and wished that he had not demonstrated his own fascination.

"Jenneth says she carries herself in a particular way that only French women do. That she does not mean to be flirtatious. And I have come to see that as entirely true."

"Has there been trouble with the staff?"

"Oh no, it is only that I worried at first. Jenneth had the

right of it, though. Madame is a lady first and circumstances have made her a housekeeper. Even without a lifetime of training, everyone agrees that she is all that one could want in a housekeeper."

Except old and ugly, James thought.

Marfield gestured to the stairs. "Would you like to see the rest of the house?"

Even as they made their way to the staircase, a knock sounded at the door. One of the field hands waited there, covered with mud to his ears. "Mr. Marfield, sir, the new dam is leaking and we need you to stop it."

"Go, Simon. I can find my way."

Marfield needed no more permission and rushed out of the house, firing questions at the boy as he ran.

James watched him go. Marfield's tour had not been as animated as Marguerite Voisson's version would have been, but he was, always, as conscientious as anyone could wish. And loyal. James wondered if Marfield's loyalty might have shifted. Did his housekeeper command a share of the fidelity that had once been only his?

He walked up the stairs, the scent of flowers rising with him. Another vase had been placed in the recess of the arched window that overlooked the garden and beyond to a glimpse of the path and the cottages to the west.

He moved down the hall and into the front room of his suite. The large desk was angled at the window and overlooked part of the garden. The room was a careful mix of comfort and practicality. As he walked closer he could see that she had filled the shelves with items that had been found in the last few weeks. "Everything that was spared was saved for a reason."

He picked up the leaden mass of Rhys's toy soldiers. Had he not told her to throw them away? Beside it, a new frame encircled the fairy drawing he had rescued from the trash.

She missed nothing. That alone gave him reason to send

her away. How long before she saw through him? It was only a matter of time, before she undermined his carefully cultivated isolation and made him want without sense or principles.

His bedroom came next and he entered with some hesitation. Nothing appeared to be out of the ordinary. Except for the fact that his room at Braemoor had been completely duplicated here.

Here was his bed, with the chip in the footboard where Morgan had kicked it in a fit of boyhood temper. They had never been able to find the piece of woodwork even though they had spent on hour on their hands and knees looking. In the end they had swabbed the spot with boot blacking and counted on no one noticing. No one ever had.

He stepped into the dressing room and found his clothes exactly as they had been stored in his dressing room despite the smaller space: his robe nearest the door, his shaving things marching along the stand. He walked back into the bedroom, wondering how long she had spent in here, making things perfect. Did she have the same fantasies as he did when she looked at this bed?

He turned his back on the question and walked over to the table by the window, even now set with a plate of biscuits and scones.

So this would be home, whether he liked it or not.

He did like it.

It had a warmth beyond the fire glowing and the spray of flowers on the mantel.

He picked up a scone from the plate of sweets and could have sworn it was still warm from the oven.

You win, he thought, *you win this battle, you managing little minx.* He walked over to the fireplace to the happy blaze that warmed the room even as the rain outside dampened the air. *I will live here.*

She could claim this as a victory, but he would win in the

end. This war had as much to do with the morals he had
been raised with as it did the aching for her that filled his
dreams.

*I do believe, Marguerite Voisson, that it is time for you
to go.*

Seventeen

Where had everyone gone? James counted almost forty-eight hours since he had taken up residence in the dower house and in all that time he had seen no more than his valet, the footman who served his meals, the occasional maid, and Prentice.

An hour or so ago, James had heard noise and found Prentice directing the lighting of the hall chandelier. That was as close to a commotion as James had observed. And he had only caught that because Prentice had difficulty reducing his baritone to a murmur.

James had had every expectation that servants would litter the place, be underfoot and in whatever room he chose to use. It had not been that way at all. For a small house it was exceptionally quiet.

He stood in the hall, outside his rooms, staring out the window at the back garden. The ticking of the clock persisted as a rhythmic counterpoint to the spatter of rain on the windows. The wet had eased up for most of the day, but it had started again late in the morning, an hour or so before dinner. The rain explained why no one was outside. There did not appear to be anyone inside either.

James headed down the stairs. The chandelier remained lit, unnecessarily so. Despite the rain, the fanlight over the front door let in sufficient light, as did the windowed doors

at the back of the hall. Was Prentice putting the housekeeper's cleaning efforts to the test?

James walked into the green salon and pushed the door
closed behind him. The latch caught but did not hold, one of
the few repairs that Marfield and Marguerite had missed.

She was avoiding him. With Prentice back at work, whole
days would go by when he would have no need to see his
housekeeper.

What had happened to the baskets left on the office floor?
She had always been so eager to share those with him. And
the menus. Every week she had brought them to him, insisting that she wanted a complete understanding of his
preferences. As if he cared what he ate. Food, enough of it,
and served when he wanted it. She insisted that could not
count as an adequate description and had bothered him with
cards and once even a recipe.

Finally, he had reminded her that food never went to
waste when you fed a staff of this size, and told her to serve
whatever she wanted. If he did not like the dish, surely it
would be a favorite belowstairs.

A fire warmed the room and he claimed the chair that
was placed so that he could appreciate the fire and also see
the door. He picked up the paper but did not read a word.

Even with no baskets to share and menus forbidden, she
had always had a dozen other questions. Why was she not at
his door three times a day?

Had he hurt her feelings? She was his housekeeper. Her
feelings were not supposed to show. They did, though, oh
how they did. He could tell when she was excited by the
way she sat on the edge of her chair, when she was amused
by the way she grinned and shook her head. He could tell by
the way she walked whether she was tired, hurried, or irritated. The most he could recall about Mrs. Lanning was her
size and how annoyingly slow she could be.

Marguerite had been crushed by his insistence that she

burn the diaries. She had brushed past Marfield and left the room near tears. She was upset, no doubt about that.

She had been annoyed with him before. She made a habit of it. Usually it did not last beyond their next meeting.

Could her upset date back to their meeting on the hill? Did she fear he would force his attentions on her again? He had done everything he could to demonstrate his disinterest.

She could be angry. She could be troubled. She could feel threatened, and all because of him. One question worried the back of his brain. If he was not interested in her, why did he care?

Because he *was* interested. More than interested. He was captivated. He had to send her away. In time, neither her station nor her innocence would be protection enough.

The front door opened. He heard it easily with the door ajar. A gush of chill, wet wind, followed the noise into the room. There had been no knock and James waited for whoever came in to announce himself.

"My mother lived here."

The marquis. James could not see him, but that voice he recognized. He began to stand up. How had the old man managed to make his way from the cottage without help?

"She did?" His missing housekeeper. Her response seemed vague, distracted. Had the old man managed to wear her patience thin?

He moved a few steps closer to the door.

"Oh dear, please do watch your step, my lord. The wet has made the floor slippery," she said.

"I will. I will. I can see it. I'm feeble, not blind."

Ah no, She had worn his patience thin.

"But here let me take hold of your arm, my dear. That way you will be safer." The old man cackled at his own joke.

James came to the door and opened it. He stood in the doorway, ready to offer his help, when it occurred to him that she would manage better without it.

Their backs were to him and as he watched, she took the old man's arm and wrapped it round hers. She was gentle, so gentle that he envied the marquis, would have traded places with him in age and time for the touch of her arm on his.

She paused next to a chair. "Let me take your coat. I wish you would have waited until the rain stopped."

"Waited! Ha! We waited two days for that drizzle to end. You've been talking about this place for a sennight. I was not about to wait any longer."

As she took the coat, the marquis sank into the chair. The housekeeper tossed the wet coat over another chair and wiped her hands on her apron.

"Where's that idiot of a butler?" Straeford called out at the top of his lungs.

"The staff have gone to dinner. I thought this first tour would be best without company."

James had been about to go to her aid again. He withdrew instead. If she wanted this first visit to be without company, he would not intrude. Indeed, he would be the worst sort of company, one sure to agitate and not calm. He walked back to the fire and held his hands out to warm them.

Why did she think this move better made in privacy? James wondered that a moment before the marquis barked the very question.

"So you can freely express your opinion, my lord."

James almost laughed out loud. As if a room full of people would keep the marquis from making his feelings known. It could well be that she wanted to protect the staff and not the old man.

"My opinion, eh? The light is very good in here."

James sat back down. Obviously she did not need his help.

"Why do you have all those candles lit during the day, girl? Cost too damn much to have them lit even at night."

"Prentice suggested it, for this occasion only. We all wanted to make this place so welcoming that you would not consider going back to the cottage."

Before the Marquis could reply, James heard the door open again.

"Mrs. Beecher!" Madame welcomed her with all the graciousness of a Town hostess. "Do move on ahead of us. You can inspect your room. The marquis' suite is through the door to the right at the back of the house."

"The back of the house?" Whatever energy the marquis had conserved he used to raise his voice. "I am to have rooms at the back of the house!"

James stood up again; sure that a mean burst of temper would follow, one that his petite housekeeper would not be able to manage. *Of course you are on the ground floor, old man. What other choice does she have?*

The marquis could not negotiate the stairs even once a day. He recalled the suite in question. His grandmother had used it at the end of a debilitating illness. His grandmother. He could barely recall her. An old, old lady whose hands shook and who insisted he call on her after dinner each Thursday. He had been so young that his nurse had accompanied him. Surely she had died before his mother left. He could not quite recall.

He waited at the door to see if Marguerite would need help.

"You are at the back and on the ground floor, only because it will be more convenient for you."

She spoke with an effortless patience that was impressive. James pushed the door shut and leaned against it, but still the latch would not hold. He was an eavesdropper whether he wished to be or not.

"There is easy access to the garden and a lovely prospect from your sitting room window. Please do not prepare a dislike before you have even seen it. Besides, my lord, no physical place can diminish who you are."

Illness had done that though she would never say so. His old man's ego was as fragile as his health. James thought back to the days before his apoplexy. He had been autocratic before, used to his way and quick to anger. While that remained, now it showed itself as the peevish demands of an old man, a person to be humored rather than respected.

Marguerite Voisson did respect him. That was what was so endearing about this little drama. Her affection had nothing to do with his rank or his wealth. She treated him as though his age and infirmity had earned her esteem.

James realized that she treated everyone with a particular mark of courtesy, even Mrs. Beecher, a woman who must be used to far less than the flattering welcome she had been given a moment ago.

And how did she treat him? As an equal. The answer popped into his head with hardly a moment's thought. *Ah, Miss Morton, despite your best efforts, her breeding will show.*

"So tell me, my dear, if nothing can change who I am, why are you moving me from the cottage, eh?"

That question brought James's attention back to them. When had the marquis rediscovered that irritating habit of debating the most unimportant subjects? Did it not show a mental acuity that they had all thought lost forever?

"We are moving, my lord, because even though it is not yet summer, winter will come and you will be much more snug here than in the cottage."

"Humph." Was his only reply. Then, "Give me your arm, and help me up out of this blasted chair."

James went back to his own chair, sat down one more time, picked up the paper, and tried to lose himself in news that he had read yesterday.

The clap-tap of Mrs. Beecher's ill-fitting shoes announced her presence in the hallway.

Not ten minutes ago he had wondered where everyone had gone. Slowly but surely they all were gathering in his front hall.

"Miss, the room is. . . ." Mrs. Beecher stopped talking as though words were beyond her, and then continued, "The room is most cunningly arranged. Why, at first I thought it too close. But after a bit I could see that you had thought of each and every needful thing and made them to fit so that it is roomier than my bigger room at Braemoor."

"I am delighted that you like it, Mrs. Beecher. Perhaps you could walk back to the cottage and encourage Justice and Billy."

Were those the names of the two strong-armed men Mrs. Lanning had found to help the nurse? Trust Marguerite to have learned them. She probably even knew their favorite colors.

"Yes, miss, I'll go and get 'em and tell 'em to get a move on. 'Tis a good thing they moved the big bed and table this morning before the rain started up again."

"You can protect the rest of the marquis' things with the old blankets. . . ." The thud of the door meant that madame was talking to the air.

"Well," her voice drifted back to him as she moved down the hall. "It is only water."

"What did you say?"

Marguerite moved farther down the hall and spoke to the marquis, words that James could not quite catch. He did hear the marquis' answering cackle.

The house quieted again and James stared at the fire, half mesmerized by the glow of the coals and flickering of flame.

She had befriended every person on his staff. And the marquis. That surprised him most of all. His father seemed a different man from the one who had stumbled into their interview more than a month ago.

She had invaded every corner of their life, his life. Would it have been that way if Prentice had not been injured and then taken sick? Or if the under butler knew how to do his job?

If she stayed on she would become only stronger. She would no longer be a high-minded busybody. He'd admitted not long ago that she was well on her way to becoming indispensable. It seemed she now was.

What had Marfield said in his quiet defense of her? "Everyone agrees that even without training, she is all that a housekeeper should be."

He would have to let her go soon, before every member of the staff followed her out the door. He would give her a year's salary and, God help him, a good recommendation. That would be generous enough. But he would send her packing. He would do it soon, very soon.

He tossed the paper down with finality, rose and walked to the door. As he stood there, the two men pushed through the door bearing baskets covered with blankets.

They must have been almost to the dower house when Mrs. Beecher left to get them. The nurse came behind them, holding one of the marquis' canes, looking for all the world like a shepherd urging reluctant sheep.

"Watch your dirty feet, don't be tracking mud down Miss' perfectly clean hallway."

Justice and Billy did not notice him. Mrs. Beecher stopped her harangue long enough to give him an ungainly curtsey.

He nodded to her. "Tell Madame that I want to see her."

"Yes, my lord."

She continued to urge the two men down the hall, not nearly as short with them. "Hurry up, hurry up, you hulks, I need to talk to Miss."

James paced back to the fireplace and then to the shelves, and glanced idly at the books that she must have ordered from London. Burke and Voltaire in uneasy company. Defoe's *Tour of the Whole Island of Great Britain*. Thomas Cook's multi-volume account of his travels.

Before he could choose a volume of Cook, there was a tap on the door. It was not Marguerite. What did it say that he knew her even by the way she scratched at the door?

The architect stood there waiting for permission to enter, his clothes dampened by rain and very wrinkled. He had disappeared two days ago on his familiarizing tour. Who would have guessed it would take that long? Graely's face glowed with a creative excitement that made James dubious even before he spoke.

"Come in. Come in. Dry yourself by the fire."

Graely looked down at his coat, "Oh, is it raining?"

James nodded. Had he wandered in the wet for the last two days? He pushed the volume back into its place and turned to the drinks table to get the man a glass of wine. The architect walked to the fire and held out his hands for barely five seconds before turning around. "My lord, it is a most wonderful ruin. It captures all the mood and feeling that so many try to create in their follies."

James handed him the wine. Graely took the glass and set it on the mantle.

"You see, my lord, this patina of age cannot be duplicated. It comes only with the ravages of time."

"Yes, I am sure it is filled with the mystery of the ages." He hoped the architect did not detect sarcasm as well as his housekeeper did. He did not want to alienate the man, at least not yet. "Yes, Graely, it is impressive. The question remains whether it can be rebuilt so that we can endure the ravages of time in some degree of comfort?"

"Why would you wish to, my lord?"

"It is what I hired you for."

"My lord, you hired me to build you a house. Yes, We did discuss the possibility of building on the ruins. However after even my first examination I can see that it is perfect as it is."

"Perfect?" This man spoke a language all his own. Where was his housekeeper? Surely she could translate.

"Yes. You must leave it as a ruin. Clear away the wood and debris so that only the stone is left. Let plants and vines claim it. It will attract people from all over."

"We are spectacle enough already."

"One of the burdens of your position, my lord."

No excuse in that quarter, James thought. Not from a man with a mission. "Where are we to build? You do have a place in mind, do you not?"

"Do you know that grove of trees? The one to the south-west of Braemoor?"

"Graely, I know every inch of this land."

"Yes, of course you do, my lord. I am so sorry." He bowed to James in an excess of regret. "That rise is the perfect site for a new Braemoor, situated so that it commands a view of the Downs. The old Braemoor would be visible too, but not dominate the prospect."

"You already have a design in mind?"

"Not precisely. I begin with a general idea of the location and the design forms in my head."

"When exactly does what I want come into consideration?"

"Why, my lord, I already know what you want. A building that reflects your family's history and consequence. A place that tells everyone that the Braedons have put their mark on this land long ago and will not be displaced, neither by the impact of war or politics."

"Or fire." James added, hoping to recall the man from his oratorical heights.

"A temporary inconvenience."

"Thank you for your insight, Graely. I appreciate all the time you put into this first examination." He turned to the fire. "I must think on this for a day or two."

"Very well, my lord." Graely seemed disappointed.

Five more minutes of obsequious banalities and Graely left for the village. Immediately there followed another tap on the door and James smiled, and just as quickly turned solemn. One did not dismiss an employee with a grin.

She walked in and stood by the door, holding a carefully wrapped bundle.

What was this? She did not look at all herself. Rather very young and dispirited, as if someone had taken her happiness and trampled it under their feet.

"What has the marquis done?"

"Why nothing, my lord." The question gave her a little animation. "He is sitting by the fire and most likely asleep. The move was quite an effort for him." She tried to smile but her expression was a mockery of her usual élan. "He seems very content."

"Come in, madame." He disliked the edge in his voice and tried again. "Come by the fire. It is much warmer over here." There, that sounded better. Make her comfortable and then fire her. Was there a gracious way to do this?

She walked across the room, came up to the fire and placed the bundle on the table by his chair. She plucked Graely's untouched glass of wine from the mantle and carried it back to the serving table near the door.

Turning towards him, she spoke from the far side of the room as though she planned to make an escape as soon as the words were said.

"I am so sorry, so very sorry." She drew a breath that came out more like a moan. "I am resigning. I am giving up my post as housekeeper."

Eighteen

"What?" He could not have heard her right. She intended to leave? She was resigning before he had a chance to fire her?

"I am so sorry. I cannot stay at Braemoor any longer."

"You're going away?" He shook his head, incredulous and furious at once. This made no sense at all. Avoiding him was not enough? Was this her next method of putting distance between them? It seemed excessive. Never mind that it had been his intention as well. Thank God she was the one who suggested it. He could see now that it was a stupid, nonsensical idea.

She belonged here. He could not imagine Braemoor without her. It had been unbearable before. After having seen her light and life fill each corner it would be even worse if she left. The staff, his father, the Marfields, not one of them would tolerate her leaving any more than he would.

She looked so forlorn that all he wanted to do was console her, cradle her close, and distract her from her heartbreak. It was a ghastly temptation.

"Leave Braemoor? Marguerite," he said with a disgust that was sincere even if his cynicism was not. "What about that tripe you handed me last week, when you said that you had found your true calling here?"

"Working here is my calling, truly it is."

Good, he thought. That straightened her spine. She no longer looked like a stray puppy expecting a kick.

"At least it used to be, my lord. Now it is different. The work that I do best is complete. There is nothing left to salvage at Braemoor. The ruin is only a ruin and this house is made comfortable. And it is time for me to move on to another post."

"Because?"

When she did not answer his leading question he went on. "I could hazard any number of guesses but your explanations are so much more entertaining."

"The truth is that I know nothing about being a housekeeper."

She was wringing her hands.

"What is this? Now I am confused. Knowing nothing about housekeeping has never mattered before." His tease did nothing to relieve her distress. "There must be something seriously wrong when my sarcasm neither annoys nor amuses you! Indeed, if you keep on like this, I will be the one in need of comfort."

Only the slightest of smiles at this sally, and it did not last. What could have put her in such a state? "Has Prentice insulted you?"

"Oh no, my lord, he has been everything that is accommodating."

"If you have his support, you can learn all you need to know from him. Indeed, he will assume much of the work you have taken on in his absence."

She looked down and when she looked up again her eyes were filmed with tears.

"Are you going to cry?" The thought shocked him. He had seen her close to tears only once before. That had been at least nominally his fault. What had he done this time?

"Come over here." He tried to be gentle but feared that he sounded desperate.

She walked two steps closer. He raised his eyebrows at her and she came all the way to where he stood. She came very slowly, as though walking to the stocks.

She stopped in front of him, her head bowed. "I am doing my best not to cry."

He could see the tears win out and he handed her his handkerchief. She accepted it, wiped her streaming eyes, and began twisting it. "I have been so happy here. Indeed, it is like a home to me. Your father is so kind to me. Mrs. Beecher is a different woman. The chef and I speak French and trade recipes. The architect is come and will make a beautiful new home for you. And I have ruined it all." The tears stopped. She looked at him. "I have done my best to deceive you and I can not bear it anymore. I had every intention of never telling you. Except I find that I cannot keep the truth from you. I have worked so hard to earn your trust and now I have ruined it."

"Has Jenneth Marfield tutored you in drama? It would do Goldsmith credit."

She did not see any humor in the tease.

"Did you say that you had deceived me?" He was so distracted by her theatrics that he had almost missed the confession. "You lied to me?"

She nodded and tears came anew.

"Tell me, and tell me without tears. I am more than tired of asking questions."

"Lord Crandall," She drew a deep breath. "I have read the journals."

She raised her hands to her breast, looking like a penitent telling the worst of her sins. "I read them despite your specific order to destroy them. I know that you will send me away, most likely without a reference. And still I cannot keep this from you. I cannot lie about something so important."

Her heart was breaking right before his eyes.

"My God, Marguerite!" Relief made him irritable. "This melodrama, these theatrics, this threat to leave is all because you read the diaries?"

She nodded, quick, short, sharp nods.

"Of course you read them." He spoke very slowly and with emphasis as though stating the obvious "My dear girl, that is not news at all, not at all. If you were a spy for Napoleon, were going to marry the marquis, set fire to Braemoor yourself, any of these would be news."

Good God, could melodrama be catching? With an effort, he stopped his rant and spoke calmly. "But reading the journals? Marguerite, I expected nothing less."

She took a step back in shock. "You did?"

"Do you think I'm a complete fool? When I told you to burn them, do you think I expected you would obey me?"

She nodded very slowly.

"What joy!" He laughed. "Congratulate me! I know you better than you know yourself! Just this once, but even once is very satisfying."

She straightened and lost her haunted look. "You made it a test?"

"Of a kind." He prepared for a burst of temper.

"And you are happy that I failed?"

"Not happy. No, but, all in all, more pleased than upset. I never doubted that you would read every word and even memorize the more meaningful passages."

She looked better, her color had returned, the guilty look gone.

"Oh, I do so thank you, my lord, for not being angry. They are a wonder, truly they are. Lady Gwyneth wrote all about your childhood and how you would tease your brother and. . . ."

"Stop right there."

"But, my lord, there are such wonderful stories. And there

are the most amazing revelations. My lord, you have a brother!"

"Marguerite, I have two brothers." He spoke with some exasperation, more annoyed with himself for responding to her than for her misstatement.

"No, my lord, I mean another brother. Your own mother, Lady Annabelle. . . ."

"Stop!"

She did, with a huff of annoyance.

"My mother died in childbirth within a year of leaving here. I know it, the marquis knows it, and no doubt Lady Gwyneth had her own proof or her father would never have let her marry. Annabelle's bastards, whether they survived or not, are of no interest to me whatsoever."

Marguerite pressed her lips into an unbecoming thin line.

"Yes, I can see you must physically restrain yourself from telling me more. Please refine the practice, madame. I am not interested."

"Very well, my lord; however, I must say one more thing. I cannot burn Lady Gwyneth's journals. I will not. I am returning them to you." She spoke with conviction. "If you want them destroyed you must do it yourself. And even if you do destroy them, then there will be stories that I must tell you. Some things are too important to leave to fate."

"You will stop talking and listen to me, Marguerite. We do not need more drama." He gestured to the chair across from his. "Sit down."

When she sat, he did the same.

"Where do you think my sister Maddie discovered her fairies?" He would not lose his temper over this. She was close enough to an outburst herself. One of them had to remain calm.

"Maddie's fairies? Like the ones in the drawing?" She did not wait for his answer. "They came. . . ."

"Straight from my very creative stepmother's imagination. She made up stories for her children and made up impossibly happy endings. And she did it because the marquis made our lives a misery."

As usual, whenever he spoke of his family, he had her complete attention. Satisfied with his own composure, he went on.

"We lived for the times they went to London. The others missed their mother. That was more than made up for by the fact that our father had gone with her. Mrs. Lanning was less irritable, Prentice would let us play in the billiard room even though it had been labeled strictly off limits, even Harold, the hall porter, never complained when we knocked and ran away a dozen times in one day."

Marguerite nodded. "You are right that she made up stories."

He glanced at the books and back at her. "You believe what I'm telling you?"

"But of course. However, they are so clearly different from her journal entries. If you look, you will see. Her stories have elegant drawings with them and, indeed, the largest volume is almost entirely tales of fairies and children who discover each other in the wood."

He could not convince her, no matter how cogent his argument, that these books were no more than novels. The worrisome thing was that she had half convinced him that they had value.

"And you have brought up another important consideration, my lord. These diaries were written by Lady Gwyneth, and while you may not want them, it is possible that Lord Morgan or her other children might."

"You are saying that they are not mine to destroy?"

"Yes, my lord." She sensed a trap, he could tell by the way she looked askance at him.

"If these are not mine to destroy, how are they mine to read?"

"Because to her mind you were as much her child as all of her natural children. You will see that if you read the entries." She leaned closer to him, "My lord, she loved all the marquis' children, not only those she bore. . . ."

"Emotional drivel, that is all this is." He interrupted her without compunction, raising his voice only a little. "I will tell you only once more that I do not want to hear a word about these books. Not from you or anyone."

"Bien sûr, my lord." She repeated, with great calm. And then added in English, "I can respect your wishes. Indeed I will."

"Are you trying to convince me, or yourself?" *That was easy,* he thought. *Too easy.*

She ignored his question for one of her own. "But still I must ask, did you truly *want* me to read the journals?"

"No, not want, but I had every expectation that the lure of family history would be too great for you to resist."

Wrong answer. She stood up, any hint of servility replaced by aggrieved anger.

"And you could not simply give me permission to read them? You could do no more than set up temptation and hope that I would sin!"

He stood up too. "You are making entirely too much of it."

Her pink cheeks were flushed and pleasure had nothing to do with it. "My lord, you are the only person I know whose idea of generosity would put me through such anguish. If you intended to make me a gift of the journals why could you not simply say so?"

She did not shout, she never did. He did hear an outrage in her voice that matched his growing annoyance.

"Madame, you go too far." He came closer.

"Oh yes, now you are very much your father. You think if you assume all the *hauteur* of your title I will not press you further." She walked from behind the chair and stood in front of him with her hands clenched at her sides. "Very well, I will not. I will bow to your wishes." She gave him the most mocking of curtsies and turned to leave the room.

"No." He spoke with great calm, though it took effort. He stopped her by the expedient of taking her by the shoulders and holding her in front of him. Touching her was the most hellish delight he had ever endured. His grip tightened ever so slightly. It was either that or pull her into his arms.

"No matter in what manner I gave you the journals, I expected more gratitude than condemnation. Why is it that you are never satisfied?"

Her eyes fell and he wondered if she could see the pulse beating in his neck as he could feel hers hammering. "What more do you want, Marguerite?"

"Everything, not these little tiny bits of yourself. I want everything you are." She whispered the words but he heard them. Had she meant him to? She raised her eyes as she spoke and her heart was there for him to see, for him to take. "You have so much to give."

He did not waste one moment more. He had longed for this that night on the hill and she had said no. Today he would not give her the chance.

They were so close it was the merest breath of distance to reach out and taste her mouth. Her lips were soft, her touch hesitant. His was not. With that first intimate contact he captured for his own her warmth, her generosity, her *joie de vivre*. They were his. He pulled her more fully into his arms as her essence filled his heart.

He held her body against his, felt the gentle pressure of her breasts, the warmth of her hands around his neck, the response of her mouth, as he demanded more. She gave as was her nature and he gave to her, an entirely new experience for him. He gave her pleasure, longing, the promise of more heady delight.

He made to end the kiss, and then tasted once more, a test

to see if the first were real or an intoxication of his body. She opened her lips to him and he tasted her sweetness. As he did, he was gripped with a fear as intense as the pleasure. He put her from him, very carefully. They stood apart not touching, each drawing less than steady breaths.

Her breathing grew more measured, though her eyes were still dazed and her expression showed as much surprise as pleasure. He found it an amazingly erotic combination.

"That was not precisely what I meant, my lord," she said unsteadily.

Her voice was a bare whisper and he made to step closer, stopped himself and shook his head instead.

She raised her face to his. A smile framed her words. "That was not what I meant, before, when I said that I knew you had so much more to give."

"Oh my dear liar, that is exactly what you meant." He stepped back farther, away from her lips, her eyes, her heart. He made his voice practical. "It does answer at least one question though."

"Oh yes, my lord, it does."

She answered him with such enthusiasm that he wondered if they had the same question in mind.

"I meant that we have both wondered what a kiss would be like."

"There was never any true doubt of that was there, my lord?" As she spoke she nodded slowly, with saucy impudence, as though he had only part of it right.

"Not since that night on the hill when you would not leave me alone." He tried to be stern. It came out teasing.

She shook her head. "Not since the day that Lord Morgan interrupted us."

Transfixed by her smile, he nodded, forgetting caution. "Not since the day when I saw through your disguise and held your hand."

"Since the beginning?" She spoke on a breath of pleased laughter.

"Yes." He turned from her even as he made the admission. He could do what he had to do only if he did not look at her and see her heart in her eyes.

"Now that we have shared that elusive kiss, we can go on as we have before."

He wanted to turn back and judge her reaction, but did not. Instead he picked up his wineglass and took a sip, and another. "It was after all, only a kiss."

"I would be insulted, my lord, if I did not know that this time you are the one lying."

He turned back to her in surprise. She looked offended. He weakened. "It was an entertaining kiss. Vastly so."

She gave him a measuring look, so filled with seductive reproach that he wanted nothing more than to show her how much more entertaining their next kiss could be.

This would not do. Not if he was to behave as he ought. "Madame, if my stepmother ever taught me anything it was that one does not take advantage of those of a lesser station. It might be done in some households, but not this one."

He chose the words quite deliberately. Let her think he saw her as nothing more than a servant. That her birthright counted for nothing here in England. He would use it to put distance between them. "My kiss was insult enough, madame."

She sobered, her expression neither one of anger nor of happiness, any lingering sensuous warmth replaced with uncertainty.

"I will take this no further and you are to forget it as well."

She looked down at her hands, held tight in front of her. "As if we can control our dreams."

"We will go on as we have before."

"This is what you want?" The question in her voice called him a liar.

"Yes." He looked straight at her, speaking the single word with the chill voice and cold eye that had stood as his best protection for most of his lifetime. "You are my housekeeper and nothing more. That is exactly what I want and as it should be."

When she looked up at him, her expression a mix of hurt and denial, he did not look away, but let her vulnerability harden his resolve. He felt more a cad than a gallant. Did she not understand that he did this for her own good?

"You have a home here, Marguerite. I would do nothing to endanger that. Prentice can show you how to get on. It will be years before the new Braemoor is ready and by then you will be so well educated that even your Miss Morton would be impressed."

It was a mistake to try to explain. He knew it the moment she stepped toward him, the softness back in her eyes, one hand reached out to him.

"It is only," she stopped and tried again. "I had hoped that we. . . ."

James was so afraid of what she might say, what she might offer, what he might take, that he shook his head and turned his back to her. He raised the glass again and finished the last of the wine with a long swallow.

Turning, he handed her the empty glass, determined to show her that they could go on as they had before. "Tell Prentice to come to me."

She took the glass and somehow managed not to touch him in the process or even look at him. She hurried to the door, stopped and turned around. "I want you to know. . . ."

"I am not the slightest bit interested in what you want me to know. I thought I made that clear." He turned away not only to hide his own embarrassment from her, but also so he would not see how his rudeness would hurt her. A cad and a coward. Let her see that. Let her believe it. Hopefully she would never realize that her attempts at deception were pitiful compared to his.

He knew the moment she left the room and poured himself another drink.

Would Prentice explain to her that you did not leave a room until you were dismissed and that you did leave it as soon as you were? James hoped not. She was no more his servant than he was her lord and master.

He sat by the fire to let the warmth seep into him. He was cold. Fear did that to him.

That kiss. Oh God, it had stripped his soul bare, compelled him to face truth. He was no more immune to love than his besotted brother Morgan. His father had not beaten it out of him. His mother's betrayal had not killed it.

He had denied it, hidden from it, taken lovers to convince himself that sex was all he needed. This one kiss had shown him the truth. He was as vulnerable as any man, as open to longing, pain, the inevitability of loss.

Had he convinced her that life would go on as before? How absurd. He should have dismissed her. He should have, at least, accepted her resignation, but he could no more do that than he could send the marquis away or burn those foolish journals. What would he do? He reached up and tried to press away the beginnings of headache. He would avoid her if she did not avoid him.

He would find other lovers. He would. He would not try to understand Marguerite Voisson. Was that even possible? No more than she could ever understand him, God willing.

Nineteen

Marguerite ran down the path. The rain made a good excuse but had nothing to do with her rush to Jenneth's cottage. The echo of James's kiss was like an aphrodisiac, so insistent, so evocative that all she wanted was to feel his lips again. Even as she ran, she chanted the same phrase over and over. "What a fool I am! What a fool. What a fool."

Jenneth answered the door with a look of concern that eased when she saw Marguerite. "Come in. Come in." She stepped back and Marguerite crossed the threshold, stopping long enough to shake the rain from her skirts.

"You were knocking so hard that I thought it was one of the workers with another emergency." Her momentary ease vanished. "Is something wrong with the marquis?"

"Oh no, he made the move very well." She drew deep breaths to slow her heart. "That seems days ago."

"What is it then?" Jenneth spoke with a quiet calm that Marguerite found so comforting.

"Lord Crandall." The very act of saying his name brought tears to her eyes. "He lies, Jenneth. I am certain he is lying. Oh, please what am I to do?"

Jenneth's took her hand, drawing her inside. "You will sit, take tea with me, and tell me what has upset you."

She spoke with such maternal concern that Marguerite let herself be led to the second chair by the fire before she remembered that Jenneth's husband was most likely awaiting his own tea.

"Oh, Mr. Marfield! Surely he was looking forward to tea with you."

"He is asleep, Marguerite." Even as she spoke, Jenneth stepped into the kitchen and brought out the tea. "He has spent day and night on that drainage and new dam. He is in desperate need of rest. I do not expect him to awake until morning, indeed I would not wake him except for the most serious emergency."

"My knocking." Marguerite spoke with sincere regret. To her horror two tears tracked down her cheek.

Jenneth fussed with the tea things and did not look at her. Marguerite hurriedly fished a handkerchief from one of her pockets and wiped her eyes.

"Tonight we could throw the tea things against the wall and he would sleep through it. He is that exhausted, my dear."

Jenneth went back into the kitchen and returned with a plate of biscuits, checked the teapot, and settled in her seat. "The tea can steep a little longer. Can you tell me what has so upset you?"

The few minutes of fussing had given Marguerite time to calm, not completely, but enough that she could wonder if Jenneth was the right confidante. She was hardly objective where the viscount was concerned.

"Jenneth, I understand why you cannot care for Lord Crandall. I wish I could find a way to make you see him more kindly." She stood up again, paced the room, and came back to stand close to the fire. "Have you ever thought that his experience of other actresses may have been every bit as disappointing as your experience of the ton?"

Jenneth was gracious enough to consider the question before answering. "I hardly think that likely. His kind have all the power and I had none."

"I am sorry. I do not mean to insult you in any way. I know none of the details of your London life so it is presumptuous of me to seek any concession for him." Marguerite sighed. "If only you could see him as I do."

Marguerite stared at the ceiling and refused the tears. She paced the length of the room and came back to her chair.

That kiss meant something to him. It must have done. How could he be unmoved when she had felt the earth shift? Had he tried to protect her out of a misguided sense of responsibility? Or could it be that his much wider experience made their kiss amusing and nothing more? Which of the possibilities was worse? She needed advice and she needed it badly.

"I can see that you are upset, Marguerite. Please sit down and I will listen."

Marguerite nodded, sitting down again. "Jenneth, he is very protective of those he cares for." She reached for her tea but her hand was not quite steady. "You believe that it is out of a sense of obligation, but he has no obligation to me."

"No, I would say he has more of a responsibility than an obligation." She emphasized the word responsibility as if she knew what was coming.

"Neither word is very appealing at the moment." Both made the possibility of a future unlikely. She tried another tack. "Jenneth, Lord Crandall is the one who suggested that you move to the dower house."

"No!" Her one word held vehement disbelief.

"Oh yes," Marguerite warmed to the subject. "Mr. Marfield told me so when we were first discussing the possibility of renovating the place. And when your husband refused to live there, it was the viscount who suggested that you combine two of these cottages into one."

"Marguerite, how can that be? I thought Lord Crandall

had determined to do everything in his power to make my life a misery."

"There, you see? If you have misconstrued his behavior in this situation, could it not be that you were wrong the other time?"

"Hardly."

"Was it only that one occasion? When he offered you money to cry off on your engagement? You must tell me the truth and not try to spare my feelings." She moved to the edge of her seat and prayed that she would not hear a story that would destroy her own belief.

"Only that once, Marguerite, when he came to my rooms in Town. But it was such a vulgar thing to have tried."

"And I am sure he has regretted it ever since. He keeps so much to himself, his regrets, his disappointments."

"You would know more of that than I."

"Yes I would, for I see him daily and you do not. He goes too far in his wish for privacy. He would even prefer that people not suspect his generosity." She was thinking of his gift to her of the diaries. "It is so very like him not to care what people think, or pretend not to care."

She had calmed enough that she could sip her tea. "His offer of money to you was wrong, but I believe, truly I do, that he only had what he thought were Mr. Marfield's best interests at heart. The viscount has known so little true affection. How could he know that yours was a love match?"

"But, Marguerite, it was not."

"Not a love match?" Marguerite forgot her own concerns at this bald announcement.

"That's right." Jenneth closed her eyes and bowed her head. "I did not love Simon when he asked me to marry him." She picked at the edging on the napkin in her lap. "He was quite infatuated with me and I was desperate enough to take advantage of it. Lord Crandall knew that, I'm sure he did."

"How could he?" If he did, then Jenneth's dislike did indeed have deeper roots than the one incident. What woman would want a constant reminder of a man who thought her mercenary? "Had you met the viscount before, Jenneth?"

"Oh no, but he is well known in the *demimonde*. He has a reputation as a generous and considerate lover, though always remote, detached. Even his longest relationships have never been more than practical *liaisons*. He knows those who are of the same mind as he and avoids the others."

"Hardly romantic."

"No, my dear, romantic is not a word I have ever heard associated with Lord Crandall."

"So you had not met him, but knew of him?"

"Precisely. The theater manager told me that Lord Crandall had made inquiries and, even though I was puzzled, I told the manager that I would see him. We hardly move in the same circles. It should have been obvious to anyone with experience of the London stage that I was struggling to establish myself out of necessity rather than inclination. I needed money to live and acting was my only means of support. Or the only means I was willing to consider until I met Simon Marfield."

"If you will forgive me, Jenneth, Mr. Marfield hardly commands the kind of fortune that would make you comfortable."

"Oh yes he did. He offered the blessed security of a wedding ring and respectability." She twisted the ring on her finger. "I was as eager to grasp an opportunity as any other actress: my opportunity was a marriage license. Lord Crandall was right to think of me as no better than the lot of them." Her head was still bent.

Jenneth's embarrassment was so palpable that it gave Marguerite pause. She did not ask the first question that came into her head. *If that is so, why did you not accept the money Lord Crandall offered?* Instead she reached over and drew the napkin, now twisted and damp, from her friend's hand.

"But Jenneth Marfield, you are so obviously in love."

"Yes." Jenneth's expression softened considerably.

"It is a very personal story, but would you tell me, please?"

Jenneth laughed, "Well, I see that I must or you will think me as greedy as Lord Crandall does."

"Nonsense. It is impossible for me to see you that way. This is hardly the lap of luxury and you could have lived in the dower house if appearances were important to you."

"But I do live in the greatest comfort I have ever known! You have no idea how comforting respectability can be when you have lived without it."

She did know a little of that, but settled for a sympathetic nod. "You are comfortable now, but that is hardly the beginning and I am quite determined to hear every word."

Jenneth twisted the ring on her finger and began. "Simon saved my life."

Marguerite leaned forward and grinned. *"Bien,* you have not forgotten all the drama you learned. Did he save your life, truly?"

"Yes, he did, in many ways and indeed, quite literally."

"Then we must both thank God that he was in that place at that very moment." Satisfied that this would be every bit as romantic as she had hoped, Marguerite sat back, still attentive, prepared for a long tale. Was it not amazing the stories each heart held?

Jenneth set down her teacup and composed herself. Marguerite did her best to be patient while her friend organized her thoughts.

"It seems a lifetime ago, Marguerite."

Marguerite felt selfish. Was this a tale better left in the past? Before she could ask, Jenneth began her story.

"I had been in London for three months. I had found a little success on stage and it was becoming more and more difficult to dismiss the attentions of the men who came backstage every night. They brought gifts and flowers and would follow me from the theater. All I wanted was to earn a living, an honest, honorable living. No matter how often I said that there were one or two who refused to believe it."

Jenneth sat lost in thought for a moment and then continued. "One night two men waylaid me at my front door. They tried to force me into a carriage. No one paid any attention to my calls for help, no one except this one man who ran up, paused, and, in a very gentlemanly way, asked me if I needed assistance."

Jenneth laughed with true amusement. "I will never forget the contrast between his eagerness for a fight and the good manners he used in asking first if it was what I wanted."

Marguerite thought it very romantic.

"When I first learned his name, he had a bloody nose and a black eye and I am sure he ached in places too personal for me to inquire about."

"Mr. Marfield fought them?" Marguerite shook her head at the thought, all approval at his gallantry.

"Yes. He fought them, two of them. And he won." She said that with unladylike satisfaction.

"Simon came back the next day and offered to escort me to and from the theater. I have no idea how he found out that I was an actress or where I worked. My landlady might have told him. She was always very talkative."

She twisted her wedding ring and sat silent a moment. "After that attack I was afraid, so afraid that I welcomed his protection." She looked at Marguerite. "In every way."

They became lovers? Marguerite could hardly believe it of the staid Simon Marfield. He must have fallen hopelessly in love.

"We had two weeks. Then he told me he must return here

to Braemoor and he asked me to come with him as his wife."

"And you said yes."

"I did. I knew it was selfish. I determined that if I had to put on the best performance of my life, he would never know anything less than comfort and respect from me."

Jenneth picked up her tea and took a sip.

"Oh that is so noble, Jenneth, of both of you, but I know there is more. For anyone can see that the two of you share feelings deeper than respect."

"I owe Lord Crandall that." Jenneth said it with a smile. "When he came to me and made that offer he seemed quite confident that I would accept. I can laugh now when I recall his expression as I refused the money. I was as ladylike as the circumstances would allow. Which only made him the more insulting. He finished by saying that if I thought to have him offer me more money, I had made the wrong gamble. He was so cold. It frightened me more than a show of temper would have, but I would not be swayed."

Marguerite had seen that same coldness herself more than once. Today it had hurt her much more than it had frightened her. She pushed the upset aside. She would hear the rest of Jenneth's story. "So, you rejected Lord Crandall's offer."

"Yes, yes, I did, and decided that I must tell Simon. I would not have our marriage begin with deception, especially if it would endanger his position at Braemoor. But I was so afraid that Simon would value Lord Crandall's regard more than mine."

"Perhaps telling Simon of it was a test on your part, a test of his attachment."

"It could be, Marguerite. It could be. Simon's insistence that he would leave Braemoor before he would forsake our engagement was like being recalled from a half death."

"Did he confront Lord Crandall?"

"I have never asked. He did tell me that the viscount had agreed not to stand in the way of the banns and that his position here was secure.

"When it was over and my mind and heart had calmed enough for me to think rationally, I did wonder why I refused the money and the independence. One day, I was pouring tea and Simon took my hand and kissed it, as though pouring tea was the kindest most wonderful thing anyone had ever done for him."

Her eyes glimmered with emotion. "At that moment, that silly little moment, I understood that I loved him, that I could not imagine life without his generous spirit, his loyalty, his green eyes, and every sweet gesture that gives my life meaning."

Marguerite nodded, her own emotions awakened.

"I realized that you can be with a person for days, weeks, even longer than that, and realize love has been there all along and you have not appreciated it. Only God knows why we can be so blind."

They sat in silence except for the delicate sniffs of repressed tears.

"It is a long recounting, Marguerite. I hope you have found it worth hearing." She paused a moment. "Now you must tell me what brought you here like a fox with a pack of dogs at your heels."

She could hardly refuse when Jenneth had been so frank with her, but she did not expect her friend to be as happy an audience as she had been. "It's only that someone has done the kindest thing in the world today and left me so terribly confused."

"That Prentice is such a genuine fellow."

Marguerite laughed, "Not Prentice, Jenneth."

"No. I know who you mean. It is only that I can hardly credit Lord Crandall with anything remotely like caring."

"It is as I said before. He hides his feelings with arrogance and sarcasm. But that is another matter entirely. You would understand him better if you had ever experienced his kindness."

"And you have?" Jenneth sounded more than skeptical.

"He hired me! That alone is more generous than anyone else had been for the four months before."

"Marguerite, I have no wish to insult you, but I think he would have hired anyone who walked through the door and wore a dress."

"Yes, well, perhaps that could be true." Marguerite tried another tack, more pertinent to her current dilemma. "It could also be true that kindness is not the best word to use. He will talk to me though, Jenneth. And though he does his best to hide it, I hear loneliness and longing for his family." And love, though she would not yet say that out loud.

"Do you think so?" She considered Marguerite's explanation. "I would not have believed it before the fire. But one thing I have learned while the marquis lived so close is that the old man is more burden than support."

Thank you, God, Marguerite thought. Perhaps there is hope that Jenneth could learn to see Lord Crandall in a kinder light. "He does care. Too much. He learned from childhood what it is to live without love and to see how the world is changed by it."

The fire was fading, though the room was still warm enough; it must be growing late.

"He loved his mother and his stepmother and lost them both. Is it any wonder that he keeps the secrets of his heart hidden?"

She put her cup down and gave voice to the words that were as much wish as belief. "That uncaring façade is only pretence and the very reason that I think I must be very much in love with him."

At Jenneth's distress, Marguerite decided that her friend did not need to hear about the kiss. "Please do not worry.

Romantic history is filled with dozens of stories of unrequited love. I am not so vain that I think I am the first housekeeper to ever feel such affection for her employer."

"It can not be easy to keep your feelings secret."

"Bien, it may be that I will not have to. It may be that he. . . ." She stopped, not quite ready to put the heart-hungry wish into words. "I will tell you this, Jenneth. I have experienced enough love and loss to understand that we are fools to deny love when we find it. It is meant to be acknowledged and shared."

"Has he said anything?" She asked as if afraid of the answer.

"Oh no. Far from it." So far from it that he denied it completely. She could say that with complete honesty. *I am the one who has hopes.*

"Marguerite, you must listen to me. You must." Jenneth took her hand and spoke with urgency. "You cannot endanger your post here. It would be worse than folly to put your heart before more practical matters. Please tell me that you will not."

Marguerite bit her lip, loathe to lie but not willing to give up this new dream.

"What you are contemplating would never be tolerated here. Prentice would not allow it. He has a rigid morality that comes direct from his training here at Braemoor. He would be hard pressed to tolerate it in a member of the senior staff."

"You came for my advice and you must listen to it," Jenneth insisted.

"You made the choice to give yourself before you were certain of marriage."

"My situation was completely different. It never endangered my livelihood. It is what is expected of an actress. And you will notice how few friends I have because of that. You are the only one who calls. I should have warned you against coming, but I so longed for a friend that I was selfish."

Marguerite would have spoken, but she did not let her.

Jenneth let go of her hand, but her words lost none of their intensity. "You have a life you value here. People look up to you. They trust you. You have made a difference in so many lives, the marquis, Mrs. Beecher, even that stupid under butler, Cludde, tries harder when you smile at him."

Jenneth sat back in her chair. "Marguerite, if nothing has happened, if he has made no proposition, it will take nothing more than a firm resolve to go on. If he is the gentleman you insist, he will leave you alone. Please, listen. You will ruin so much more than your own life."

"Ruin is too strong a word." Marguerite's protest was half-hearted.

"Ruin is exactly the word." Jenneth spoke with urgent conviction. "Once your relationship is known, the only home you would have as his lover is a London house for as long as you please him. Marguerite, you would have to leave Braemoor. You know you would."

"Leave Braemoor? He means more to me than this place ever could but I thought, I hoped. . . ."

"Yes, you would have to leave. You cannot expect to keep the respect of this household if your own moral standing is compromised."

"Oh dear heaven." Marguerite stood up, now close to tears. "This is not at all what I wanted to hear."

"This may not be what you want to hear, but you came because you knew I would tell you the truth and the hard truth is what you must pay heed to."

Jenneth stood too and took Marguerite's hands. "My dear friend, I would tell you this even if Lord Crandall were my own much loved brother. I do not need to hold him in esteem to know what our world would think of such a *liaison*."

Marguerite nodded, unable to speak.

Jenneth pulled her into a tight embrace. "Please, we are here for you, both of us. Never, ever think you are alone."

A steadfast friend could be such a consolation. But for now, all Marguerite wanted was the solitude of her cottage and her grief.

Twenty

James heard the voices as he came down the stairs. The open stairwell was as good as a hall porter at announcing guests. This time, though, the company was not in the hall, but in the green salon.

Graely. He had completely forgotten that he was supposed to meet with him today. That would make him late for his meeting with Marfield.

The salon door had fallen ajar as usual and he could tell by Graely's ingratiating tone that he was talking to someone with whom he wanted to find favor.

"A building that reflects your family's history and consequence. A place that tells everyone, without words, that the Braedon family put its mark on this land long ago. . . ."

At least Graely had this part of his presentation down to the word. Who did he want to impress? He knew the answer before he stepped into the room. The marquis.

It was impossible to avoid the marquis in a house this size. Yesterday James had come upon him working his way through the post on the hall table. Pieces of correspondence littered the table and floor and when he saw James he threw the rest at him, "Bah! No one writes an intelligent hand any more."

Mrs. Beecher found him not a moment later, all apologies, as she coaxed the grumpy man back to his suite.

". . . neither by the impact of war or the trivia of politics."

"You want to build a new house on that rise to the south?"

James pushed through the door, running a litany of curses through his head.

The architect turned to him with an effusive welcome. The marquis ignored him. He was seated in the chair that James considered his, staring into the fire while he worried the head of the cane at his side. If you could ignore the badly-tied cravat, sagging stockings, and dirty jacket, he looked every inch the lord of the manor.

"Braemoor always was an intolerable place. Gwyneth hated it, every stone cold wall and rotten piece of paneling. And it as good as took her from me. Her sickness was made worse by that cold dark winter." He stamped his cane on the floor. "You could not warm the place. I all but burned it down trying to keep her room warm enough."

"My lord." A quiet and very calm Marguerite Voisson stepped closer to the marquis. She looked over at James, her face a mix of anxiety and apology.

She looked tired. Was she getting enough sleep? Or was it the awful gray-black dress she wore that drained the color from her face? She could at least wear a more flattering cap. The one she had on now was a mite too big and managed to emphasize the shadows under her eyes. Had the demands of her work kept her from bed? He hoped so, he was already beset with twelve kinds of guilt. It would double if that mad moment had stolen her *joie de vivre*.

She walked over to the marquis, and even in those few steps exhibited the grace that set her apart from every other housekeeper in the country. She bent close to the marquis, but spoke so they all could hear. "My lord, it breaks your heart to recall that loss. Will you not consider the present and what the architect is speaking of?"

To James's surprise, the marquis did not take her to task. Instead, he obeyed her, settling back in his chair and easing his grip on his cane.

James moved closer, but stayed on the far side of the table that stood in the middle of the room, now filled with papers and books. His presence rarely did less than enrage the marquis.

"Good morning, my lord." Graely spoke to James with the artificial good humor of a man afraid of trouble. "I brought information to help you with your decision and was delighted to find that I could speak with the marquis as well."

"Yes, Graely, I have no doubt that you found it very enlightening." James looked at Marguerite. "Where is Mrs. Beecher?"

"She has gone to the village to collect a medicine that the marquis must have. I offered to bear him company until she returns." She gave him a brief curtsey and turned back to his father.

A curtsey? Not only quiet, but submissive, too. He did not like it. Especially if it was his fault. He watched her as Graely chattered on. Anxious, apologetic, and subdued. It could be an attempt to keep both him and the marquis in check. She had nothing to worry about from him. The marquis? Well, even before the apoplexy his mood had been hard to measure.

James turned to the architect who had paused to consider a note in the margin of the drawing at hand. "The idea of relocating the house has merit, Graely. We will discuss it later. I am to inspect the new drainage and the dam with Marfield in an hour." He was amazed at his own conciliatory tone. Apparently Marguerite and Graely were not the only ones who wanted to keep the peace.

"We will do this now!" the marquis insisted, turning from his contemplation of the fire and raising his voice to bridge the distance between him and the other men, and half the distance to the kitchen as well. "No more debate is needed. It will be too expensive. The answer is no!" He picked up his cane and whapped it against the marble fireplace, as if his bellow could not be heard.

James looked at Graely and said, very quietly, "We shall talk later."

Graely nodded, glanced at the items on the table, and left the room as quickly as a near run could carry him. Marguerite had moved as well. The submission had disappeared, though anxiety was still very much a part of her expression. She stood in the middle of the room, her worry capped by a defensive stance, like a mediating fairy standing between two turf-challenging stallions. She had best have magic power, he thought, or she was likely to be the first casualty.

James watched her look from him to his father. Did she have to think about which one of them was more likely to explode? That was an insult to be sure. There was no denying the relief he felt when she turned to the marquis.

"You have only this moment told us how much Lady Gwyneth hated the place. Will you not at least consider the possibility of what Mr. Graely proposes?"

The marquis' laugh was breathy. "I rid the room of him, I did. He says he learned from Paine and if Paine trained him, he will assuredly think in grandiose and extravagant terms. You should have seen the house Paine designed for Norfolk. Worksop in Nottingham. Norfolk's sons died, the Duke died, and the rest of the building died with him. Too much money."

She nodded as though she understood every detail of the Duke of Norfolk's reckless spending. "I am sure that your son can convince Mr. Graely to preserve all economy if that is what you wish."

James watched the old man's face harden. He tapped the cane on the hearth and shrugged. "Tell Crandall he can move the house, if he can do it without bankrupting us."

Marguerite glanced away from the marquis and looked at

him. *It's done.* She did not say the words. They flashed from her eyes. She turned immediately back to the marquis.

"Your son is standing right here, my lord. You could tell him yourself."

James shook his head. *That one concession is victory enough, Marguerite. Don't ask for more.*

"The boy never listens to me."

James walked over to where his father sat and stood before him. "Sir, if we do move the building and I can coerce Graely into economy, would you tell me what style you favor?"

The marquis pursed his lips and a muscle in his jaw flexed. "None of that romantic claptrap that Ridley favors. Fonthill Abbey is a monstrosity."

"Yes, I think we are agreed on that." It could not be this easy. "I would say that we both favor the more classic style of the last century. It is, after all, what Paine did so well and if Graely trained with him we should be satisfied."

The marquis answered with little more than a grunt, followed by a muttered, "You handle it."

There was a scratch at the door and Mrs. Beecher came in. The marquis saw her and struggled up from the chair. "Beecher, come help me. I want my dinner."

His father stopped as he passed and inspected James from head to foot. "Those riding clothes are an insult to everyone in this room. Go change."

James held his tongue and waited until he left the room before turning to Marguerite. "How old does he think I am?"

Marguerite's disappointment echoed his. "He is still inclined to confuse time and place. It has been so long that I fear that might not change. More often than not he thinks I am Lady Gwyneth."

She crossed the room. He watched her as though she was a work of art come to life for his enjoyment. He might deny himself; deny them, the pleasure of a kiss, he would be damned before he would give up the simple pleasure of watching her cross the room.

He spoke to her back. "It sounds as though he has taken to Graely's idea, but it is entirely possible that the marquis was playing with us. Today he gives me what I want and tomorrow he will insist that he said no such thing. And that has nothing to do with illness. He has always been that way. Indeed, he seems much improved."

She looked over her shoulder and turned slowly towards him. "Do you think so? I see him so often and long so for his good health that I cannot be sure what is truth and what is wish. In all honesty his temper is still deplorable."

Her expression was earnest when he would have wished for happy.

"Nor will it. He has always been inclined to become angry when every little thing does not go his way." He riffled through the papers. He could make little sense of the drawings that Graely had left behind. "My tenure may be temporary. If he continues to recover he may demand to take control of the estate again."

Marguerite took one step closer to him. "That will never happen, my lord. Today is one of his good days. More often than not he sleeps more than he is awake and is happy to live in the past."

The silence stretched between them, still she did not leave. He looked up from the papers he had been fiddling with. Their eyes met. She held his gaze for only a moment.

Was this the way it would be between them? Less than easy and not even a smile as a reward for his virtue? "Come here and look at this drawing. I can make no sense of it."

Marguerite walked over, stood at the other side of the table and peered at the sketch. He watched her cap and the tendrils of dark, dark hair that curled around its edges. He smelled the vanilla scent that she favored or brought from the kitchen with her. He wanted to touch the delicate skin at the back of her neck, but did not.

Reaching out, she stopped short of taking his hand and merely turned the sketch around. "You had it upside down."

She was at the door again in a moment. James waited for her to stop and turn for one parting comment. He hoped that things between them had not changed so much that she would leave without that last word.

She did turn and he could not restrain his satisfaction. He would never call her predictable, even if there were some things that he had come to expect.

The smallest of an answering smile began. It grew slowly, lighting her eyes, pinkening her cheeks.

Absolute panic gripped him. The same fear he had felt yesterday. The same certainty that this was not meant for him, that if he gave in to the joy and claimed it for his own it would be ripped from him with callous hatred by some vindictive angel of an upright God.

"Madame Voisson, if my father is going to continue coming into public, hire a valet for him so that he does not look like a clown ready for a farce."

The glow of joy vanished as quickly as it had appeared. "Very well, my lord."

She waited, actually stood there until he would dismiss her.

"Did you have more to say, madame?" What had it come to that he had to ask?

Her face softened a bit. "It was the most wonderful thing to see you and your father truly speaking to each other." With that she left the room.

James spoke to the empty space. "I did it for you."

Twenty-one

"Good morning, Marguerite!"

Marguerite looked up from closing her cottage door to find Jenneth sweeping her walkway.

"Why are you sweeping, Jenneth? Is Kitty ill?"

"The day is so perfect that I told her I would do the sweeping and if she hurried with the kitchen chores she could have a half day. I will do the village errands and she can visit her beau."

Jenneth propped the broom against the wall and walked the few steps toward her. "How are you?"

"Very well." Marguerite looked up at sky, and examined the trees, knowing that if she looked at Jenneth, her friend would see the lie in her eyes. "The nice weather makes everything easier, does it not? We needed the rain, but wet for a sennight is quite enough. And it rained days before that as well. It must have been a wonderful test of the new drainage system."

"Marguerite," Jenneth put a hand on her arm to stop the chatter, "tell me the truth."

Marguerite shook her head. "I am fine." She spoke with an angry edge as though she took the question as an insult. "I am sorry, Jenneth. I cannot linger. I have two projects underway and the staff needs my direction." She hoped her smile did not look as stiff as it felt.

"Indeed." For a moment Jenneth sounded exactly like

Miss Morton had when she had caught her in a lie. The swift rush of longing for a simpler time, added one more weight to Marguerite's already burdened heart.

"If you are in a hurry, I will walk with you." Jenneth took her arm and they began down the track that led to the dower house.

The sweet smell of spring, the bird song, and a friend by her side were as much pleasure as Marguerite had known in the last fortnight. She looked up again, refusing foolish tears that were a luxury she only allowed at night.

A tiny dunnock flew up from under the hedge nearest them and they both looked up, trying to espy its nest.

"This morning I counted at least five different kinds of bird song." When Marguerite looked at her, Jenneth confessed. "I had been sweeping that walk a good while. I did not want to miss you."

With that allowance, Marguerite realized that Jenneth was truly worried about her. "I have not counted the bird songs, Jenneth. Indeed, I had not even noticed until you mentioned them, but they are everywhere, are they not? A ritual as old as spring."

A flock of house sparrows swooped overhead as if to verify Marguerite's observation. She squeezed Jenneth's hand. "'Tis a shame that the ritual of man and woman cannot be as simple. If only it was as easy as trilling a song and waiting for an answer." Marguerite put her lips together and tried to whistle. It came out tuneless and breathless. "Whistling is not a skill that I have ever been able to learn."

"Hardly one a lady should count on to impress."

"Oh, I can do one!" She stopped short and Jenneth did too. "That shrill whistle the boys use to call attention. The one where you put your fingers just so."

"No, can you? Show me."

Marguerite could not resist the dare. The shrill sound distracted more than one bird from its morning routine and they both laughed.

"If you do that again, you will have every dog in the area here within minutes." Jenneth rubbed her ear. "Finally I see a smile. I have missed them."

They started up again, lifting their skirts to avoid a puddle and stepping gingerly over the muddy patch around it.

"Jenneth, I am fine. I am doing my work. For a fortnight I have kept busy every minute of the day." She paused and then told her friend the truth she most wanted to hear. "I never see him. He never asks to see me. The days go by quickly enough, the night hours much more slowly."

She could feel the tension drain from Jenneth.

"I took what you said to heart, Jenneth. I have a useful place here and I would not risk it for something as trifling as a moment's pleasure. 'Tis only that sometimes the world seems empty without him, without even a glimpse of his face. I worry about his headaches. Are they better or worse? I wonder if he is enjoying the dower house or only tolerating it. It is only at night that I dwell on these things. Not that I wish to, but in the dark there are no other distractions."

She sighed and shook her head. "I sound as heartsick as your maid describing the way her beau looks in church on Sunday. And she can only see the back of his head!"

"No Marguerite, you do not sound a bit like Kitty, for she knows no discretion and will tell anyone who listens."

Jenneth let go of her arm and bent down to pick one of the flowers that bloomed by the side of the path. She handed it to Marguerite who tucked it in her bodice. Jenneth pulled one more and tucked it behind her ear.

"Prentice has asked after you."

"Oh dear." Would she be the next source of gossip? How awful.

"Darling, you know that you are not very skilled at hiding your feelings. He fears you grow bored with life here."

"Never!"

"That is what I told him. I tried to convince him that it was only the spring and melancholy for your old life."

"As if I would ever go back to Yorkshire. Now that the Osgoods are gone there is nothing there that I miss." She turned to Jenneth. "But I do appreciate your efforts."

Entering the dower house garden through the back gate, they walked toward the house on the most direct path, avoiding the ones that angled to the right and left and then angled back again.

Marguerite let out a breath of a laugh. "Well, that explains why Prentice has been pressing me for ideas on ways to run the house more smoothly! He insisted that is the one great virtue of a change in the senior staff.

"He would ask and then never seem excited about my ideas. Every time I broach one he asks me to give him details on how it will be done and the cost."

She stopped and turned to face Jenneth, with her back to the house. "Now I see. He is only trying to keep me busy." She walked backwards for a few steps. "It is very sweet, and so like a man."

They were near the door and Marguerite shook her skirt and began to scrape her shoes on the mat.

"We had an argument over it."

"You lost your temper with Prentice?"

"Only a little. I told him he did not need anything more than good eyesight to see that it would make sense to move the laundry to one of the buildings closer to the dower house."

"It hardly matters what you were discussing. You angry is enough to explain his worry."

Someone opened a window above and the voice of a footman drifted down to them. Marguerite took Jenneth's arm and they walked a few steps away from the house.

"Prentice need not worry, nor anyone else. I am well

enough and have no plans to go anywhere but my cottage each night. With Prentice returned to work, there is no reason for me to see Lord Crandall at all. I come early to do my business here at the dower house while he is out riding and by the time he is ready for breakfast I am in the kitchen discussing recipes with the chef. It is only that none of it is as much fun as it used to be." She shrugged. "How can I convince Prentice not to worry?"

"Try to smile more, Marguerite. It is what they all look for, how they measure your happiness. They miss it as much as I do."

With an affectionate pat on the cheek, Jenneth hurried back down the path and her planned outing.

Smile more? You are the actress Jenneth, not I. If she had any hope that her future held more than her work, then perhaps she could. If that was not to be, she would make the most of employment that she did truly enjoy and learn to smile again. Although not today, but in time.

If every other day she had managed to avoid Lord Crandall, the moment she walked in the door Marguerite knew today would be different.

The shouting came from the dining room, arrowing down to the bottom of the stairs where she was putting her bonnet on a peg. At first she thought that the marquis and his son had come to blows. As she hurried up the narrow flight of stairs, she could hear only one person shouting and it was too young a voice to belong to the marquis.

Who could the viscount be shouting at? Surely not his father. From what Mrs. Beecher had said, they had not seen each other above once or twice since their discussion about the new location for Braemoor.

Robert hovered uncertainly outside the dining room door. She grabbed the pot of coffee from him and before he could do more than whisper, "Oh, ma'am, that room is no place. . . ."

She pushed through the door and into the room determined to protect either the marquis or his son, whichever needed defending.

"Put that damn paper down, James, and listen to me a damn minute. I tell you, you cannot do it! I will not hear of it! Why must you insist on that spot?"

The shouting came from neither James nor the marquis. It was an unknown, though not unfamiliar face. Could this be the youngest Braedon, Lord Rhys?

She should leave. An argument between brothers hardly needed her intervention, but the longing to see him, if only for a moment, replaced common sense with impulse.

Marguerite moved down the table to where James sat and warmed his coffee, pouring another half-cup. He wore one of her favorite coats. The gray made his eyes look brighter, his face softer, if that was possible with such sharp cheekbones and so noble a chin.

He looked up from the paper when he recognized a female hand, her hand. "Are you come to rescue me?" He whispered the words, the paper an effective shield from his brother. "Or are you only curious?"

His smile took the bite from the words and Marguerite decided he was happy to see her. Nearly as happy as she was to see him. He looked rested, bother him. He looked as though he had spent the last two weeks at ease and in good humor. As though her absence had not made a whit of difference in his life.

The viscount put the paper down as she walked to the end of the table where the stranger stood at a place that had been well used. Plates crowded the cover, showing crusts of the cheese and toast that the viscount favored for breakfast.

When she went to pour the young man more coffee, he sat, silent and irritated. She poured the liquid, put the pot near his elbow and made her way to the door. There was a problem with just one glimpse. It was not enough. It only made her long for more.

"A moment, madame. Let me introduce my younger brother, Lord Rhys Braedon. Rhys, this is Braemoor's new housekeeper, Madame Voisson."

Rhys had enough command of his manners to rise and make a brief bow. Marguerite made him a curtsey and murmured, "My lord" and walked over to the server for a completely unnecessary examination of the trays.

Lord Rhys had the look of his brother Morgan and a little, even, of this brother. She could see it in the determined and, at the moment, angry set of his jaw. Had James looked like this as a younger man?

Most likely it was a look they both had inherited from their father. Was Lord Morgan the only one to have been spared the temper that made life so interesting and occasionally so very irritating?

"Rhys, please do not let madame's presence inhibit you. There can be no doubt she has heard every one of the last hundred or so words you shouted at me." He reached up and pulled at his earlobe. "On the other hand, I think I may be deaf."

"You heard what I said." Rhys glanced at Marguerite. She pretended to be totally engrossed in the empty muffin platter.

"Do explain it again, in a civil tone, if you please, so that madame can understand. She has come in here to protect one of us, but I do think that she is having trouble deciding which one of us needs her help or, perchance, *deserves* her help, is a better word."

"I came because I feared it was the marquis who was upset." Marguerite straightened as if an inch more would give her command of the situation. Sometimes it did.

"Yes, I know. And now that you can see it is only Rhys, you are filled with curiosity." His tone imbued the words with such affection that she did not even feel the sting of the criticism.

"I am telling you, James, that if you do this, I will never come back." Rhys leapt to his feet, threw his napkin into his chair and walked to the door with all the anger of a man belittled. "I will not come back for father's funeral, or for your wedding, not for any reason. I will leave for good."

James did not comment, nor did Lord Rhys wait for him to. He stomped from the room without the slightest show of courtesy to either James or Marguerite.

She began to clear his place, studiously avoiding the viscount's end of the table. She had two plates in hand and was almost to the door when she completely lost the battle with her wiser self and turned back. "You should not have given him such a set down in front of a servant."

"If he paid attention to anyone besides himself he would see that you are far more than a servant and possibly his most valuable ally. I gave him a chance."

"A chance so veiled in insult that he would have had to be one of the magi to make sense of the compliment."

The door opened and Robert came in. She held out the plates to him, but he was looking from her to the viscount and did not even notice her outstretched hand. She cleared her throat quietly and he took the plates with an embarrassed blush. He left without collecting anything else.

"You see, you are learning." The viscount spoke with satisfaction.

"My lord?"

"That tiny clearing of your throat. Robert, was it not?"

"Yes."

"A good housekeeper needs very few words. And I see that you have mastered one way to avoid them. Very nicely done. It drew Robert's attention without embarrassing him outright."

She walked back to the edge of the table and picked up

the cup and saucer Lord Rhys had not touched. This was
more than the glance she had hoped for. It was perilously
close to a conversation. She would gather the covers, walk
to the door and leave him to his coffee.

Twenty-two

Leave the room. She ignored the voice of good sense and sat down in Rhys's chair.

"You have advice for me?" He spoke from behind the paper. When she did not answer he lowered it and looked at her with resignation.

She gave up trying to look severe and smiled at him. It felt so right to be with him again.

James set the paper aside and reached for his coffee. "Rhys is furious about my decision to relocate Braemoor." He paused and added, "You know he is a man of science."

Marguerite nodded. "The marquis mentions him frequently. He seems both intrigued and embarrassed by his son's intellect."

"Which Rhys has used to his advantage. For years he inveigled my father to invest in one hare-brained scheme after another. This time he insists that the rise that Graely suggests we use for the new Braemoor is the only suitable place on the whole property for an observatory."

"But you have hundreds of acres."

"Closer to thousands."

"Surely he appreciates that the needs of the family are more important than his?"

"Oh, my dear, the demands of science are more important than the best situation for our home! How dare you think otherwise! Science would always come first. Beyond that, he is twenty-two years old. Need I say more?"

"When I was your brother's age. . . ."

The viscount cut her off with a breath of laughter, "Marguerite, you *are* his age."

"I am not. I am at least several years older."

"I do beg your pardon." He bowed from his seat, a mocking gesture. She could tell that he did not believe her

"He is twenty-two, you say? I am years older than that. And if you add my experience of the world I am even older than you are."

"Another lie, Marguerite." He looked so amused that she knew it had been a foolish thing to say. "And let me add, purely for the sake of debate, that your experience of the world is not broader than mine, only different. And I can prove it."

Oh, she loved the bickering. Was that possible? No matter, she did.

"You can prove your experience, my lord?" She considered a moment. "So can I. Have you ever eaten weevil-ridden biscuit?" She leaned forward, her chin raised in a dare that he best it.

"Have you ever had dinner with anyone as highly placed as the Prince of Wales?" He sat back and relaxed, as much as saying that this would be no contest at all.

She sniffed. "We no longer have a true king in France. And I would never dine with Napoleon or any of his brothers. They are all pretenders."

"Your answer is no?" He angled his chair so he could cross his legs.

"I've often wondered about the boy who shared the bottom of the boat with us when we came to England. But he was a *duc* at best, so, no I have never dined with anyone of such exalted station."

The viscount looked triumphant.

"That does not make you the winner, my lord. There are other measures." She thought a moment. "Have you ever slept on hay?"

"The very thought makes me itch."

"As well it should." She shuddered. "I would never call it restful."

"Have you ever slept the clock around?" He asked with a rakish look.

"I could have slept for a day after that night in the barn." She resisted the temptation to ask if he had been alone.

"My dear madame, I feel for you."

"Aha! Sympathy must count in my favor and add at least five years to my natural age. For you so far, I feel no sympathy. I am thinking, however, that you do deserve some. Dinner with the Prince must have been very tedious."

"We had several very attractive dining companions." He added in a show of honesty.

"Then no sympathy whatever." Not when there seemed to be an endless line of women to see to his needs.

She thought again and waved her hand in triumph. "Have you ever met a man with twelve tattoos?"

"Twelve? Was he naked?"

"Of course not. It may be that I exaggerate. But his arms were covered and he even had one on the back of his neck."

"Have you ever met a woman with one tattoo?" He asked as though he was certain that she could not possibly equal the feat.

"Have you?"

He nodded slowly. "And she *was* naked."

When Marguerite had to repress a blush, she decided she must end this and stood up.

"Sit down, or did I embarrass you?"

"It is a silly game, my lord." She remained standing taking pleasure in the defiance. Had he been playing a game or trying to prove that he had had legions of lovers and a lifetime of company that did not include her? Silly to feel slighted by it. "And I should be with the chef and you, yes, you must make peace with your brother."

"Peace between us is rare." He stood up and dropped his napkin on the table. "Rhys will be happy enough when I tell him that I have negotiated the purchase of some property for his observatory."

"Highton Rock?"

"Are there no secrets here?"

Oh, yes, she thought, *there are.* Your heart is such a tightly held secret that I will never understand it. Why are you so afraid of showing your generous heart, even to those you love? She shook her head. "Everyone wonders why you should wish to purchase such an useless piece of land."

"You mean word has not traveled back from London of our near fistfight last year when Rhys insisted I trade prime farm land for that pile of rock?"

"No, it would have explained everything. I will be sure to tell them all at dinner today." He laughed. At least one of them was in a good humor. At the door she turned back.

"While I am telling the staff perhaps you should be telling Lord Rhys of the purchase. Why keep it a secret from him?" It was a stupid question. He kept his generosity a secret, as if appreciation would take all the nobility from the gesture.

"I will not tell him until it is settled, the papers signed and registered."

"How long will it be before you see him again? It could be that he will make good his vow to leave before you are able to tell him." Even as she spoke they heard the pound of riding boots down the stairs and the slam of the front door.

"I will be in London within a sennight. Even he could not plan travel that quickly."

"You are leaving?" She hoped she sounded surprised even though it was hurt that sharpened her voice.

"Ah, Marguerite, you do not know everything, after all."

It was no longer amusing. He was leaving.

"The Season will be in full sway. I may well stay for a month or more." He came closer, so close he was only an arm's length away.

A month here without him, with spring moving to summer, with the moon full and beckoning. As much as she loved Braemoor, it would be empty without him.

"Have you ever been to London, Marguerite?"

He reached out and took the flower from the spot above her breast. He tucked it in his lapel. Even though there were at least three layers of material between her breast and his hand, her whole body responded to his indiscreet touch.

"Have I ever been to London?" She shook her head and prayed, without having the slightest idea what she prayed for.

"You must come sometime."

She could feel a blush, still not knowing whether to call this a proposition or not.

"You could learn a great deal there." He paused, a long deliberate beat, "from Mrs. Martin. She has kept house there for years."

"I should like that, my lord. I should like that very much." If he meant to amuse her with this repartee, he had failed. She was torn between anger and tears that he could treat her with such casual humor.

"Marguerite?" She looked at him and he was not smiling. His face was as serious as hers. "Have you ever wanted what you could not have?"

Thinking of his kisses, mesmerized by his haunted eyes, she nodded.

"Have you ever had a dream so heartfelt that it woke you calling a name?"

She nodded again. Just last night, she thought.

"Have you ever found what you thought never to have almost within your grasp?"

He did not wait for her answer but reached for her. She went to him with such relief and welcome that she did not know whose idea it had been.

She poured the longing and frustration of these last lost days into the kiss. He took all she had to give and gave his own want and need in return. Loneliness disappeared, replaced with joy and her heart's demand for more.

He pulled her tight against him. It was not close enough. His cravat and her fichu gave way to greedy hands. She kissed his neck and cheek.

The power of his wanting undid her. As he held her, claimed her, she knew she would be willing to give him whatever he wanted and more than he asked. They blended together in a way that made her forget everything else save the erotic promise of his touch. The pleasure of their kiss was as nothing compared to the pleasure they could share.

He lifted his head, tasted her ear, and claimed her mouth again. The flower crushed between them gave off a delicate scent that would forever be a part of this moment of magic and folly.

The fragrance reminded her of Jenneth, of reality, of the time and place of this lapse, of Robert on the other side of the door.

She would give it all up, she would.

But as his kiss ended, the echo of Jenneth's voice and one cold reality compromised the certainty of her commitment. "He will keep you as long you please him."

Jenneth's words were as sobering as the bright light of day that showed them both disheveled and aroused.

He laughed a little and reached out to replace her fichu, gently tucking it back into her bodice, letting his hand linger a moment on the curve of her breast.

She reached up to straighten his cravat, pulling the edges up along his neck, tucking the folds each into the other. She let her hands trail down his coat front before she moved away. It did not break the spell that held them, but she knew that she could run for a mile and it would not be broken.

James stepped back and when he spoke it was not a lover's voice. "Come to London. Come with me."

He made it less than a command, but she heard the arrogance, the effort he made to control his heart, and her.

She shook her head and he misunderstood her.

"You will come. I was a fool to deny it last time. And you would be an even greater fool to deny it now."

"I would come with you, my lord. I would come with James Braedon in a moment. I would build my life around him and give him my heart and my love."

He stiffened.

"Yes, I can see that is more than you want." She moved two more steps away and made an effort to straighten her cap. "You see, my lord, I never learned to give only a part of myself. I give you everything I am. And only to you. Not one little part of me will I give to Viscount Crandall, to the man who is too much his father's son."

He came to her and took her into his arms. He molded her against him, pressing her against the high-backed chair so that her body was in the most intimate contact with his.

"I can make you want me, Marguerite."

She welcomed the pressure of his hardness, reveled in the arousal, and lost herself in its sweetness. She closed her eyes and he kissed her again with a driving reckless hunger that sparked a wanton response she could not control. When she would have begged for more, here and forever, he stopped and looked at her.

"Marguerite, I can make you want me past reason." His voice echoed with a triumph as sobering as a gunshot would have been.

"You are the only one who ever doubted that, you *imbé-cile!*" With a small scream of pure rage she pushed him away. She ran to the door and stopped, trying to control the labored breathing that came from anger not passion, she insisted to herself. She kept her back to him, looked down to make sure she was presentable and reached for the doorknob.

She turned to him one more time. He watched her with a hard expression, his eyes narrowed, his lips a thin line that belied their passion.

"You think that you know so much more of the world than I do." She shook her head. "You are wrong, so wrong. My world is infinitely larger than yours because I allow love into it, something you will never understand."

Did he realize how much his seduction had hurt her? So much that she was willing to hurt him in return?

"There is one more thing, my lord." She stopped long enough to steady her breathing. "If I am ever your lover, know this now: I will be your last."

Twenty-three

She pulled the door closed and tried to convince herself that her rage would keep the tears away. The chef would distract her. Yes, she would go to him and slice whatever needed slicing and talk with him of France in the old days. The very familiarity of it would remind her of her place here. She would not let her life be limited by a man who did not see her love as a gift. Who would not welcome it beyond the bedroom.

Convinced that self-righteousness had overwhelmed her other sensibilities, she made her way to the stairs. Before she was halfway down the sound of pounding echoed from the front door. Marguerite hurried back up, looking for Prentice.

The butler had reached the door when the noise stopped abruptly and Rhys came in ahead of a laborer who was out of breath and incoherent.

Rhys hurried past to James who had just come from the dining room.

"Marfield is hurt. Badly." He drew a deep breath. "He's alive, but there is a lot of blood from a head wound."

"Where is he?" James spoke even as he moved towards the door.

"They are bringing him down the lane from the fields."

Marguerite followed, her first thought was to fetch Jenneth.

James stopped at the door and turned back to his brother. "Rhys, ride to the village for the surgeon. Find him, wherever he is."

"Yes. Right. Good idea." He was gone.

"I'll go find Jenneth." Marguerite made to hurry past him. James stopped her with a hand on her arm.

"No, wait. We want to see how he does first."

They looked at each other, neither willing to put their fear into words. She nodded.

"Tell Prentice what we will need," James tossed the words at her as he rushed out the door.

She hurried over to where the butler stood, still holding the door open as if it would not stay without his hand. "Would you bring cloths and water, please?"

Prentice ran to the back of the house without protest.

By the time she reached the front door, she found James directing the men with the litter bearing Marfield.

"Inside, bring him inside. Into the first room on the left."

In the chaos of the next few minutes Marfield was moved into the green salon, and onto the table after it was swept clear of the drawings and papers that covered it.

He was unconscious, his head wrapped with a dirty cloth soaked through with blood.

James looked at her. She nodded. "I can help until the surgeon arrives. I did learn some things from Mr. Osgood."

He stepped back and she began to uncover the wound. Marfield moaned and James moved closer.

"The moaning is a good sign, my lord." Marguerite continued the slow unwinding of the bandage and spoke without looking up. "It means that he is not very deeply asleep."

James grabbed the man who had run ahead with word. He still hovered in the doorway. "Go to his cottage and bring Mrs. Marfield." The man made to turn away and James grabbed him by the arm. "Listen to me. Do not alarm her.

Tell her he has been only slightly injured, but you knew she would want to come."

The man nodded. James let his arm go and he took off at a run.

"Mrs. Marfield is not at her cottage, James." Marguerite looked up from her careful ministrations. "I have only this moment recalled that she went to the village this morning."

"He will find her." James came closer. "I only hope he finds her before the stories do."

Marguerite pulled the last of the rough bandage away from Marfield's wound and, as she expected, it began to bleed again. She pressed her handkerchief against it. It was wholly inadequate to the task. Fortunately Prentice returned with a jug of water, a bowl and a handful of cloths of various sizes.

She pressed one against Marfield's head and looked at James. "He will do, my lord. This is the sort of wound that looks worse than it is. The surgeon will be here shortly. There may be other things that require your attention."

"You want me to leave?" He spoke with angry insult.

And she thought she had been so diplomatic.

"Madame, you may think me the most uncaring of men, but there is nothing more important to me right now than Simon."

"I know that, my lord. There are others who care as well. They are waiting outside and your reassurance will relieve them. It would be useful as well to find out exactly what happened. I think this is only a head wound that bleeds much, and can be put to rights, but I am not trained and I could be wrong."

"All right, all right," he agreed with frustration. "I will go." With one last glance at his friend, he left the room.

She sent Prentice off for blankets and finally let herself look closely at Marfield. His face was gray and his clothes were soaked with blood. It looked like a lot of blood even knowing such wounds as she did. It was frightening, and one reason to remove his clothes before Jenneth arrived.

He must have fallen into water, besides being blood-soaked, his clothes and hair were wet. That was an even more pressing reason to undress him. He needed to be warmed so that his head wound did not progress to something worse. With her free hand she began to pick out the bits of stone and twigs from his hair.

The door opened and she turned to see the marquis standing there. He came into the room leaning heavily on his cane, looking curious and confused. "Is that blood?"

"Yes. Yes, it is, my lord." Where was Mrs. Beecher? How could three people not keep track of one charge? "Will you sit down, sir, until Billy can come for you."

He waved his cane in denial and came closer, his eyes darting from her to her patient.

"I know who that is." He looked at her with nothing less than rage in his eyes. "What is that bastard doing here?"

"Please, my lord. It is Simon Marfield. He has been hurt."

"Get away from him." He made to take her arm, but she moved around to the other side of the table. "I am not going to make this same mistake twice."

Did he think her Gwyneth was about to cuckold him as Annabelle had? "I am Marguerite Voisson, the house-keeper." She was about to call for help, when Justice appeared and with surprisingly gentle hands urged the marquis from the room.

No sooner had they left when Prentice returned again, this time with an armload of coverings and the surgeon behind him. He was a competent man, and the force of his personality filled the room.

Marguerite was shooed away as they made to treat Simon. She stood outside the door waiting for word and then hurried to the front door certain that Jenneth would be arriving soon.

It was the same delicately beautiful spring day, now filled with memories that would each have been worthy of their own spate of time, not crammed together in less than an hour. James's declaration. No, not a declaration. How she wished it were. His proposition. For that was all it had been and knowing him as she did, all it would ever be. Even that might be enough if he would acknowledge the truth hidden in his heart. How could he kiss her and hold her heart in his hands and still not realize that they were meant for each other as surely as two lovers could be?

If he could not see it, there was no future for them that would leave her soul whole.

At the moment, though, that paled in comparison to the loss that Jenneth Marfield faced. Why were they taking so long? She paced back to the doorway and could hear concern in the surgeon's voice, though she could not make out his words.

Prentice stood near the door, with his back to her, effectively blocking any view of the activity inside.

She saw Jenneth hurrying down the path as the surgeon came out into the hall and announced "Marfield will do."

Jenneth must have heard some version of the accident, but maintained her calm if only because the surgeon let her in to see her husband immediately.

After a brief description of the wound, the surgeon expressed every confidence that his patient would recover then ruined it all by stating that "the longer he sleeps the worse it will be."

Marguerite urged the surgeon to the dining room for refreshment and made to leave Jenneth alone with her husband when her friend turned to her.

"Where is Lord Crandall?"

She looked angry, so angry that Marguerite pushed the door closed as far as she could. Before she could answer Jenneth went on.

"He is not here, is he? He is off entertaining himself with another pointless indulgence while Simon works day and night to make the Braedons richer and richer. He has spent weeks on that stupid drainage project so that Braemoor can claim a few more acres. Lord Crandall has no notion of how hard Simon works or how much he cares for his regard."

"He went to find out what happened, Jenneth. I asked him to go. And that was after he ordered Simon brought in here and sent for the surgeon."

"Mrs. Marfield, Simon means as much to me as my brothers do." James spoke from the doorway and both women turned toward him in surprise. "He is not just a land steward. He is a friend, one I count on for more than his ability to make me richer. I have too few true friends to take his hurt lightly."

Jenneth looked blankly from one to the other.

James nodded. "What you said about my excess is undoubtedly true, Mrs. Marfield, but for today at least, my only indulgence was breakfast with my brother, Rhys."

Marguerite had never heard humility in his voice, never once before that she could recall. He was upset over Marfield's injury, to be sure, still his contrition did seem out of all proportion humble.

Jenneth was trying to recall exactly what she had said. She raised tear-filled eyes to the viscount. "I am sorry, my lord. It is only that he looks so awful."

"He does. And I am the one responsible. And even with the surgeon's optimism, you are only reacting as any loving wife would."

His understanding made her cry. At the same moment a hoarse voice called "Jenneth?" and her husband had her complete attention.

James waited a moment and then left the room. Marguerite waited longer to make certain that Simon was indeed talking to his wife and hurried down the hall after James.

He stood at the back window looking out onto the garden.

"That was very kindly said, my lord."

"It is the truth. She is right. This is all my fault." He looked away from the window, but not at her. "Simon was in the drainage ditch resetting certain of the tiles. He slipped and hit his head on the edge of one of them. He pulled himself from the water, then collapsed on the bank."

He looked at her and she saw that he was as ravaged by emotion as Jenneth had been.

"Do you know why Simon felt the need to reset those tiles? Because when I rode out to see the project last week I asked why they were set the way they were. I wanted to show my interest in the work he did, that I valued it. He took it as criticism. That was why he was resetting them today."

"You are not responsible for every thing, my lord." She wanted to hold him, console him, but stood instead with her arms tightly folded. "You are not responsible. This is above all the worst kind of conceit."

"A very generous lie, Madame. You have said yourself that I never give a gift or a compliment directly. That it would take a wise man to find the praise because I bury it so thoroughly."

"Those of us who love you understand your meaning." She took one step closer and did not drop her gaze.

He looked at her for a long measuring moment. "Thank you for your help today. It comes as naturally as your sweetness and your smile."

Without waiting for an answer he left her, going out the front door and away from the house.

Twenty-four

The quiet of evening settled on the house. James could hear Prentice moving up and down the stairs. He'd heard a door open and close. The last of the maids had left for the day. No doubt his bed was turned down and warmed, the fire in his room a welcoming glow. Whatever the hour, it was entirely too early to go upstairs.

The tea at his elbow cooled and he picked up the post that had been left earlier in the day. Invitations, and very few of those. He tossed them onto the table without interest. When he returned from London he must make himself more available. If he was going to spend most of his time at Braemoor he had best find a way to entertain himself here.

Marguerite Voisson could entertain him. She had for weeks. That simple pleasure was so much more complicated now, though. His last ill-conceived kiss had changed their relationship and while he might long for the carefree chatter of her first few months, he longed even more for what could be.

His London trip felt more like a sentence than an escape. He should go. He had to go. He had to be away long enough to find some way to cope with her nearness and not take advantage of it. Of her.

"If I am ever your lover, I will be your last." It sounded more like a threat than a declaration. Or maybe he should call it an ultimatum. More than the words her expression, both sultry and challenging, had announced that she would be all the lover he would ever want or need.

It could be true. He could spend a lifetime with her and not grow bored. He would be occasionally annoyed, more often amused and generally enchanted, and never bored.

So why did a trip to London and its hedonistic distraction seem so essential? There were a dozen practical and moral reasons to deny his heart. Even a certain etiquette entered the picture. None of those were the core of it.

She would give so much more than her body. She would give him her heart and even part of her soul. And expect the same from him.

He hesitated because it meant commitment, whether as mistress or wife.

"My wife." Saying it aloud made all things possible. His father's order that he not marry was nothing more than one man's efforts to perpetuate his misery on the next generation. James had only ever agreed because adding marriage had seemed tantamount to adding another dimension of hell to his world.

Now that the shadowed face of his bride took on the black hair and sparkling eyes of Marguerite Voisson, the word had far more appeal.

Her love, her hand in marriage, might make his world happier, but what did it guarantee hers? Braedons did not always take the care they should of the hearts in their keeping. Proof of that was his very selfishness in considering it in spite of what it would cost her.

He looked at the journals that were neatly stacked on the table next to him. Gwyneth and her lord. How had she coped with the hurt and the selfishness? He could recall without reading a word her patience, her endless calm, her surprising playfulness.

Her love for the marquis. It endured through all the hurts. He had never seen it falter. No wonder the sick old man confused Marguerite with his second wife. They had much the same loyalty. And hearts so generous that deliberate insult was an effort. "My world is bigger because I allow love into it." *Yes, my darling it is. Is there room enough for two?*

He reached for the topmost volume. Could he find a message here? He opened the first page with a desperate hope that it held the key to his future.

The house was so quiet. Marguerite looked up from the mending in her lap. The marquis sat opposite her, in a light doze. She settled more quietly, knowing well enough that if she moved from her seat he would awaken irritable.

It was one of his more stubborn conceits that he should remain awake for several hours after tea, maintaining the pretence that he was more than a man in failing health. She would grant him that wish. Everyone had his fantasies.

With each mended pillowslip she added to the pile at her elbow, Marguerite's sadness deepened. No tears. She would save them for later when she was abed.

Would James always have her heart, even if he would never give his own? Would a gesture be enough for her, or did he have to say the words? "I love you." Had any woman ever heard them. No, she was sure not.

Would trust be enough? What if he read the journals?

She had left bookmarks in her favorite places: small strips of paper on which she had drawn a heart, or an initial. There was a fairy to mark a charming story about Maddie. She had drawn a house for the story of Morgan's and Rhys's escapades in the dower house and a ship for yet another story. She'd found sorrow, joy, and secrets. All waiting to be claimed by another Braedon generation.

If he read them, to please her, for his own insight, for whatever reason, it might be the first step, almost enough to give them both a tomorrow that would be more than another day of loneliness.

She reached for the scissors and knocked them off the table. They chinked on the hearth and the marquis awoke.

James fingered the strip of paper. This one was adorned with a ship. Not a ship precisely, more like a small fishing boat, the kind that you might find close in to shore or in a fishing village.

Was that where she was from? He had never asked. He had always assumed that she came from one of the towns close to Paris, where her parents could dance attendance at court as the King demanded. Was home closer to Brittany or perchance Marseilles? She was well-schooled so it would be hard to tell in her turn of phrase. Near Brittany, he decided.

He opened the page wider and began to read:

How can he be so stubborn, so cruel? William is his son, his completely legitimate son and still he will not allow him to stay. He flew into a rage at my suggestion and told me to leave lest he should be so angry he would strike me for my insistence.

He never would, but he needed time to come to terms with the news. It is not often a man finds he has a ten-year-old son, by a wife who abandoned him for another. He insists that the boy is not his, but one look at his face is the proof of it as are the papers that accompanied him. Annabelle had seen to that and done it on her death bed.

I will not even try to imagine how awful that must have been. To die so far away and knowing that you must put your husband's son in the care of your lover.

For ten years, he cared for him as his own. Was it out

of love for Annabelle or or out of a sense of responsi-
bility? His surrogate father is dead and he has been
sent to us. My husband is sending him away. He will
not trust me enough to tell me where, only that he will
live or die on his own.

James lowered the book and shook his head. He knew
what the boat symbolized. One more child, sent from
France, abandoned by death. God in heaven, how had Marguerite kept this to herself?

"Children are such a burden." The marquis spoke with an
irritated edge to his voice. "Why do we have so many?"

Marguerite settled the scissors on the table and turned her
attention to the marquis. He thought she was Gwyneth. It
could not be healthy, though, to live so much in the past.

"Why so many children? Certainly because you wished
it, my lord. And they must be a joy to you."

"Joy? Only because they give you pleasure, my dear. I
only wanted more sons so that James would not inherit."

"But no matter how many children you have, sir, he will
inherit." Had illness confused his basic understanding of in-
heritance or had hatred done it long before?

"He can inherit, there is nothing I can do about the en-
tailment, but if he never marries, never has children, her
blood will die with him. Did I not tell you that before? I
have forbidden it. I want no bastard inheriting the title. It is
bad enough that he bears the name."

This was too much. Her own emotions were too closely
involved. She could not be a part of this misuse of his son.
"James is very much your legitimate son. It is entirely
wrong to wreak vengeance on James for his mother's sins."

"Bah! You sound just like her. Never loyal, never a moment of fidelity, birthing nothing better than bastards."

Anger surged through her. To argue with him was pointless. He would not recall it tomorrow or even a few moments from now.

With a fiercely concerted effort she calmed herself. She stood up to replace the candles that were guttering, hoping that the movement would distract him from his tirade.

"I gave you no permission to leave. Sit down."

He roared the words and the very command in his voice compelled Marguerite to resume her seat. "I was not leaving. I was only going to replace the candles."

The marquis took his cane and swept the candle and its stand from the table. It crashed to the hearth and the candle rolled harmlessly toward the fire. "There, it will distract you no longer."

The room was not much darker but the anger simmering between them turned sinister. Marguerite shivered. She could get up and walk from the room. He could not stop her. He did not have the strength or dexterity.

She rose again. "My lord, I am leaving. I will send Mrs. Beecher to attend you."

He looked at her with a calculated hatred.

"You bitch. You never did keep your place. You do not leave the room until I say!"

His confusion was as frightening as the malevolence in his eyes.

"Sir, sir, I am Marguerite Voisson, the housekeeper."

"You are a slut, Annabelle. A housekeeper. Ha! Whose house are you keeping? Who are you whoring for tonight?"

She stepped away from the chair, as intent on making an escape as much as finding assistance. He stood up far more quickly than she had thought possible.

"You've come back to see that boy you sent to me, is that it? He is dead."

"Dead? Your son William is dead?"

"Yes, drowned years ago and as dead as the sea could make him."

"How do you know he is dead? Who told you?" It hurt to hear him speak so callously. What made a father like this? Selfish. Heartless. Her pain for the long-suffering James and even the long-lost William brought a small moan of distress. "How can you speak this way of your own son?"

Reaching for his cane, he raised it and swung it at her. "You lying bitch. I saw you with that man today. The boy was a bastard. He was!"

The cane struck her on the shoulder and she gasped with the pain. The blow was forceful enough that she stumbled toward the hearth and almost lost her balance.

He moved closer, blocking her escape. "I will beat you, Annabelle, beat you to God damn death." Spittle gathered in the corners of his mouth. She could see the madness in his eyes.

He raised the cane and hit her again. This time she cried out in fright as she sidestepped the blow. It did little more than whip along the side of her skirt, tearing it, but leaving her unharmed.

As she moved past, he reached for her hair. He grabbed her cap. The pin held it long enough for her head to be pulled slightly toward him. He took his stick and used it to trip her. Marguerite fell hard to the floor. And he laughed.

"You won't get away. Not this time. I will tie you to the damn chair and punish you until you beg."

He looked around the room. For rope? His eyes widened as he saw the fire. "I'll burn this house down and you in it. I lost Gwyneth when Braemoor burned. This time I'll rid myself of a woman I hate as much as I loved her."

As he bent toward the fire and stuck his cane into the flame, Marguerite screamed, "No, no, please God, no. You cannot." Terror had her speaking in French. She tried for the

English words, but French was all that came to her. That and memories of another fire that had destroyed her world.

"Speak English, you bitch! Have you lived with your French lover so long that you have no English? It makes no difference. Fire speaks every language and shows no mercy."

With his attention riveted on the smoldering cane, Marguerite tried to get to her feet. She wanted to call for help, but her breath came in short gasps and her cries were little more than whimpers.

She watched him as she struggled to her feet, afraid that if he saw her move he would turn the red-hot cane on her. For the moment his whole attention was on the chair she had vacated. Jabbing the cane into the center he laughed in wicked satisfaction as the wool began to smolder. He pushed the cane back into the flame and brought it out flaring like a torch.

This time he jabbed at the chair until it was alight in several places. He looked around for his next kindling as Marguerite finally found her feet and began to run across the room. The door slammed against the wall and James burst into the room. Hysterical relief drained her strength and she collapsed into his arms.

He held her in a grip so tight that it hurt, then held her away from him and scanned her face. She looked worse than she felt she was sure, with her cap gone and her hair streaming down her back. No matter, she craved the refuge of his arms. She wanted to lose herself in him and forget the memories and the moment. Even as he set her very gently aside, she knew that could not be, not while the room was lit with the unhealthy glow of red and gold flames and the threat of worse.

"Vite, Vite, je vous en prie, James, I beg you stop him."

James was already pulling a curtain down. He took the long heavy piece of velvet and swung it at the flames that had blackened the chair and were beginning to singe the rug.

Fear for him overrode her fear of the fire and Marguerite grabbed the vase of flowers near the window. Her hands shook and her knees threatened to buckle as the stench of burning wool and singed wood filled her nostrils. Despite her terror, her aim was true and the water reduced the last of the flames to a hiss.

With the threat of fire gone, James turned to the marquis. The old man raised his cane, little more than a charred stick. "You can die with her, you bastard!"

James stopped the blow by grabbing the cane and pulling it from the marquis' hand. The marquis turned back to the fire and pulled one of the tools from the stand nearby. He swung round with the poker, the full force of his strength behind it. James stepped back and the poker caught only air.

With a scream of rage, the marquis hoisted it like a sword and rammed it forward. James sidestepped that as well and ended the fight by grabbing the poker above his father's hand. James pulled it from him and threw it into the corner behind them. It fell with a thud and the room grew quiet. The two stared at one another for a long minute.

Finally, James spoke in a half-whisper. "What have I ever done to earn this? How can any one man hate so much?"

As the marquis' gaze fell, James looked away from his father and over to her. "Is this in my blood, too? Is it?"

She shook her head as tears filled her eyes.

Suddenly people filled the doorway: Prentice, Justice, Mrs. Beecher.

For Marguerite there was no more than the two: father and son. Meeting as equals for the first time.

James looked down at the man who had fallen into the chair despite the wet that still dripped from the back of it. Marguerite blocked the doorway so that James and his father had some privacy.

"This is the end, father. This is the end." He waited. The marquis did not answer him. "They will take Braemoor from you. And you have brought this on yourself."

James took a step closer and Prentice pushed into the room. Marguerite stopped him by grabbing his arm. "Leave them alone a moment more."

James bent down to the marquis and spoke gently, as though he were the parent now, caring for a difficult child. "I am sorry it has come to this, but make no mistake that it is over. You will be cared for and safe, but no more love will be given to you than you have shared. That is the legacy you have earned. And, God help me, more than you deserve. I will be your son in name only and nothing more."

"Go to hell." The spittle flew from his lips and spattered his son's cravat.

James pulled out his handkerchief and wiped his shirt-front as he stood. "No, my lord, I have just come from there and I will never go back."

He looked toward the doorway and Marguerite stepped aside. Without words, Mrs. Beecher and Justice moved into the room.

James spoke to them with the same calm he had used with his father. Despite the quiet tone, his voice carried command. "See to his needs. Do not let him cause any more harm. Restrain him only if you must."

Marguerite wished she had half his self-control. She could no more stop her tears than she could stop the shivering that racked her body. James came to her and it only made the tears worse. He swept her into his arms and carried her from the room.

Twenty-five

The fire in the green salon was far more welcoming than threatening. He sat on the sofa, still holding her in his arms, cradling her as though she were much loved, his own treasure, one he had come close to losing.

"Mon Dieu, mon Dieu, it was as though I were a child and in France again. He so reminded me of that horror." She raised her head and looked up at him. The tears locked in her throat made her voice a hoarse whisper. "The marquis became the man I found in our own library when I crept out of the hiding place Papa had put me in. When the marquis raised that cane it was that man with a torch, as though the fire had lit his eyes and burned away his soul."

She tried to hold back the sobs but they would not be restrained. Burying her face in his chest she let the tears come, too upset to be embarrassed, to want anything save the security of his embrace.

He began to rock her as one would a child and the movement awakened her to his heartache.

She looked at him again, more angry than tearful. "How could he treat you that way?" Fury edged her clogged throat and cleared her voice. "How could he speak to you that way? He would have killed you if he could."

He kissed her forehead. "Calm yourself, sweetheart. He is an old man who has built his world on hatred and now must live in it."

"You are his son. His child. His flesh." She began crying again and had difficulty in getting the words out. "How can you stay so calm?"

"One of us must." He even laughed a little. "I promise that when you are yourself again, I will come to you crying and begging for comfort."

She shook her head. She tried for control and was pleased that when she spoke again it was with quiet conviction and not hysteria. "You are all that is the best of him. How can he not love you? How can he not know how hard you have tried to please him?"

"Oh my darling girl, I have seen how much you have longed for a family. But they are not all sunshine and love."

"I wanted it for you, James. I wanted you to know a father who can love and give life, not hatred and death."

"Thank you, Marguerite. That comes direct from your generous heart. But some families are so dark that it is better to be alone."

She straightened and looked at him, her heart full of dismay. "No one can live without love. It has been the marquis' ruin. I know I cannot live without it. For this last year after the Osgoods died and before I came here, I was so lonely that I thought I would die of it. James, you cannot live without it. How will you manage?"

He looked at her with such tenderness that she felt foolish for even asking. "I will find love with someone else."

The kiss was gentle, a consolation that tasted of tears and heartbreak. That soon changed, as her heart was made whole by the promise of passion. She gave herself to him and he did not refuse what she offered, and he gave with a generosity that made her hope.

The kiss would end, must end, but the echo of it stayed with them. He stroked her hair and she reveled in the sweet contentment of that simple contact.

"Marguerite, I want only you. I can say I love you, but I must trust you to teach me what that means."

She leaned away from him and could not help grinning. "Having your love is wonderful. I was only waiting for you to realize it as I did. But trust. You said trust? Do you mean that?"

He nodded and she accepted it as though it were an oath.

"It was the one thing that Gwyneth longed for that my father would never give her." He lifted the book from the table nearby. "It ruined his life. He would have had it ruin mine."

"You have read them! You read the journals!"

He gave a slight nod, as though embarrassed to admit it.

She kissed him, *she* kissed *him* for the first time. She gave him reward and gratitude and the beginning of a love that she had kept inside for far too long. "Oh, I love you for that, I truly do." She pressed kisses to his cheek and neck, found his mouth again and teased his lips. He began to laugh in the middle of this sensual assault and she pulled back.

"If I had known this would be the reward I would have read them much sooner."

She shook her head and turned serious. *No you would not have,* she thought. *For even now I wonder how ready you are for love?* It was too fine a moment to test so she merely snuggled closer and waited for him to say more. When he remained quiet, she asked, "You read of William?"

"Yes. Annabelle's son and, if you would believe her, my brother." He said the words with a kind of doubtful wonder that made him seem so vulnerable.

"Your father spoke of him tonight. He was angry and hardly in a sound mind, but James, he said that William is dead."

"Ahhh." He said no more for a moment. "It does not surprise me." He was quiet so long that she wished she had not told him. When he spoke again it was with a resigned kind of grief. "Someday I will make inquiries, but not until I am sure the marquis will not interfere."

There was a scratch on the door and Marguerite scrambled from his lap. She moved to the drinks table and was doing her best to look like a housekeeper when James called "Enter."

It was Prentice. He came into the room, came over to Marguerite and presented a tray on which sat her much abused cap.

She looked at Prentice who seemed both distracted and distressed. She took the cap. In a minute she had twisted her hair into a knot and had the cap affixed with the pin that still dangled from it.

When she turned back to James he was staring into the fire, not looking at her. She bent her head and considered him for a long moment and turned back to Prentice. "Thank you." She whispered. "Would you leave us?"

He did not want to, she could tell. He opened his mouth to speak, and then shut it. He left the room with a doleful expression and an empty tray.

Marguerite whirled around and waited for James to look at her. They had shared enough heartache for one night. There was so much more to be discussed, not the least of which was what would happen to the marquis, but right now they would escape all that.

Happiness bubbled through her as though it had been hidden in her cap and was hers again. She gave James a conspiratorial wink when he finally looked her way. "Please, my lord, there are ears everywhere here and the smell of smoke I can notice even in here. Can we go out, for a walk, to the rise, to your favorite spot? I have not been there in weeks."

"As if there is no one outside to spy on us?" He shook his head, but stood up readily enough.

They slipped out the front door. Prentice had disappeared.

They could hear voices at the back of the house. Good, Marguerite thought, Prentice was supervising the clean up of the marquis' rooms. By rights it was her responsibility and she considered briefly, very briefly, going back to help.

Any such idea disappeared the moment James took her hand. He did not tuck it into his arm, but held it with his, running his thumb over her knuckles as they walked. The moon rose through a mass of low clouds. The faint light was all that they needed since the path was so familiar to both of them.

They stopped near the tree and looked out over the old house. No guards paraded the grounds. It looked abandoned and no friendlier that it had months ago. James let go of her hand, taking her arm instead and turning them so they faced the site of the new Braemoor.

"Marguerite?"

He did not look at her and a *frisson* of fear clouded her joy.

"Marguerite, who is Monsieur Voisson?"

She was so relieved that he'd asked such a simple question she blurted out the answer without forethought. "Monsieur Voisson was our cat."

"Your husband is a cat." He said it so matter of factly that she thought he might actually believe it.

"He was the cat that Mr. Osgood kept in the kitchen."

"Ah Marguerite," He bent down and kissed her very quickly, very lightly. "If it please heaven, may you never run out of stories. And how did you come to marry the cat?"

"When I went for my first employment, I mentioned that the only worry in moving to York was what I would do with Monsieur Voisson." She laughed and he did too.

"My new employer was delighted to find that I was married, as though that promised a more steady employee and she said that he must come with me, of course. Thus Monsieur Voisson went from cat to husband. I said my husband was too unwell to travel and, I am sorry to say, he died before he could come to York with me. A widow was even more appealing to my employer and it was then that I decided that it had advantages for me as well."

"And what became of the cat, Monsieur Voisson?"

"Ah, the local apothecary adopted him and renamed him Tom."

He pulled her into his arms and held her a little away, shaking his head in awe. "Now I see that you have a long and practiced career as a liar. It is one your most endearing traits."

"Perhaps so, my lord." She did not even try to hide the huff of irritation. "Do you think we could use the word storyteller? It is so much kinder and much closer to the truth, truly it is."

A chuckle rumbled between them but no more agreement than that.

James pressed his forehead to hers. "Prentice was your chance, Marguerite."

"Yes, he was."

He leaned back. "Prentice wanted very much to rescue you from your impulse."

"Hardly an impulse, my lord." She was feeling slightly testy. He could hear it in her voice.

She pushed out if his arms and held on to his hands for a long moment. "I love you." She paused, let go of his hands but still held his eyes. "Some part of me has always loved you. And you love me."

He nodded.

"Once they know that, they will understand everything."

She turned from him, laughing aloud and twirling around, so delighted that she could not contain her pleasure.

She walked up to him and stood before him. She made herself look into his eyes and the smile that was there, if not on his lips, gave her courage. "It will be so easy."

"Too easy." He nodded.

"And such an adventure."

"Marguerite, I suspect that loving you will always be an adventure."

"Oh, I do hope so." She moved closer. "And I do believe that there is a way we can contrive to keep our passion a secret. Why we can be lovers for years and I wager that no one need ever know."

He did not reply. Despite his silence, she knew his curiosity was at its highest.

"You see, all day long I will be your housekeeper." She leaned closer to him and explained. "Your very good, very competent housekeeper. A true model. We will almost never see each other. Why should we? But at night, ahh at night, I will slip from my cottage to the ruins of Braemoor. There I will put on the white gossamer shroud and hood that will surely make me look like a ghost. I will come to you in the dower house late in the evening and if anyone ever does see me they will think that I am the ghost of Braemoor always wandering and looking for a new home."

"Brilliant, my dear." He took a step back as though trying to visualize her as a ghost. "And so like you. And, yes, you are much more a storyteller than a liar. How could I have ever thought otherwise?"

"You agree?" She could barely contain her excitement.

"I would agree with almost anything that will bring you more fully into my life, my heart and oh yes, my bed. But I cannot agree to this plan of yours, for I have my own fantasy and only you can make it happen."

"Yes?" She did not want to go to London. So much needed doing here.

"You must marry me."

She was stunned into silence. The night sounds grew louder and she could even hear voices drift up from the path nearby. In a less than a moment all was quiet again. Nothing had changed.

She shook her head, slowly, sorrowfully and his teasing smile faded. "I am your housekeeper, James. It is impossible."

"You are Braemoor's housekeeper for the moment." He waved that complication aside as though it were a bit of dust. "You are a housekeeper only by the force of circumstance. There is not a body here at Braemoor who does not know instinctively, if not in fact, that you are better born than I am."

"That may be, but my life changed forever when I left France. I accepted the truth of that long ago."

"I have wondered for weeks now, Marguerite, why Miss Morton did not try to place you with one of the noble *émigré* families once you were in England."

"I refused to leave her. By then, she was as much a mother to me as my own *Maman* had been. She arranged it somehow. I was too young to care about how she managed it, only that I did not have to leave her."

Once again he felt immense sympathy for her Miss Morton and a flashing disappointment that he would never meet her. "We must name one of our children for her, *ma chère.*"

"That would be lovely, James." Marguerite's smile was tinged with sadness. How she wished Miss Morton could know. "Her name was Caroline."

"Did you not tell me once that the difficulties of your life were sent to prepare you for your future? They brought you here, Marguerite. Yes you came here as a housekeeper. But that was nothing more than fate's way of bringing you to me."

She smiled. The smile grew to a grin, and then she sobered again. "Your brothers will think you caught in a spell."

"Morgan is caught in the same spell and Rhys couldn't care less what I do as long as it does not impede his plans."

"Your friends will laugh."

"Not once they have met you." He took her hands. "Marguerite, if I have learned nothing else from watching the Marfields it is that love comes in strange disguises and we are fools to let the surface distract us. I tested their commitment when I first met Jenneth and came away disgusted with myself. The only good that can come from that embarrassment is to learn from it."

"But we share so little."

"Ah, my darling girl, we share so much. I want to spend a lifetime showing you."

He pulled her into his arms, but did not kiss her.

"I want to be your lover. I want to be your only lover Marguerite. I want to be your last lover." He kissed her. "As I want you to be mine."

Epilogue

They stood on the site of the new Braemoor, holding hands in the late afternoon light. The spot had been cleared of the bushes, the birds dislodged to new homes, the flowers trodden into the soil, their seeds hopefully sown elsewhere. There were stakes in the ground and they walked the length of one side, along a building that only Graely could envision, but James and Marguerite could imagine.

They reached the far side of one wall, the corner of the home-to-be that was as far from the old Braemoor as the new building would be in spirit. They walked on toward the back path James had taken so many times, the one that would be the new drive. As they came closer to the trees they stopped and turned back to try to envision the prospect.

"Why did they not build the first Braemoor there?"

James did not answer her. Instead he pressed her against the trunk of a tree and kissed her. It thrilled her every bit as much as the first kiss had or the hundred since. And no less than the next thousand.

He lifted his head, his body still pressed intimately against her. His ardor drove all questions from her mind, save one.

"Have you ever made love outside?" She stood on tiptoe, arousing him still more and tickling his ear with the whispered question.

"I live to indulge your every whim, my darling wife, but

Graely is climbing up from the other far side and I would not share any part of you with him."

Marguerite stepped away and smoothed her skirt and tried to straighten her cap, though she only succeeded in tilting it over one ear.

James reached up and set it right, easily imagining the long stream of hair that he could lose himself in later.

Graely huffed up the path, waved to them and stopped to look over at the site.

"A wonder is it not, my lord?" He bowed to Marguerite. "My lady."

He had adapted to Marguerite's changed status with as much ease as the rest of the staff.

"I hope the guests who are coming for your picnic will respect the site, my lord."

"I am sure they will, Graely. There will be men posted to show them where they may step and what the plans are."

He nodded, somewhat mollified. "If you will excuse me, my lord, my lady, I am going to inspect the day's work. If you will join me, I can explain what the next step is."

"In a moment." James nodded affably. "Thank you Graely."

He walked off and Marguerite tucked the wildflower she had picked in her husband's lapel. "Prentice tells me that almost everyone invited is coming tomorrow."

"So they can meet you."

It had been his idea to invite the neighborhood for a *fête* as though that would secure their highest approval of her. Truly everyone had been most charming so she had every expectation that James was right, but not for the reasons he had listed.

"You are still more cynical than I would like, James, if you think that an endless supply of food and drink will bring everyone round."

He would have answered her, but she raised her hand to

stop him. "I think the picnic an excellent idea, for once they have seen our obvious devotion all gossip will be gone."

James laughed. "To be replaced by immediate speculation regarding the birth of our first child."

A young boy ran up to them. "Mr. Graely implores you to come quickly, my lord, before the light fades. There is something he must show you."

Marguerite patted his arm. "Hurry on, James. Keep the man happy. I will follow right behind."

The boy ran back up the hill and James followed more slowly. Marguerite watched her husband and breathed a prayer of thanks so heartfelt that it brought tears to her eyes.

James had worried so much more about appearances than she had, insisting on the banns being read rather than opting for his true first choice: a special license.

The announcement in the London paper had drawn the attention of some of the *émigrés* who had known her parents and they had been everything that was kind. Some had written of their memories of those days, letters she treasured as much as she treasured Lady Gwyneth's journals.

Moving back in with the Vicar had been a wise move, especially since his wife had managed to convince everyone that Marguerite had been in regular contact with them for the last few months and everything was as proper as could be.

As soon as the marquis had been sent to live on one of the Straeford estates in Wales, Mrs. Lanning had all but gone down on her knees to secure her old job, all the while implying that she had been on leave and that Marguerite had been acting more as hostess than housekeeper.

Marguerite came upon Graely and her husband, their inspection complete, watching the sun set in a great rainbow of summer blue and pink.

The two turned to greet her. She eyed the stakes driven

into the ground in a kind of engineering code that Graely read as simply as they might a book.

"It is a wonder, Graely," James said, "but my true question is how long will it take you to build it? Will I live to see it complete?"

Graely did not answer, obviously lost in a creative brainstorm. He took two steps away before he recalled his manners. "Good night, my lord. My lady. Tomorrow will be a holiday for the men, as you wish. I will be here to be certain that all is secure."

James nodded his thanks.

"As for how long it will take." Graely thought a moment. "You will live in it, my lord, there is no doubt of that. You, your lady and your children. It will be an estate that will speak of pride and wealth, that I promise you."

He wandered off walking between some stakes, around others as though there were already walls and halls in place.

James and Marguerite stood in silence, surrounded by what could be. Twilight glimmered in the sky and the first stars winked on.

Marguerite leaned against him and James put his arm around her shoulders before he spoke. "I want it to speak of more than Braedon pride and wealth, Marguerite. I want it to be more than the old Braemoor was. I want that as much as I want a family." He sounded more confident than defiant.

She smiled to herself. He still was not wholly convinced that this life could be his. "We will have it, James. Graely can build the house and we will fill it with life and love." She reached up to kiss him. "We can and will be a family." She took his hand. "We already are."

ABOUT THE AUTHOR

Life on the Chesapeake Bay continues to suit us perfectly. Especially after the heartache of September 11, the Bay seems the best place to be to heal and embrace life once again. Each day of the writing of *His Last Lover* was dedicated to one of the victims of the attacks, taken from the *New York Times* "Portraits in Grief" and the *Washington Post*.

My life will continue to be inspired by Casey Cho, Jeff LeVeen, Odessa Morris, Asia Cotton, Anthony Demas, Edmund Young, Donna Marie Bowen, Danielle Kousoulis, Arlene Fried, Dan McGinley, and the hundreds of others whose lives touched mine after their death.

I can be reached by email at MaryBlayney@aol.com.